ULTRABALL
LUNAR BLITZ

ULTRABALL
LUNAR BLITZ

JEFF CHEN

KATHERINE TEGEN BOOKS
An Imprint of HarperCollins Publishers

Katherine Tegen Books is an imprint of HarperCollins Publishers.

Ultraball #1: Lunar Blitz
Copyright © 2019 by Jeff Chen
Library of Congress Control Number: 2018938806
ISBN 978-0-06-280266-8

Typography by Joel Tippie
18 19 20 21 22 CG/LSCH 10 9 8 7 6 5 4 3 2 1

First Edition

For Tess and Jake, who always want to hear a story

OPEN TRYOUTS

STRIKE SAZAKI WAS the best quarterback on the moon. He had led his team to the Ultrabowl three years in a row, but each game had ended in agonizing defeat. This was finally the year his Taiko Miners would go all the way.

It had to be. The future of Taiko Colony depended on it.

Strike swallowed hard as he bounded down a tunnel leading to the home field of his Taiko Miners. He rounded the curve, Taiko Arena rising in front of him. Even though he had walked this tunnel from the locker room to the arena hundreds of times over the past four years, the awesome sight still made his breath catch. Taiko Arena was housed inside an enormous cavern whose walls were fused airtight. The arching roof was dotted with three-hundred-year-old lighting panels dating back to the first lunar mining colonies. Dust danced in the fluorescent light. Hundreds of gray-brick benches rose high on either side of the playing field, like the snaggleteeth of a monster leaping out of the ground.

Strike focused on the Miners' slogan—*Miners Together, Miners Forever*—freshly scraped into the high walls of the stadium in twenty-meter-tall letters. He closed his eyes, his face screwing up in agony. This preseason tryout wasn't going like he'd hoped. Finding a new rocketback 1 for the coming season was proving to be even harder than he had thought.

He jolted when someone bumped into him. Rock, his trusty rocketback 2, barely noticed that he had rammed into Strike. Rock mumbled a nonstop stream of consciousness as he scribbled furiously in a little notebook, pausing only briefly to scratch his stubbly black hair.

Strike caught the back of Rock's blue jumpsuit before his friend wandered out of the tunnel onto the field. Strike motioned toward the small group of recruits sitting in the stands. "You absolutely sure about this?" he asked.

Rock circled various numbers in his notebook. "Chang could be a good rocketback 1. I need to collect more data on him."

"Chang," Strike said, eyeing the lone adult in the crowd of kids. "That guy is ancient. He's so old, he sat on Neil Armstrong's baby." He shook his head. "No. I meant . . .

his baby looks like Neil Armstrong. Wait." He pinched his lips together, straining in thought.

Paging through his notebook, Rock ran a finger down a long list titled "Clever Insults," written in tiny block handwriting. "That guy is so old, he babysat for Neil Armstrong."

"Yeah, that's it," Strike said. He put an arm around his best friend and smiled. Rock's compulsive habit was annoying at times, but it sure came in handy. Rock cataloged and analyzed everything, from sixteen different types of jokes, to the moon's water supply levels, to every Ultraball stat on record. Rock even kept track of all the poops he took. In eight years of being roommates, Strike had never seen Rock without his notebook.

They walked onto the field, heading toward the near sideline. The Miners' five Ultrabot suits were neatly lined up along the clear protective barrier separating the stands from the field, the blue mech exoskeletons gleaming under the spotlights. The motley bunch of recruits was gathered in the front row of the stands. Every single pair of dark brown eyes was locked onto Strike.

Strike hesitated before speaking. A few of the kids he knew. A grimy-faced one had been a hero last month after his quick thinking prevented a mine shaft from collapsing onto fifteen boys and girls. Another hung around Strike's apartment building, scrounging and stealing to stay alive. A third Strike remembered from years ago, when he,

Strike, and Rock all lived together at the Tao Children's Home. Strike nodded to him, hoping for his sake he'd play well enough to make the team. To escape a life working down in the Taiko mines.

Strike pulled out a gray hardtack bar for himself and flipped another one to Rock. He gnawed on his as he studied the stooped-over adult, Chang, who was even shorter than most of the kids around him. The child-sized Ultrabot survival suits were the only ones that NASA had managed to deliver before Earth went nuclear ten years ago, so only kids had ever played Ultraball. The pint-sized Chang was an oddity, an adult still small enough to fit inside an Ultrabot suit. But could he fit in with four teammates less than half his age?

Maybe if he can take a joke, Strike thought. He nudged Rock. "Hey. Chang is so old, he babysat for Neil Armstrong."

Chang let out a chuckle. But he jolted when Rock erupted in machine-gun laughter.

Rock's snickering abruptly halted. "You see, Neil Armstrong landed on the moon almost four hundred years ago, so that would make you comically old," he said. "And if you babysat for Neil Armstrong, that would make you even more comically old. That's why the joke is so funny."

Chang's forehead furrowed. He sneered at Rock and let out a derisive snort. "Bunch of kids making dumb jokes," he said, shaking his head. "Better than breaking my back down in the mines, though."

Strike's eyes narrowed to slits. His arms tensed up, trembling. A raw fury burned through his body. "Get out."

Chang froze in shock. He shrank down as all the kids around him turned to stare. "Really? You want me to leave?"

"You heard me," Strike said through clenched teeth. "No one makes fun of Rock."

Looking around for support but finding none, Chang stumbled over his words. "I was just goofing. I didn't mean it. I can't go back to the mines. I can't. Come on. Give me another chance. Please."

Strike folded his arms across his chest, stony-faced.

Chang's tone changed, his fists tensing. "Don't be dumb, Strike. You know I'm the best one here. You need me. Bad."

Strike bristled at the word "dumb." He set his jaw, clenching his teeth. He jerked his head toward the exit airlock.

In the dead silence, everyone continued to stare at Chang. The man slowly got to his feet, his hunched shoulders making him look even shorter than he was, and slunk down the stairs toward the exit. "Frak!" he yelled as he trudged across the field. "A thirteen-year-old kid running the show is just idiotic." The airlock squealed as it opened, and Chang disappeared.

"I think that might have been a mistake," Rock whispered to Strike. "But thanks."

Strike nodded. He scanned the others, landing on the kid who had been at the Tao Children's Home with them. "Jin-Lee," he said. "Suit up for more reps."

The skinny little boy jumped off his bench and bounded down the stairs. The rest of the kids let out deflated sighs.

Rock's forehead wrinkled as he choked down the hardtack bar packed with nutrients and calories but no flavor. "Odd choice," he said. "But I suppose even if Jin-Lee isn't star quality, he might be a decent rocketback 2."

Strike's hardtack bar suddenly became even harder to stomach than usual. He held up a hand, signaling Jin-Lee to wait in the stands. Gripping Rock's shoulders, he took a deep breath. "For the last frakkin' time, I am not replacing you. You're my RB2. That's the way it's always been. That's the way it'll always be."

"*LunarSports Reports* brings up valid points." A corner of Rock's mouth twitched. He flipped his notebook to a page covered with miniature numbers and showed Strike. "The facts are clear. I am the Miners' weak link. For the good of Taiko Colony, you ought to cut me. I insist that you take this opportunity to find both a new rocketback 1 and a new rocketback 2."

Strike turned and pretended to study his Ultrabot

suit, his gut tightening into knots. Almost every Ultraball analyst from *LunarSports Reports* to the *Touchdown Zone* to the *SmashMouth Radio Blitz* ranked Rock as the worst rocketback in the league. But Rock wasn't just Strike's RB2. Rock was the smartest person Strike knew, having gone to school all the way through fifth grade—after Earthfall, most kids in Taiko Colony dropped out as soon as they were strong enough to work in the mines. Plus, Rock helped run the Taiko Miners, taking care of all the things Strike screwed up.

Most important, Rock and the other Miners were Strike's only family.

"Look, you butt-sniffing turd," Strike said. "The people of Taiko Colony made me the coach and general manager of the Miners. It's my call, and I say you're my RB2."

"But the fate of Taiko Colony—"

"Could you just go rescue Nugget from Pickaxe? I need my crackback 2 in one piece." He motioned toward two squat boys wrestling with each other by the fifty-meter line. The older brother was sitting on the younger one's head, attempting to fart on him.

Strike yelled out to the far end zone, where five kids in yellow jumpsuits were milling about next to their yellow Ultrabot armor. "Ready to get started again?"

Supernova, the quarterback of the Farajah Flame-throwers, gave Strike a thumbs-up. The Flamethrowers went to their Ultrabot suits, starting the process of transforming themselves from runts into machines of war.

As Rock went to retrieve the Miners' crackbacks 1 and 2, Strike touched the mech suit of armor he had piloted for three years. Ultrabot suits weren't much taller than him, but they were built like tanks. Strike's hulking exoskeleton had served him well, taking him and the Taiko Miners all the way to Ultrabowls VII, VIII, and IX. He slapped the impactanium plating, still undented after years of use. The punishment of Ultraball was nothing compared to what the suits had been designed for—a week of survival against nearly anything, giving NASA time to launch a rescue mission—but big hits were big hits.

Strike motioned for Jin-Lee to come down and join him. After Strike unlatched the clasps of the number 8 suit, panels opened with hydraulic hisses. He stepped into the foot mounts and placed his arms into the side slots. The suit winched closed and locked him in. The helmet rotated forward and lowered into place, squishing his hair down as it sealed shut. Flexing a bicep, Strike tried not to focus on how tight the Ultrabot suit was getting. A thought had been running through his mind every day lately: *If only NASA had sent up some adult-sized Ultrabot suits before Earthfall.* As soon as he outgrew his Ultrabot suit, Strike's days playing the greatest game in the history of humankind would be over. He had to win an Ultrabowl for his teammates before that happened.

Readouts flashed on the heads-up display, his power level at 37.6 percent, his visual targeting system online, and his glove magnetization at full strength. Strike ignored the barrage of other data he didn't understand. The futuristic robot suit was in stark contrast to the moon's scrambling frontier environment, the twenty-one United Moon Colonies still figuring out life after Earthfall. The Ultrabot suits were almost magical, one of the high-tech remnants from before that fateful day ten years ago.

Green lights blinked inside Strike's helmet, indicating that he was locked and loaded. He waited until the others were suited up. He gathered them into a huddle, gazing through his helmet visor at Rock, Pickaxe, and Nugget, his sworn brothers. If Strike could lead them to an Ultrabowl victory, he would set them all up for life. But if he failed at any point along the way . . . Strike pushed the horrible thought out of his mind and forced a smile to his face. "Miners together?" he said over the Ultrabot suits' comm system.

"Miners forever!" came back the united response.

Strike waved to the Flamethrowers in the other end zone, their suited-up quarterback raising his yellow robotic arm in acknowledgment. Strike picked up the solid steel Ultraball, the Ultrabot suit allowing him to heft the fifty-kilogram ball like it was a pebble. He smacked it between his hands, adrenaline leaching into his veins.

His entire body tingled with glee. So much about life on the moon was miserable, but every time Strike got into his Ultrabot suit, he became the luckiest kid in the world all over again.

The five Flamethrowers jogged to the fifty-meter line, where the two teams met. Supernova flipped his helmet visor from reflective to clear. "Getting scrimmage time on your field is awesome," he said. "Tough to get used to these crazy field pits." He looked over his shoulder at the deep craters all over the field, some hidden, camouflaged, or booby-trapped—the home-field feature of Taiko Arena. "You getting what you need out of this scrimmage?"

"I think so," Strike said. He forced a smile at Jin-Lee.

"Season's coming up quick," Supernova said. "Don't go easy on us anymore, okay? Let's go full speed from here on out."

Strike nodded. "I bet this is the year you break the Torch's Curse. Maybe even go all the way. Well, to make the Ultrabowl. Not win it." He grinned. "We'd have to put the beatdown on you guys if we met up there."

"It'd be an honor to face you in the Ultrabowl," Supernova said. "But I'd just be happy to break the curse and finally give our fans a winning season." He motioned his team to huddle up.

Strike brought his Miners together by their forty-meter line, slapping Jin-Lee's helmet. "Earn yourself an Ultraball name, okay? We'll come up with something awesome if you make the team."

"I will, Strike," Jin-Lee said. "What's the play?"

"Enough of the basics," Strike said. "Time to see how you handle a slingshot V." His mouth curled into a wicked grin. "A fake slingshot V."

Jin-Lee's eyes widened for just a moment before he nodded. "I got this, Strike."

"Good. Back left corner of the end zone. I'll zip it in to you after I scramble. Show me what you got. Pickaxe and Nugget, send him flying."

"Oh yeah," Pickaxe said. "We're gonna rocket you to the roof."

"We need a great fake out of you, Jin-Lee," Strike said. "Really sell it. On two." The Miners broke the huddle, Strike striding up to the Ultraball, his boots clomping on the hard-packed turf. Rock set up beside him, and Nugget and Pickaxe took their places ten steps behind. Deep in the backfield, Jin-Lee got into a three-point stance. It was the classic slingshot V formation, with Nugget and Pickaxe preparing to whip Jin-Lee forward at meteoric speed.

On the other side of the line, Supernova immediately recognized the formation, signaling to his teammates with his arms raised into a V. He waved his two crackbacks in, both champing at the bit to leap over Strike and Rock and break up the play before the Miners could load the slingshot.

"Oxygen," Strike yelled. "Mad Mongol blue, Mad Mongol blue!" He pointed to Nugget as if directing him to do something, but the words were just fake signals. As Supernova looked backward in confusion, Strike screamed, "Hut hut!"

Snatching the ball off the ground, Strike scrambled behind Rock, who got pounded by the two charging Flamethrower crackbacks. One of them tried to hurdle up and over, but Rock locked a magnetized glove onto his boot, whipping him down to the ground with a booming thud.

In the backfield, Jin-Lee had raced forward, leaping like a superhero. Pickaxe and Nugget grabbed his hands and launched him forward. Right in Jin-Lee's path, Strike held the Ultraball high and let it clang into Jin-Lee's magnetized gloves as he flew by. The Miners had executed a perfect slingshot V.

The Flamethrowers' two rocketbacks backpedaled to the corner of the end zone where Jin-Lee was flying, ready to spear him but good.

Except that Strike hadn't let go of the ball. Casually jogging backward with the ball tucked away, he looked over his shoulder at Jin-Lee, watching with everyone else. As the Flamethrowers scrambled to pursue the rocketback zooming through the air in a blue blur, Strike burst into a hard sprint. He pounded the turf behind Nugget, who was now his lead blocker.

A moment later, Supernova caught on to the fake and jerked around, swiveling to race after Strike. The rest of the Flamethrowers charged in with their quarterback, all five of them targeting Strike like laser beams.

Still behind Nugget, Strike juked to avoid an oncoming Flamethrower, and then pushed Nugget into another before spinning away. A third defender locked a magnetized glove onto Strike's shoulder plate, but with a hard chop, Strike broke the guy's grip.

The last two Flamethrowers raced in to corral Strike, the situation seemingly hopeless. But Strike suddenly planted his back foot and charged right at one of the oncoming defenders. He jumped high and heaved a monster pass. A split second later, the defender blasted into Strike's chest plate, slamming him backward. Warning lights flashed on Strike's heads-up display, but an Ultrabot suit could dampen blows five times as hard as this one. He jarred only a little as he slammed down onto his butt.

The speeding Ultraball soared through the cavern toward Jin-Lee, who was playing possum in the back corner of the end zone. He'd only have to leap ten or fifteen meters for it, an easy jump, even for a rookie. If he remembered to engage the electromagnets in the suit's gloves, he'd only need to get within centimeters before the steel Ultraball snapped into his hands.

Strike swore under his breath when Jin-Lee kicked off

the ground into a tremendous leap. "Too high!" he yelled.

Jin-Lee realized his mistake right away, windmilling his arms to slow himself down. But he still soared so high that he had to reach down between his legs to snag the Ultraball. It smashed into him like a cannonball, the force of the impact throwing him into a front spin. He managed to hold on, but the Flamethrowers would have plenty of time to race in underneath to prevent him from getting a foot down for the score.

Flamethrowers and Miners sprinted toward the end zone, the swarming mass jockeying for position, smashing elbows and fists into each other's helmets in bursts of blue and yellow. Supernova was the first one there, leaping to crash into Jin-Lee when he was still two meters off the ground. He launched a barrage of roundhouse punches, fiery yellow missiles aimed at the Ultraball. Jin-Lee held on, but as more and more defenders clanged into him, it was all he could do to curl up around the Ultraball and yell for help. A Flamethrower rammed in with a spearing punch, threading through limbs to land a fist into the Ultraball. It popped high into the air, straight up toward the roof.

Strike pushed away from the pile before anyone else. He ran toward Pickaxe, who bent down with hands cradled together, knowing exactly what Strike wanted. Strike jumped up as Pickaxe launched him, zooming ahead of everyone else. He grabbed the Ultraball as he zipped by.

Pretending to curl up like Jin-Lee had, he made like he was going to try to fall back to the turf for the touchdown.

But as two Flamethrowers rocketed up at him, Strike reared his arm back and aimed at the other side of the end zone, where Rock was streaking. His targeting system locked onto Rock's number 5 suit, and Strike threw a bullet. The ball was nothing but a silver blur as it shot across the field. It cracked into Rock's magnetized gloves, its fiery momentum jerking him forward into a wild spin. Rock cradled it into his chest plate and he rolled and bounced uncontrollably before smashing into the clear impactanium barrier separating the field from the stands. All his limbs splayed out, turned nearly upside down, he held up the Ultraball.

Jin-Lee ran up to Strike. "I'm so sorry. I should have jumped lower. It would have been an easy score. I'll do better next time. Please. I promise, I will." Although his visor was still set to reflective, Strike could almost see the tears of desperation running down Jin-Lee's cheeks. Making the team was his only way out of working in Taiko Colony's mines.

"It's okay," Strike said, even though it wasn't. Jin-Lee could probably be a decent Ultraball player. But he didn't have the killer instinct of a rocketback 1.

Strike jogged over to Rock, flipping him right side up and helping him to his feet. He signaled for a private conversation, unlatching his helmet. The giant dome clicked and then rotated back over his head, the helmet comm system going quiet. Rock did the same.

"Seven points," Strike said. "Good work."

"Any rocketback could have made that front-roll catch," Rock said. "And a lot more efficiently. I used a full 2.4 percent of my suit's power on that single play. I really think you should replace me. For the good of the team. For Taiko Colony."

As if Strike didn't have enough to worry about with finding a rocketback 1, he knew that Rock was probably right. The weight of so many people's futures crushed down upon his shoulders. "Could this day possibly get any worse?" Strike muttered.

"Oh, absolutely," Rock said. "We haven't even come close to number one on my list of worst moments ever."

Strike slowly nodded. It was hard to imagine that anything could be worse than what happened eight months ago at last year's Ultrabowl.

But Rock's prediction might just come true.

2

THE MELTDOWN GUN

STRIKE AND ROCK trudged through the tunnel leading into the locker room. Strike slapped the wall, echoes pinging back and forth between the airtight surfaces. The rest of tryouts hadn't gone well. More accurately, they had stunk. "What do you think?" Strike asked.

"No clear answer," Rock said, his head buried in his notebook. "Hassan and Ichiro are the front-runners."

"Yeah, I guess so." Strike paused. "But I'm still thinking that Jin-Lee might be our guy."

Rock looked up in surprise, then consulted his notebook. "Not only did Jin-Lee mess up that sure touchdown, but he dropped one of your passes. He also had a hard time following some of your play calls."

"But the last pass he caught was spectacular. How many people can make such a smooth one-handed front-roll grab like that?"

"The safe choice—"

"The safe choice won't cut it," Strike said. "There's something in Jin-Lee. A spark. A flame." The fragile little boy had black hair so wispy you could see his scalp through it. He probably hadn't ever eaten a full complement of ten hardtack bars in one day. But that made the kid hungry, and hunger drove people like nothing else. Jin-Lee knew that Ultraball was his only salvation.

Strike had been that same kid three years ago.

Rock's pace slowed as they neared the door at the end of the tunnel. "Are you considering Jin-Lee because you think he'll help us win the Ultrabowl? Or because of your loyalty to the Tao Children's Home?"

Rock knows me too well, Strike thought. "Why can't it be both? We need a moon shot if we're going to win the Ultrabowl. We need to find a rocketback 1 with as much game-changing ability as TNT."

Strike's fists balled up. It was the first time he had said his former teammate's name out loud in months. He swore that it would be the last.

"Strike?" Rock said. He waved a hand in front of Strike's face. "Are you okay?"

"I really think Jin-Lee could replace you-know-who," Strike said through gritted teeth. "With a lot of practice, he could be spectacular."

"Well, that is a possibility," Rock said. "But an unlikely one."

Strike took a deep breath, reaching for the big green button on the control panel. *Rock's probably right*, he thought. He always was.

The metal airlock door rasped open, and Strike froze at the sight of a grizzled man and two kids sitting on a locker room bench, all of them wearing the bright red jumpsuits of North Pole Colony.

The old man got to his feet, an angular black weapon strapped to his side. Raiden Zuna walked tall, with a bold swagger, platinum chains adorning his jewel-studded jumpsuit. A gleaming Governor's Star was displayed prominently on his chest. Not only was Zuna governor of North Pole Colony, the richest of the twenty-one United Moon Colonies, he also owned the North Pole Neutrons, winners of three straight Ultrabowls. Behind him stood two short boys who were the most famous superstars on the moon: Fusion and Chain Reaction, the Neutrons' quarterback and rocketback 1. "Pretty ugly tryouts today," Zuna said.

"Only if you think pretty is ugly," Strike spluttered. "Pretty as yo mama's nuclear fallout. I mean, ugly as her fallout. Rock, help me out!"

Rock flipped through his notebook, nearly fumbling it. "L-l-let's see," he said, stealing nervous glances at the

Meltdown Gun strapped to Zuna's side. "Yo mama's so ugly, she uses nuclear makeup for fallout. I mean, nuclear fallout for makeup. You see, that's funny because—"

Zuna burst into laughter. "That's almost as terrible as those recruits you tried out today. But not quite."

Strike flushed hot. "We have some good players to choose from. How did you get into our locker room, anyway?"

"Colony Governors go wherever we want," Zuna said. "And you don't fool me. None of those kids can take you to an Ultrabowl victory. Certainly not Jin-Lee Wu."

Strike's jaw went slack. The government watched everyone and monitored all transmissions, but Strike had only talked about Jin-Lee privately, to Rock. "How did you know I was leaning toward him?"

"I have eyes and ears everywhere." Zuna leaned against one of the lockers, stroking his bushy salt-and-pepper beard. "You and I know both know that the Miners have no shot this year with any of those scrubs who showed up today."

"We've found ways to get to the Ultrabowl," Strike said. "This year will be no different."

"But you're going to lose to my Neutrons yet again." Zuna crouched so they were eye to eye. "Look. I like you, Strike. You got guts." He stared at Strike like a weapon locking onto its target. "I want you to be my new quarterback."

Strike jolted. "You want me to play for you? As a Neutron?"

Zuna nodded.

Strike had been a die-hard Taiko Miner his entire career, and he would never take a deal from the man who had supposedly paid off TNT to throw last year's Ultrabowl. But being a North Pole Neutron was the closest thing to being a god. "What about Fusion?" he asked. He shot a look at the baby-faced boy doing his best to hide in a corner of the locker room.

"Never mind about Fusion," Zuna said. "I'll set you up in North Pole Colony with a cushy pad and a fat salary. Be smart, Strike. You know the North Pole Neutrons will win our fourth Ultrabowl title in a row. I'm giving you the opportunity to become part of our dynasty. Join Neutron Nation. Join my alliance. This is your only chance to escape that crumbling rathole you call a colony."

Strike gulped. When Taiko Colony's main oxygen recycler failed during last year's Ultrabowl, it had looked like the underground colony was done for. It was only Raiden Zuna who had given Taiko Colony a chance for survival, making a bet with the governor of Taiko Colony: Zuna would loan out North Pole Colony's spare oxygen recycler for a year, and if the Miners won the upcoming Ultrabowl, he'd let them keep it.

If not, Raiden Zuna would become Taiko Colony's new governor.

Strike glanced silently at Rock, who paused before raising his eyebrows. After living together for eight years, Strike knew exactly what Rock was thinking: *The logical choice is to accept Zuna's deal.* But for all its mounting problems, Taiko Colony had been his parents' home before they died in the Fireball Blast mining accident eight years ago. It was where Strike belonged.

"Thanks," Strike said. "But no thanks." He motioned Rock ahead and walked down the hall of lockers.

Chain Reaction, the Neutrons' star rocketback 1, moved to block him. "Strike," he said, his weasely face twitching as if he'd smelled something deliciously rotten. "Don't be dumb. Me and you would make up the most powerful offense in history. With me as your primary receiver, you'd not only break Torch's records, you'd shatter them. You'd finally get one of these." He shoved a bony fist into Strike's face, three platinum Ultrabowl rings glinting. Chain Reaction was all skin and bones, with weird bald spots dotted across his patchy black hair, skin peeling all over his face. But no one cared about that, because the three-time league MVP was the best rocketback of all time. "Think of the fame. The fortune. The glory."

Strike pointed to Fusion, whose hands were jammed into his jumpsuit pockets. "You'd seriously just toss your own quarterback aside?"

"Fusion's going to quarterback his own team," Chain Reaction said. "Once Mr. Zuna gets control of Taiko

Colony's five Ultrabot suits, he's going to move the team and rename it the North Pole Fusion. Awesome, huh?"

Zuna smacked Chain Reaction across the back of the head. "Idiot. I told you not to talk about that."

Chain Reaction cringed, his hands held protectively in front of his face. "I just thought it would help him make up his mind."

"I pay you to score touchdowns, not to think." Zuna smoothed out his fiery red jumpsuit, flashing his diamond-studded rings as he conspicuously touched his three Ultrabowl Champion patches. He shrugged at Strike. "You have to admit, moving the team makes sense. It's basic economics. The Miners are losing money. Taiko Colony is getting poorer and poorer every day. How long until it collapses?"

Heat rose through Strike's body. The Miners were Taiko Colony's rallying point, one of the few sources of joy and hope in people's desperate lives. He turned to Fusion. "This is what you want? To steal Taiko Colony's team?"

Fusion ground his toe into the locker room floor, his forehead wrinkled in agony. "I just want to play Ultraball, that's all. I do what Mr. Zuna tells me to do. Sorry, Strike."

"What do you think you're doing?" Zuna yanked Fusion to his side. "Neutrons never apologize."

"Yes, sir." Fusion shirked away. "Sorry, sir."

Zuna turned to Strike. He lifted a fist, his arm flexed

and quivering. "You are one of the strong ones. Join me. Neutron Nation will bring forward a new era of wealth and prosperity. Think about my offer." His eyes narrowed. "Think seriously what the future must bring."

Strike exchanged confused glances with Rock.

"You're too young to remember life before Earthfall." Zuna unholstered his Meltdown Gun and waved it in the direction of the dead planet somewhere above. "It was magnificent. Anything we wanted, Earth shipped it right to us, the heroes spearheading humanity's expansion across the solar system. But everything changed when Earth went nuclear. So many people think that everything will just work itself out. But the wise man faces reality and does what needs to be done. Neutron Nation will see to that. Join me in my mission to save the moon."

Strike's nostrils flared. All he ever wanted to do was just play Ultraball and win a title for his Miners. Why did so many people try to get him involved with all this other junk? "C'mon, Rock, let's get out of here." He shoved past Fusion as he stormed toward the rear exit.

Zuna called out to them. "I hear the line for hardtack bar distribution is extra-long today. Even longer than the water distribution line. Have fun waiting for hours. What are you down to—eight and a half bars a day? How do you poor folks even get by on that?"

Strike tried to deny Zuna the satisfaction of a reply, but he broke stride. Taiko Square was exactly where he and Rock were heading, to wait in the distribution line. And Taiko Colony's ration had just been cut from nine hardtack bars per day to eight and a half.

How was it that Raiden Zuna was always one step ahead of everyone?

3

THE TORCH'S CURSE

Strike and Rock emerged from an airlock into the immense cavern that housed Taiko Colony, where all the moon's ore was mined. Each of the twenty-one underground cities that made up the United Moon Colonies produced some important resource—New Beijing Colony making hardtack bars, North Pole Colony generating solar and nuclear energy, Tranquility Colony building heavy machinery, Guoming Colony recycling the moon's waste—and an unfortunate by-product of Taiko Colony's mining was a huge amount of dust kicked into the atmosphere.

Although an acrid haze coated Taiko Colony in a blanket of gloom, it wasn't nearly as bad as it had been in the past. Ever since Raiden Zuna's people had installed the loaned oxygen recycler last year, the air was more like mist than smog. Sitting in the center of the gray-brick buildings making up the cityscape, the giant oxygen machine was spotlighted underneath a bright fluorescent ceiling panel, its motors and pumps chugging along at a low hum.

A lump formed in Strike's throat as he thought about the bet the governor of Taiko Colony had made with Raiden Zuna after last year's Ultrabowl. But Governor Katana hadn't had any other choice. Without the new oxygen recycler, Taiko Colony's oxygen supply would have run out within days, the main airlock door automatically sealing to prevent the problem from spreading. Taiko Colony would have died then and there, leaving three thousand people to scramble away, scattering through the Tunnel Ring connecting the twenty-one underground colonies, or even heading out for the uncharted Dark Side of the moon. Hardly anyone would have taken in the refugees. After Earthfall, the once-prosperous moon had broken down into survival mode, every colony for itself.

As Strike and Rock made their way toward the city center of Taiko Colony, a group of adults in the beige jumpsuits of Peary Colony came running at Strike and Rock, jockeying for position. Most of them had *LunarSports Reports* patches sewn on, but there were also reporters from *SmashMouth Radio Blitz* and the *Touchdown Zone.*

"Get ready for the stupid questions," Strike muttered.

Rock nodded, pulling out his notebook and opening it to a long list titled "Most Idiotic Comments from Reporters."

All the reporters, camera operators, and photographers spoke over each other as they elbowed to get in front. "Hey, Strike," one of them asked, sticking a microphone into Strike's face. "Still fitting into your Ultrabot suit?"

"What do you think about oddsmakers giving you only a thirteen percent chance of winning the Ultrabowl?" another shouted.

"Do you think Rattler or Hammer Fist is prettier?" yet another said.

At this last question, Strike turned to tell Rock to start writing. But Rock was already scribbling.

A *LunarSports Reports* person elbowed his way in, everyone else deferring to the big shot and his team of cameramen. "Vikram Cho with *LunarSports Reports,*" he said, holding his microphone out to Strike. "Let's get down to the question in the forefront of everyone's minds: Did you find a new rocketback today?"

Strike and Rock exchanged glances. Strike began to stammer. "Well . . . uh . . ."

"Can you comment on TNT's failure to score during the final play of last year's Ultrabowl?" another reporter blurted out. "Did he really throw the game?"

Rage surged through Strike, his hands curling into fists. He spit out the words he had repeated so many times over the past months. "I told you. I'm not talking about that traitor."

"How do you respond to the reports that he's been sighted in the Tunnel Ring?" the reporter asked. He pulled out a blurry picture of a boy in a grimy blue jumpsuit riding a tunnel tram. "What would you do if you found him?"

Strike clenched his jaw. The boy's jumpsuit hood was pulled over his head, but there was no mistaking who it was. Strike ripped the picture out of the reporter's hands and tore it into shreds. "I'd frakkin' kill him."

Smelling blood, the *LunarSports* reporter pressed his microphone in close. "That's it, Strike. Give me something I can really use. Do you really think you have a chance to win the Ultrabowl this year? The oddsmakers say no."

A guy with a wiry black-and-white goatee stepped in front of Strike. "Let me handle this one," he said. "Of course the Miners are going to win the Ultrabowl. Strike is going to save Taiko Colony." He stuck out his chest with pride, his platinum Governor's Star gleaming bright. He pointed to all the Miners' player decals stitched on below his star, Strike's number 8 front and center. "Our Miners have learned from the defeats over the past three years.

This is finally the year that our boys raise that Ultrabowl trophy. Isn't that right, Strike?"

Strike's face burned even hotter. As if he weren't nervous enough being on camera, it was ten times worse with the governor of Taiko Colony also pressing him with questions. His forehead beading up with sweat, Strike spluttered as he tried to muster a show of confidence. "Uh . . . does a hardtack bar smell?"

The reporters all looked at each other. One pulled out a gray hardtack bar and sniffed at it. "Sort of, I guess."

"There is a trace odor, but it really isn't offensive," Rock said. He flipped open his notebook. "What Strike meant to say was, 'Does a hardtack bar *taste bitter*?' The answer is obviously yes, thus making the joke incredibly hilarious." He fired out an explosion of laughter, making everyone jump.

"That's what I meant," Strike said. "I just got all mixed up and . . ." He nearly cried with relief when a dark-haired woman pushed through the crowd: Nadya, his neighbor across the hall in his apartment building. Nadya had been the first person to welcome Strike and Rock when they moved into the building three years ago. In her twenties or thirties, she looked out for Strike and Rock when she wasn't working down in the mines as a shift foreman.

"All you reporters leave Strike alone," Nadya said, waving the crowd back. She turned to the governor. "With all due respect, Governor Katana, Strike has enough to worry about without extra pressure from you."

"I'm not pressuring him," the governor said. "I'm just reminding him of what's at stake. Winning the Ultrabowl is the only way to save Taiko Colony."

"Strike knows what's at stake," Nadya said. "And there is another way to save Taiko Colony."

"Don't be ridiculous," he said. "Ten million Universal dollars is an impossible amount of money. There's no chance we could buy Zuna's oxygen recycler outright and call off our bet. The only realistic way to save Taiko Colony is for the Miners to win—"

"Please, sir," Nadya said through gritted teeth. "Stop pressuring Strike."

Under Nadya's fierce glare, everyone slunk away, people around Governor Katana mumbling about how the Miners had to win it all. The governor looked back over his shoulder at Strike and threw him a thumbs-up sign, but he tugged at his goatee in worry.

"So many people bugging you," Nadya said, shaking her head. "I'll keep them off your back. You have enough on your mind as it is."

"Thanks," Strike said. He stiffened when Nadya put an arm around his shoulders. A small part of him wanted to lean into her hug, but he had to protect himself. His mom had died in the Fireball Blast. TNT's mom had gone away. He couldn't let it happen a third time.

A guy from Strike's apartment building pushed in close

to Strike. "I can get three-to-one odds on the Miners winning the Ultrabowl," he said. "Those are great odds, aren't they?"

"Buzz off, Jamal," Nadya said.

Strike stared at the cavern's high roof in exasperation. The worst part about playing Ultraball was all the people pumping him for information so they could place bets on the games. If there was one thing more popular than Ultraball, it was betting on Ultraball. And people gave him way too much credit—Strike barely knew what "three-to-one odds" meant, much less if it made for a good bet.

"Come on, Strike, be a pal," Jamal said. "Gimme something I can use."

"I told you, quit it," Nadya said. She elbowed the guy hard in the ribs, and then escorted Strike and Rock away.

Strike mouthed a silent thank-you to her.

Arriving at Taiko Square, Strike stopped in his tracks as he spotted a huge line coming out of the main government building. It went down the road, turned the corner, and disappeared. Lines for weekly hardtack bar distribution were the norm, but this was even longer than usual. And by the looks of things, the delivery from the hardtack factory hadn't even arrived yet—no rovers, no one wearing the green jumpsuits of New Beijing Colony.

"Gotta get back in line," Nadya said. She pointed a threatening finger at the people crowding around Strike.

"No questions about tryouts. No questions about betting. And turn off the radios. Those *SmashMouth Radio Blitz* guys are giving me a headache."

"But Berzerkatron and the Mad Mongol are giving the lowdown on the Neutrons' new crackback 2," one guy said, his radio held to his ear. "This girl is supposed to be unbelievable."

"Who cares what those idiots say?"

"I care. They're former Ultrabowl MVPs. They know what they're talking about."

"Just turn the radios off for a couple of minutes," Nadya said, her jaw set like iron. "Berzerkatron and the Mad Mongol are on for twelve hours a day. Give Strike a little break."

People grumbled, but several of them holding small radios clicked them off.

With a wink at Strike, Nadya joined a friend who had been saving her place.

Someone toward the front of the line shouted, waving his arms. "Hey, Strike! Rock! You guys can cut in front of me." By the sound of his voice, the little kid had to be younger than Strike, but his dark brown face was powdered with gritty gray dust that made him look like he was a grandfather.

An adult with scraggly black hair shoved the kid. "No cuts."

"But that's Strike."

"He could be the captain of the Blackguard for all I care."

People sucked in a collective breath, stepping away from the man. Insulting the Blackguard could get you thrown into prison.

But the kid held his ground. "Give him a break. Strike is Taiko Colony's only hope."

"We have no hope. So no frakkin' cuts."

The boy raised a fist and stepped toward the man. "You take that back. The Miners are going to win the Ultrabowl."

"It's okay, everyone," Strike said. "No cuts." As badly as he wanted to save himself hours of waiting around, he'd feel terrible about cutting in front of all these people who broke their backs in the mines to earn their hardtack bars, water ration, and tiny amount of U-dollars.

Strike walked toward the rear of the line, and people of all ages held up their hands for him to high-five. He forced out a sickly smile through the surging waves of nausea. Why did everyone have to put all this pressure about Taiko Colony's future on his shoulders?

And who knew—Raiden Zuna was creepy, intimidating, and crooked, but he had made North Pole Colony the envy of the moon. Before Earthfall, all twenty-one underground colonies had flourished as highly planned utopias, each one a melting pot of people from countries all over the Earth. But the ten years since Earthfall had seen North

Pole Colony and Taiko Colony move rapidly in opposite directions. While kids in North Pole Colony continued to get normal educations at least through high school, most kids in Taiko Colony dropped out of elementary school as soon as they were strong enough to work in the mines, or even earlier so they could beg for hardtack bars. Governor Katana was one of the few governors who wasn't corrupt, but under him, Taiko Colony had crumbled into the armpit of the United Moon Colonies.

Maybe it's time for a change, Strike thought.

"Strike," Rock whispered in his ear. "Back there. Is that Torch?"

Strike's heart raced upon hearing the name of his boyhood hero, the legendary QB for the Farajah Flamethrowers. Strike's memory was usually terrible, but when it came to Ultraball, every detail got burned into his brain. Images flashed through his head, Torch in his yellow number 7 Ultraball suit, stampeding through an electrical disruptor zone, lit up by a firestorm of crackling sparks. Torch had blasted three defenders off their feet on his way to scoring a spectacular touchdown in the first play of his Ultraball career. He had only played one season four years ago, but the superstar had set records that still hadn't been broken.

"Can't be Torch," Strike whispered to Rock. "He's not wearing a Farajah yellow jumpsuit. And why would he be in Taiko Colony, waiting for hardtack bars . . ." He trailed off as he reached the tall boy, slumped over, his hair a wavy black curtain hiding his face. "Torch?"

The teenager turned farther away from them. "Got the wrong guy," he mumbled.

Stepping closer, Strike sucked in a breath. "Torch," he said with awe. "You were my idol."

"I'm telling you, you got the wrong guy."

"If it hadn't been for that interception in the Ultrabowl—"

"I can't take that back, all right?" The teen grabbed Strike and yanked him away. He looked over his shoulder to a little girl. "Save our place in line, okay?"

When they were well away from anyone else, Strike cleared his throat. "I didn't mean to bring up bad memories. It's just that you were my favorite player. If it hadn't been for that one interception, you would have been a legend. You still should be a legend. It was just one throw."

Torch pinched his eyes shut. "It was a terrible frakkin' throw, and it cost us the Ultrabowl. It cost me everything." His fists trembled. "Stop calling me Torch. Torch is dead. I'm just Taj Tariq now."

"But you were the greatest," Strike said. "You nearly pulled off the impossible." Against all odds, Torch had led the Farajah Flamethrowers all the way to Ultrabowl VI, in what was supposed to be a rebuilding year. But during the last minute of the big game, Torch had tossed an ugly interception, allowing the Tranquility Beatdown to seal the victory. It had been Torch's first season playing Ultraball, and his last. Ever since then, Flamethrowers fans blamed their team's streak of losing seasons on the Torch's Curse.

The tall boy sighed. "You're probably the only person on the entire moon who gets that, Strike. Everyone else remembers just one thing: the interception that cost the Flamethrowers the title. The throw that cursed the team." His voice cracked. "That's all I heard about for weeks. Months. Years. People kept on writing all sorts of horrible things on my door. Death threats, saying that I had to be killed to break the Torch's Curse. My sister and I finally had to leave Farajah Colony." He pointed to the tiny girl still in line, coughing and sniffling as she wiped her nose on her jumpsuit sleeve. "None of the heat generation factories wanted anything to do with me. I couldn't even get work as a boiler room monkey. I was lucky to land a job here in the mines last month."

Strike blinked. It was crazy to think that this shattered, slumped-over teenager had once been Torch, the sensational quarterback who had been destined to carry on the Farajah Flamethrowers' dynasty. During his one season, he had been featured in *LunarSports Reports'* Top Ten Plays every Sunday night. There had even been serious talk about Torch running for governor of Farajah Colony. He had been headed toward becoming one of the most powerful people on the moon. But because of a single play, he was now waiting in line for hardtack bars, breaking his back down in the Taiko Colony mines.

That same miserable life awaited Strike and his teammates if they didn't win the Ultrabowl. It didn't matter that they had made the big game three years in a row.

No one cared about the losers.

"I'm one of your biggest fans, Mr. Tariq," Rock said. "Strike and I watch your game film every time Taiko Commons broadcasts it. The slingshot V reinvented Ultraball. How did you even think of it?"

A tiny smile crept to the former quarterback's face. "It's been years since anyone's brought that up. Me and Dragon, we used to stay up all night dreaming up plays."

Strike bit his lip as memories bubbled to the surface. Torch and Dragon had pulled all-nighters to dream up new plays—just like he and TNT had done.

"We never thought we'd use that play," Torch said. "It was complicated. But we needed something huge. Unexpected. You should have seen Dragon's face when I called it—"

"To win your semifinals game against the Neutrons four years ago," Rock said. He consulted his notebook. "You lined up behind Dragon and Barbeque, all three of you deep. Napalm long-snapped you the ball. You charged forward and tucked it in before Dragon and Barbeque slung you into the sky. You slammed into the back wall of the arena and fought all five Neutrons while falling into the end zone."

Strike and Torch watched each other as Rock recounted the play, both of them grinning. A surge of emotion connected the two quarterbacks, a bond that only a select few people on the moon could ever understand.

"You single-handedly changed the game of Ultraball," Rock said. "Before then, it was hardly different from Earthball."

"Now superjumps and slingshots are a standard part of every team's playbook," Strike added. "You were the greatest mind in Ultraball history."

Light from the flickering roof panels glinted off a sheen in Torch's eyes. "My Flamethrowers were the last team to beat the Neutrons during the playoffs. Best moment of my life. Best year of my life. Until the interception, anyway." He stole a nervous glance at Strike. "How did tryouts go? You find a rocketback 1 anywhere as good as TNT?"

The familiar dread seeped back into Strike's bones. He chewed at a fingernail, studying the tall, lanky teenager in front of him. If NASA had delivered just one adult-sized Ultrabot suit before Earthfall, all of Strike's problems would have been solved—Torch would be an ideal addition to the Miners. "Can I get your opinion on something?" Strike asked.

"Me? I've been out of the game too long. And I don't want to curse the Miners, too. I can't help you."

"You might be the only person on the moon who can help me."

Torch's black eyebrows knitted together. He stuffed his hands in his pockets and shrugged. "What do you need?"

Strike took a deep breath and leaned in. "Don't tell anyone, but tryouts didn't go well. They were garbage, actually. Only twenty kids showed up."

"That's it? Why so few?"

Strike stole glances around him before whispering, "I think Zuna threatened people to stay away. Or paid them off them. Or both. He showed up after tryouts with Chain Reaction and Fusion, to taunt us. And worse."

"Zuna." Torch spit on the ground. "He's destroyed the game. And now he's going to become governor of Taiko Colony." He flinched. "I mean, if you don't win the Ultrabowl this year."

Strike winced. "Anyway, I got two guys who might be a solid RB1. And then I got a guy who might be great. But he also might be a bomb. He's so rough. What would you do?"

Torch looked off into the distance through the haze. "That's a little like my decision with Dragon. You should have seen his tryout. He made this incredible spinning catch after launching himself off Inferno's shoulders halfway up to the roof. First time I had ever seen a superjump. It was like he was a real-life superhero. But he also fumbled twice on routine handoffs. And one of those times, he had his glove electromagnets activated. How is that even possible?" He chuckled, shaking his head. "But with all the pressure to bring home the Flamethrowers' third Ultrabowl title in a row, I had to go big or go home."

That was exactly the answer Strike wanted to hear. "Thanks, Torch. Sorry. I mean, Taj."

"You know what?" He smiled wistfully. "You can call me Torch. Brings me back to better days. When I had a whole lot more." He shoved one hand deeper into his jumpsuit pocket, clenching it into a fist. "All I have to show for a year of playing Ultraball is twenty-six U-bucks. How am I supposed to support my kid sister like this? It'll be at least another year until she's strong enough to work in the mines."

"I can work," his sister said, her sudden appearance making everyone jump.

"Jasmine," Torch said. "I told you to stay in line. Strike and I have some stuff to talk about."

"Hi, Strike," Jasmine said, starry-eyed. "You're my favorite player ever."

"Not me?" Torch said.

"Oh." Jasmine knotted her fingers up, fidgeting. "I meant, besides you. Yeah, that's what I meant. But. Um. Well, the thing is . . ."

Torch tousled her hair. "Just messing with you. Strike's my favorite player ever, too."

"How did you sneak up on us so quietly?" Strike asked, looking around. "Where did you come from?"

"I might be small, but I'm nimble," Jasmine said. "I can work as a mine shaft crawler—" She erupted into a storm of coughs, nearly choking.

People in line looked over in disgust as Torch thumped her on the back. Finally, the coughing fits died out.

"Do yourself a favor, Strike," Torch said. "Think about life after Ultraball more than I did. Come on, Jasmine. We need to get back and make sure we don't lose our place in line." He put an arm around his sister and trudged away. "Good luck with the season."

Strike nudged Rock, and they headed down the line to where it disappeared around another corner. "Hard to believe that's actually Torch," Strike said. "I mean, the guy was a legend. And he sure had great advice. We have to go big and take the risk. Let's work out Jin-Lee some more."

"But Strike," Rock said, "I really don't think that's the best idea."

"Can't we just—"

Shouts broke out behind them, and Strike swiveled to catch sight of a boy in a grimy jumpsuit running off.

Torch was splayed out on the ground, holding his side as he grimaced in pain. "Stop him! He robbed me!"

People took awkward steps away from the fallen teen. No one wanted to get mixed up with the Blackguard police. Everyone turned away, pretending they hadn't seen a thing.

Strike ground his teeth together as the thief sprinted away. "Come on!" he said, yanking Rock with him. They tore down the street in hot pursuit.

THE THIEF

STRIKE AND ROCK whipped around a corner into a narrow alley between two gray-brick apartment buildings. "Got him now," Strike said, panting. Sure enough, the thief slowed as he approached the dead end hidden in the shadows. Strike pushed Rock behind him. "Stay here."

He took careful strides toward the thief as the guy darted back and forth, slapping the walls as if looking for a secret passageway. "Just give us back the money," Strike said. "We don't want any trouble." He slowed as he neared, the thief's erratic motions unnerving him. Sometimes the smallest boys packed the hardest punches.

The thief charged. Strike flinched, throwing his fists up. But the thief leapt high, kicking off one of the close-set alley walls. He rebounded toward the other wall and zigzagged up, rising higher with each step. He soared over Strike, and by the time he passed over Rock, he was at least ten meters in the air. With a front flip, he dropped to the ground and tumbled forward, launching into a sprint.

"He just ran up the walls," Rock said, his mouth hanging low. "That's not possible."

"Come on," Strike said. They raced out of the alley, turning to follow in pursuit.

The thief tore past a row of towering apartments, all covered in grime and moon dust. He turned into another alley. When Strike caught up, he craned his neck to gape at the thief, who was scampering up the side of the building, scrabbling at narrow ledges in the brickwork. With a great leap, he vaulted to an open window ledge and caught it with the tips of his fingers, pulling himself in.

Rock stood next to Strike, both struggling to catch their breath. "We lost him," Rock said.

"You stay here and make sure he doesn't drop back out one of those windows. I'm going in." Strike headed toward the front steps of the building.

"What should I do if he comes back out this way?"

"Yell for me." Strike tried the main door, but it was locked. He kicked it in frustration.

Then a screech pierced the air, followed by the sounds of a scuffle. He took a step back as footsteps grew louder.

The door burst open, a man yelling about an intruder in the building as he ran out. Strike slipped in.

On the second-floor landing, the thief spotted Strike and tore up the central spiraling staircase. He put distance between him and Strike, racing faster than Strike had thought possible. He took the steps four at a time, only needing three giant jumps to make it up each flight of stairs. Up they went, higher and higher, ascending the thirty stories at a dizzying speed.

Strike's heart pounded, and pain seared his legs and chest. He finally had to stop at the twenty-fifth floor, gasping for breath. But the thief was trapped. Already at the thirtieth floor, he pounded at the locked door leading to roof access. There was no way out.

Taking it one slow step at a time, Strike kept his eyes trained on the thief. "Someone help me," he called out. "Please. Miners together."

Slowly, a door opened. "Strike?" a man said. "Is that you?"

"Yeah. And we have to stop that thief." He jabbed a finger at the boy, who now stood at the top of the stairs, his fists raised, ready to fight.

To Strike's relief, a man stepped out of his apartment. "Let's get him. Miners together."

"Miners forever," Strike said, a surge of pride rising in his chest.

Another door opened, and two more guys came out to

join them. "Miners together."

"Miners forever," everyone said in unison.

Over the years, Strike had repeated the mantra of the Taiko Miners over and over, but this time filled him with more love for his hometown than ever. The people of Taiko Colony were standing behind him, no matter the risk. Strike made his way up the last flights with a posse of a dozen men and women.

"Give back the money," Strike called out. "I won't get the Blackguard involved. We just want justice. You can't steal from a Miner." It was crazy to think of Torch as a Miner instead of a Flamethrower, but he now wore a blue Taiko Colony jumpsuit. And Miners had to look after their own.

The thief tried to back up at the sight of the growing crowd, but he was at a dead end. He pulled his jumpsuit hood even lower over his face. He cracked his knuckles.

Strike held up a cautious hand. The staircase was narrow enough to force the posse to head up only two at a time. They'd eventually overwhelm the thief due to sheer numbers, but a few hard kicks could inflict serious damage, even send someone over a railing, plummeting thirty floors to their death. Hardly anyone in Taiko Colony had the money to go to Salaam Colony's hospital, so Strike had to be careful to not put anyone in harm's way.

Strike charged up the final flight, screaming, "Miners

together!" He bounded up the last steps and lunged, and grabbed nothing but air.

The thief had swung himself over the railing.

Strike leaned over, watching in horror as the thief plunged to a certain death. But five floors down, he caught a foot on a ledge, slowing his fall. He kicked off other railings as he fell, managing the huge drop as if he had somehow lowered gravity. By the ground floor, he caught a step and pulled himself onto the stairs. He crashed into four guys blocking his way, bowling them over as he scrambled toward the front door. Two more guys charged at the thief, but he spun around and shot between their legs.

Strike tore down, stealing glances at people tackling the thief. Even with the kid's incredible agility and speed, he couldn't fight the sheer numbers, more and more men piling into the scrum. By the time Strike ran all the way down the flights of stairs, the thief was pinned, his wrists and ankles held tight. Strike yelled to Rock to come into the building.

One guy nudged Strike, his forehead creased with deep lines. "The Blackguard is going to come, aren't they?"

With all the noise, it was a pretty good bet that the cops would show. The Blackguard never missed a chance to remind people who was in charge—and to extract their bribes. "Someone help me tie him up," Strike said. "Everyone else go hide."

A guy raced into his apartment for rope, and people

tied the thief's kicking feet together before binding his wrists behind his back.

"Thanks for all the help," Strike said. "Miners together."

"Miners forever," came back the chant. People high-fived each other and slapped Strike on the back before scuttling away to their apartments and shutting the doors.

Rock pushed his way through the thinning crowd. "Are you okay?"

"Fine." Strike dug through the thief's jumpsuit pockets and yanked out a wad of bills, holding it up. He shoved it into his own pocket for safekeeping. "I can't believe one of Taiko Colony's own would steal."

"He's not from Taiko Colony," Rock said. He leaned over and brushed the back of the guy's jumpsuit. "He's in disguise. This jumpsuit isn't actually blue."

"It isn't?" Strike kneeled to look more carefully in the dim red emergency lighting. "You're right."

Rock wiped a layer of dirty blue powder off the thief's jumpsuit. "It's white underneath." He consulted his notebook, his face going pale.

"What?" Strike said. Ever since the very first moon colonies three hundred years ago, every colony was assigned its own distinctive jumpsuit color. "No one has white jumpsuits."

Rock stepped nervously away from the thief. "Dark Siders do."

Wild pictures flashed through Strike's head, of all the urban myths he had heard about the Dark Siders. Over the decades, waves of disgruntled people had left the United Moon Colonies for the uncharted Dark Side of the moon. No one had heard from any of them since. Everyone on the moon was dark-skinned, after centuries of people from different races living together, but the Dark Siders were rumored to have gone ghostly white. At least once a year, stories circulated about Dark Side phantoms appearing out of nowhere and disappearing into thin air.

Strike's hand trembled as he reached for the thief's hood. He yanked it back, tensing against the horror of the ghoul's pale face. But a shock of straight black hair flopped out. The guy's skin was even darker than Strike's and Rock's. "Hey," Strike said. "You don't look any different than us."

"Except that he's . . ." Rock pointed at the thief's high cheekbones and shoulder-length hair. "Sorry, I meant, except that *she's* a girl."

"Cut me loose right now and I won't hurt either of you," she said.

"Hurt us?" Rock said. "You're in no position to make threats. The Blackguard are likely on their way, and they'll escort you to Han-Shu Prison."

"Prison?" She snorted. "How am I going to help you win the Ultrabowl if I'm in prison?"

Strike froze. "What did you just say?"

"You heard me. You need a new rocketback 1, Strike. You need me."

A guy leaned out of his apartment. "Strike! Cops are coming." He slammed his door. A dead bolt slid into place. Other doors also closed, steel locks scraping shut.

Strike gaped at the girl. "How do you know who I am? You know about Ultraball?"

"Of course. Everyone on the Dark Side watches. We're not Earthers, with our heads stuck in the sand."

"Why didn't you just come to tryouts if you want to play?"

"Would you really have given a Dark Sider a shot?"

She was right. The twenty-one colonies were rapidly diverging after Earthfall, but one thing they still had in common was the legends of the Dark Siders. The first one ever to return, showing up out of nowhere? She would have been stopped at any airlock, maybe even thrown into prison for questioning. "Why do you want to play?"

"You're up against Raiden Zuna," the girl said.

Strike and Rock looked at each other. "How did you know that?" Strike said.

"Everyone knows about the bet Zuna made with Taiko Colony's governor. The Miners winning the Ultrabowl would stick it to Zuna. Bad. I want in on that."

"Why?"

"His alliance has been explosion mining and blast

fracking on the Dark Side, trying to steal our precious reserves of buried ice. He's already killed ten people." The girl's lips pulled back into a snarl. "I have to stop him."

Strike gawked at her. *Raiden Zuna, killing Dark Siders?* That was crazy talk. Although most of the moon's twenty-one elected Colony Governors were shady—especially Zuna—there was no way any of them would have done these kinds of things. But if she could help Strike finally win the Ultrabowl title he so desperately needed, who cared if she was insane?

He turned to Rock. "What do you think?"

Rock studied her, his forehead furrowed. "Miners fans aren't going to like having an outsider on their team. And a Dark Sider? People will protest. It might not even be legal." He pinched his lips tight. "It's a tremendous risk. But the potential payoff is also tremendous." He hesitated before nodding. "We should at least try her out."

Footsteps outside drew nearer as Strike's mind raced. He tugged at the knot around her ankles. He motioned for Rock to get her wrists. "Follow my lead," Strike hissed to her.

They finished loosening her bonds just before two policemen in black jumpsuits barged through the front door. Both wielded thick nightsticks, their faces shrouded by riot gear helmets. "Hands up," one said. He motioned to his partner. "Cuff 'em. Dirty little thieves."

Strike froze. In the shadows, the cops hadn't recognized

him yet. In the past three years of Ultraball stardom, he had gotten used to being left alone by the Blackguard. He had forgotten what it had been like to be pushed around by cops whose power was becoming virtually unlimited. "We didn't do anything, Officer."

One of the policemen approached. "Strike? Is that really you?" He pointed to the girl, two ropes at her feet. "Filthy frakkin' scum. Hand over what you stole and I won't break your face. Yet."

"She's okay," Strike said. "The thief ran out. We didn't see which way."

"Who's this, then?"

"Just a friend," Strike said, with a shrug. He stole a glance at Rock, who was sweating, his nervous glances bouncing back and forth between the Blackguards and the girl. Rock might have been a genius, but everyone could read his face.

One of the Blackguards stared Rock down. "Why do you look so worried?" he asked. He took out his nightstick and pressed the tip of it into Rock's chest.

"Who, me?" Rock said, his voice rising. "I'm not nervous. Nothing to lie about. I'm definitely not lying."

The policeman shoved the girl. "Turn around. Hands behind your back." He patted her down, searching through her pockets, coming up empty. He scowled and motioned to Strike and Rock. "You two. Hands behind your backs."

Strike turned around, squeezing his eyes shut as he remembered Torch's money in his pocket. Why hadn't he hidden the wad of cash? After all this, the Blackguards would walk off with Torch's twenty-six U-bucks.

The policeman stuck a hand into Strike's jumpsuit pockets. But the Blackguard just continued along, patting Strike down to his feet. "Nothing."

"Nothing on Rock, either," the other Blackguard said. "God, I hate Taiko Colony duty. Even the Ultraball stars have no money. Worthless little turds." Without a warning, he whirled and thwacked the girl in the stomach with his nightstick. She doubled over, howling in pain.

The Blackguard drew his arm back to smash Rock, but his partner stopped him. "Leave these two alone," the second officer said. "I got fifty U-bucks riding on the Miners winning the Ultrabowl. Three-to-one odds—that's going to pay off big-time." He jammed the end of his nightstick into Strike's chest. "You're also the QB of my fantasy Ultraball team. So I'm expecting lots of TDs out of you. Got it?"

Strike held his breath as he stared at the club pressing into his ribs. He nodded.

The Blackguard kicked the girl in the side, her groans echoing in the staircase. He pointed to Strike and Rock. "Even Ultraball stars aren't untouchable. The Blackguard is watching you." The two of them left, slamming the front door shut.

Strike and Rock kneeled by the girl. "Are you okay?" Strike asked.

Curled up in the fetal position, she stole a glance at the door. Her moaning slowly morphed into chuckles. Soon, she was laughing.

"What's so funny?" Rock asked. He pulled out his notebook and flipped through the pages and pages of jokes, studying them intently.

Leaning forward, the girl spit onto the ground. Out came a wad of bills.

Strike scooped up the pile. "Torch's money?" He shoved it all into his pocket before she could steal it again.

"You ought to be more careful with your cash," the girl said with a shrug.

"You pickpocketed Strike after we untied you?" Rock asked.

She nodded.

"How are you not hurt?" Rock asked. "That Blackguard walloped you."

"I was lucky it was in the stomach," she said. "A thousand sit-ups a day builds up your muscles."

"All that moaning and groaning was fake?"

"You can do all kinds of things when someone thinks they've got the upper hand." She opened her hand to display a badge.

"Is that his ID badge?" Strike said, his jaw hanging low. "You stole a Blackguard's ID badge? Are you insane?

He'll kill you."

"It'll be hours before he notices. I'm gonna go take a few things from the Blackguard storehouses and then leave his badge back here. He'll think he dropped it."

"What if he finds out?" Rock asked. "Blackguards aren't afraid to use force. Deadly force."

"Not against the Taiko Miners' new rocketback 1." She gave him a sly grin.

Strike studied her. "We still have to try you out, you know."

"You really think I won't make it?"

Strike nodded warily. "Okay. Eight a.m. at Taiko Arena. We'll work out for an hour before my two crackbacks show up at nine."

"Got it. Now if you don't mind, I have shopping to do. There are some big-ticket electronic items I've had my eye on over in Saladin Colony." She made her way down the stairs.

"How are you going to get into Saladin Colony?" Rock said. "You can't just walk through the Tunnel Ring and knock on the airlock."

"There's a saying we have: Dark Siders cast no shadows." The girl shot Rock a roguish look over her shoulder as she broke into a jog.

"Wait," Strike said. "What's your name? And we'll have to give you a good Ultraball nickname, too." One of the best things about Ultraball was coming up with awesome player names. Shinzo Sazaki had been just another orphan at the overcrowded Tao Children's Home, but once he had transformed himself into Strike, everyone on the entire moon knew his name.

"Give me an Ultraball name after you see what I can do," the girl said. She tucked the stolen ID badge into her jumpsuit pocket and took off, vanishing into the dim lights of the moon's artificial night.

5

CRACKBACKS 1 AND 2

THE DARK SIDER thief still refused to tell Strike her real name, but she earned her Ultraball name during her first play inside Taiko Arena. Sealed into an Ultrabot suit, she lined up with Rock defending her, twenty steps away. She raced forward with the ball, building up an incredible head of steam. Rock squatted and charged to meet her, but she smashed into him with a staggering *boom*. Rock went flying, skidding along the ground, toppling into one of the deep field pits.

Strike rushed to his rocketback 2 and crouched over him. "Are you okay?"

"What a hit." Rock flipped his visor to clear, his eyes in a daze. He clawed his way out of the trench. "Good thing

I'm protected by impactanium armor."

Strike offered him a hand and watched the girl, who had raced all the way to the end zone and was doing a touchdown dance. Although he still didn't know if he could ever trust a Dark Sider, there was no doubt that she was incredibly talented. "Looks like we might have ourselves an RB1," he said through the suit's comm system. "Get back here, Boom."

"Boom?" the girl said. She flipped her visor to clear, a smile on her face. "I like that."

"Let's see how you do with some basic plays. And let's work on your touchdown dance before our crackbacks get here."

"What's wrong with my touchdown dance?" She stuck her hand into the air and waved it around as she high-stepped in a tight circle. "Dark Siders know how to dance."

"Touchdown dances are meant to charge up the crowd," Strike said. "Not make them think you're hallucinating from dust poisoning."

Her eyebrows pinched together. "You don't hallucinate from dust poisoning."

"She is correct," Rock said. "I think what Strike meant to say was, 'Not make them think you're hallucinating from dust *dementia*.'"

"Yeah, that," Strike said.

"It's funny because it exaggerates how strange your

dancing looks," Rock said. He launched into a torrent of laughter, but it quickly died out as the girl stared him down.

"You're seriously making a joke out of that?" she said. "Out of *dust poisoning*?" She stuck a finger into Strike's chest. "Dust poisoning is a very serious disease. Do you know how many people die of it every year? Last year alone, the death toll—including both the United Moon Colonies and the Federation of Free Territories—was five hundred fifty-one people. That's about half a percent of the moon's total population."

"Oh. Sorry. I didn't mean to . . ." Strike looked to Rock for help, but his rocketback 2 looked as confused and horrified as Strike felt.

The girl cracked a smile. "Just messing with you." She waved the ball into the air as she shook her butt at them.

Strike nudged Rock. "What's the Federation of Free Territories? And what the frak is she doing? She looks ridiculous."

"Must be what the Dark Siders call their nation," Rock said. "And she looks pretty good to me." His face went red and he flipped his visor back to reflective mode. "Her touchdown dance, I meant. That's all. Nothing more. Let's get in some more reps before our backcracks arrive. I mean, our crackbacks."

Strike was too nervous to laugh at Rock, his stomach flip-flopping at the thought of how Pickaxe was going to react to Boom. Pickaxe was fiercely loyal to his teammates, but he hardly trusted hardly anyone else. With so much rumor and fear surrounding the legends of the Dark Siders, there was no way Pickaxe would accept Boom as a teammate. It didn't help that Pickaxe had been pushing Strike to give him a shot at the star rocketback 1 spot. To get beat out by a Dark Sider was sure to rankle him but good.

"Line it up," Strike said. "Let's see how you do with some simple pass routes. Pretend it's fourth down. Give Rock a juke and then take sideline or fly. Whatever he gives you."

"If I give her anything," Rock said.

"Oh, I'll get open," Boom said. "I'm gonna put ten points on the board so quick your helmet will short-circuit." She raised her arms in a victory pose. "Boom saves the day, on fifth down."

Rock paused. "I had assumed you knew the rules. But perhaps we should go over them. Touchdowns are seven points, not ten. There is no such thing as a fifth down." His forehead wrinkled up. "And Ultrabot suit helmets don't short-circuit."

"I think she was just kidding around again," Strike said.

Boom smiled. "I brushed up on Ultraball rules last night. Doesn't take a rocket scientist to understand the rule book."

"Yes, but it's important to understand the nuances," Rock said.

"What nuances?" Boom said. "All five players have to play every single down. Four downs to score, or you turn it over. Seven points a touchdown. Easy as that."

"No, Rock is right," Strike said. "There are other things you have to know. Like when you tackle someone in their own end zone—"

"You score seven points," Boom said. "Just like when you stuffed Fusion in his own end zone during last year's Ultrabowl. Eighth play of the game. Man, that was an impressive hit. He almost wiggled out of your grasp, but you turned him upside down and pile-drove his helmet straight into the turf."

"Huh," Strike said. "You've done your homework. I doubt anyone but Rock would remember what play of the game that was. Right, Rock?"

Rock stared off at the roof. "Yes, I suppose Ultrabot suits could short-circuit."

"What?" Strike said.

"A big enough electromagnetic explosion could short out an Ultrabot suit. Now, how big would that explosion have to be?"

Strike rolled his eyes. "Let's just line it up for the next play."

"Couldn't I just run a couple of quick calculations?" Rock asked.

"No," Strike and Boom said at the same time. They grinned at each other.

Strike got over the Ultraball, and Boom lined up to the far left. Rock jogged over to cover Boom, crouching down.

"This is gonna be an easy six points," Boom said.

Rock straightened up. "It's not possible to score six points. All touchdowns are seven—"

"Hike!" Strike shouted. He grabbed the Ultraball and backpedaled as Boom took off like a shot. She caught Rock off guard, but he jumped back into action, jamming her as she streaked by. Swiveling, he chased her in hot pursuit.

Boom accelerated, shifting her angle, heading straight toward a deep field pit at the thirty-five-meter line. It was a curving trench that wound back and forth in an irregular pattern, giving Rock a huge advantage since he had practiced around it all preseason. But Boom danced back and forth along its edge, barely staying ahead of Rock. Toward the end of the trench, it looked like she was going to fall in. But with a hard jab step, she kicked off the side of the pit and threw herself high into a backward spin, hurdling into the air, head over heels. Unable to stop his momentum quickly enough, Rock raced right underneath her.

Boom hit the turf hard, but she popped up, breaking into a sprint toward the far corner of the end zone. Strike reared back and threw a bullet of a pass, aiming two meters above her helmet. She didn't have to break stride or even adjust her path as the ball roared in. Reaching up with both hands, the ball smacked into her magnetized gloves, its momentum whipping her forward into a hard spin, sending her bouncing along the turf. Strike had put everything he had on the pass, too hot for many rocketbacks to handle. But Boom held on tight, hauling the ball safely into her chest plate as she tumbled along the ground.

"Watch the one-meter pit!" Strike yelled into the helmet comm.

Just before crossing the goal line, Boom plummeted into a camouflaged hole, disappearing through the trapdoor with a thud.

Almost perfect, Strike thought wistfully. He shouldn't have gotten his hopes up so high. No one could do it all on just their second play inside an Ultrabot suit.

Rock raced in, leaping into the pit to smother Boom and end the play. But as he dropped in, Boom came shooting out of the trapdoor. She smashed into him with a clang. Rock yelled in surprise as he flew up off his feet. The two of them tangled in midair, exchanging a barrage of explosive punches, blue gloves flashing in a dazzling array of speed and power. For a second, it looked like Rock would crack the ball loose, but as they fell, Boom crunched a boot into Rock's chest plate. In that split second of freedom, she lurched over the goal line and smacked the Ultraball down into the end zone. "Eight points!" she yelled.

From the ground, Rock propped himself up onto his elbows and flipped his visor to clear. "It's not possible to score eight points . . . ah, another joke." He cocked his head. "Right?"

"You don't think I deserve an extra point for all that work?" Boom asked.

"There are no extra points in Ultraball. Didn't I already say that it's just seven points for a touchdown . . ." He trailed off as Boom chuckled good-naturedly through her clear visor. He turned to Strike. "I really need to write these jokes down. Please?"

"Later," Strike said. He studied Boom's mischievous grin. "I have a feeling there will be plenty more, anyway."

Strike had them run all their simple plays, from slingshot Vs to passing routes where Strike ricocheted the Ultraball off a protective barrier at tough angles. Boom beat Rock almost every time. Even though Rock was an experienced defender, Boom put on a showstopping array of jukes, dives, and jumps off Strike's back to make Rock miss over and over again. It wasn't until the last play that Rock took her down for a loss, anticipating a spin move and latching on to her leg armor with a glove electromagnet.

"Okay, genius," Boom said from the turf. She flipped her visor from reflective to clear. "How'd you know I was going to cut left?"

"I based my guess on emerging patterns. When you

lead with your right foot, there's almost a two-thirds chance that you'll ultimately go left. I went with the odds."

"Huh." She grabbed Rock's outstretched hand. "Maybe this kid's not so weird after all."

Rock looked to Strike. "Can I click out of my suit now, so I can catalog and analyze all of Boom's statistics?"

"Okay, maybe he *is* weird," Boom muttered. But she shot Rock a crooked smile.

Rock reddened. Before he could say anything, one of the airlock doors opened, and two boys bounded in. "Remember, don't tell Pickaxe you're a Dark Sider just yet," Strike said over the helmet comm.

"This is insulting," Boom said. "Shouldn't your crackback 1 want to play with the best teammates possible, no matter where they're from?"

"Yeah," Strike said. "But you gotta admit, there's a lot of questions about the Dark Siders. Pickaxe isn't the only person who's going to be suspicious. Can't you just tell us a little more? Like how many Dark Siders there are in that Federation of Free Territories you mentioned?"

Rock leaned in to whisper. "There are approximately ten thousand people living on the Dark Side."

Boom narrowed her eyes. "How'd you know that?"

"You said there were five hundred fifty-one deaths from dust poisoning last year, and that was about half a percent of the moon's total population," Rock said. "Given that there are about one hundred thousand people in the UMC, the rest of the math is easy."

"Huh," Boom said, looking off into the distance. "So it is. Easy."

"Uh, yeah, easy," Strike said. He wasn't sure he could do that math even with the help of Copernicus College's supercomputers. "Just tell us a little more about the Dark Side."

She shook her head. "The only thing that matters is that I will win you an Ultrabowl."

"I have to agree with Boom," Rock said. "The facts are clear. She represents our best chance of winning the Ultrabowl, no matter if she's a Dark Sider or a girl or an outsider or what."

"So you don't care that I'm a girl?" Boom asked.

"No. Wait. Yes." Rock gulped. "What's the right answer to your question?"

Two dark-skinned boys bounded in from the entrance, a tiny one and his taller older brother. Pickaxe and Nugget had been Strike's two crackbacks for three years now, all of them having started as Ultraball rookies at the same time. Along with Rock and TNT, they had been the Fireball Five, nicknamed after the Fireball Blast mine explosion that killed all their fathers and two of their mothers. The Fireball Five had gone to the Ultrabowl in their first year, an astounding feat for a team of five rookies. Reaching the next two Ultrabowls as well, they deserved a place in history. But just like Torch knew all too well, no one cared about the losers.

Pickaxe ran a hand through his short black mohawk as he eyed Boom. "You give any more thought to my idea?" he asked Strike.

Strike unlatched his helmet, the dome rising and over his head. He locked eyes with Pickaxe, hoping he would sound believable. "I can't move you to rocketback, because you're too valuable at crackback 1. You got my blind side."

"Don't you think we need a star rocketback more? I can do this, Strike. I'm your man."

"I need you keeping me safe. There's nothing scarier to a QB than a blind-side hit. You're my enforcer. My muscle. Without you at crackback, the Miners are going nowhere fast."

Pickaxe grinned. "Guess I'll have to stick to crackback 1, then, right, little bro?" He grabbed Nugget, shoving his armpit into his little brother's face. "What's that? I can't hear you."

Nugget slapped at his brother's hands, his face turning red as he slithered his way out of his brother's grasp. "You suck. And you smell like you've been swimming inside one of Guoming Colony's waste recyclers. And eating out of it, too."

"I'd shower more often if a certain little turd eater didn't steal my assigned bathroom time slots."

"You'd still stink even if you showered every day." His eyes squeezed shut, Nugget rubbed his face with both palms. "You burned away most of my nose hairs."

"Lemme get the rest of them for you." Pickaxe aimed his butt at Nugget before tensing up and ripping a fart. He burst into laughter as his brother gagged and punched at him.

Strike cracked up at the brothers. "All right, Pickaxe," he said. "Cut it out before you take a dump on his head."

"You need to check your jumpsuit," Nugget said, swatting at his brother's butt. "Something that smells that bad has to be solid."

Strike's nose wrinkled as the stench hit him. "Or liquid. Seriously, Pickaxe, there's something wrong with you." He pulled his helmet down, smiling both at Nugget's look of disgust and the fact that his Ultrabot suit's air filter had kicked on. "Come on, suit up already."

Pickaxe and Nugget went to the sideline to get into their Ultrabot suits. "Okay, Boom," Strike said. "Show Pickaxe and Nugget what you can do. Everyone, line it up. Sideline left, fake fly, cut in." A standard play, no flips or superjumps or anything, but a solid performance by Boom would start winning over Pickaxe.

"Line me up on the other side, Strike," Pickaxe said. "Give me a shot at the RB1 spot. Come on."

It made no sense, but Pickaxe was one of the Fireball Five, one of his sworn brothers.

"Okay," Strike said. "One play to show me what you can do. Sideline right for Pickaxe. Boom, cut over for a lateral after Pickaxe makes the catch."

"Really?" Pickaxe said. "All right!"

"Lemme defend him," Nugget said, jogging over to guard his brother. "Please?"

"Let him, Strike," Pickaxe said. "I'll flick the little man away like he was a dingleberry hanging off my butthole."

"Got some serious dingleberry problems, do you?" Nugget said, frowning with mock sympathy.

"Okay, you two, get to the line," Strike said with a grin. The brothers' never-ending stream of smack talk always kept things fun. Strike engaged his glove electromagnets and grabbed the solid steel ball as everyone lined up into their positions. "On two. Hut hut!"

Pickaxe immediately got jammed by his brother, Nugget digging in to drive Pickaxe backward. Strike could almost see the glee on the short boy's face. In an ideal world, Strike would have made Nugget his crackback 1, but that might have pissed off Pickaxe to the point of quitting.

"Stop it," Pickaxe said, swatting and punching at his brother. "Give me a chance to make my move."

"How about I give you a chance to smell my butt?" Nugget said.

"Let him through," Strike said.

"Fine," Nugget said. The play was busted, as Pickaxe

was way behind where he was supposed to be, but Strike tossed him an easy floater anyway. The brothers' legs tangled, and Pickaxe tripped.

Nugget vaulted over his brother. "Interception coming up," he said.

Cutting in, Boom pumped her arms, getting her Ultrabot suit to full speed. She charged toward the Ultraball, still high in the air.

"Oh no you don't," Nugget said. "That's mine."

Boom jumped early, vaulting high toward the ball. Caught off guard, Nugget leapt as well, but Boom sailed higher, easily twenty meters into the air. She snagged the ball as Nugget tackled her legs. But with a snakelike twist, Boom writhed out of Nugget's grasp. On the way down, she grabbed his wrist and whipped him around, smashing him into Rock, who had been charging in. As she landed, she took off in a burst of speed. By the time she crossed the end zone, she had left everyone in the dust.

"Dang, what a play," Strike said, racing in.

"Got a hand from Nugget," Boom said. She hit him playfully on the wrist she had grabbed.

Rock burst into gunfire laughter, making Boom flinch. "Are you okay?" she asked. "Seriously, what's with that laugh?"

"I'm better than okay," Rock said. "That's such a great joke. I have to write it down." His helmet clicked, popping up with a hiss.

"Hey!" Strike said. "We've talked about this a hundred times. Write it down later. I never want to see anyone out of their suit while on the field, even if it is just practice." During games, a player getting out of their Ultrabot suit on the field resulted in an automatic forfeit.

"But it'll only take a second," Rock said.

"No."

"What if I forget the joke?"

"I'm sure she'll have more," Strike said. "Okay, everyone, let's line it up and work through our playbook. Nice try, Pickaxe, but I really do need you at crackback."

"I didn't really want to play RB1, anyway," Pickaxe grumbled. "Everyone knows that the most important position on the field is crackback 1."

"Except for quarterback," Nugget said. "And rocketback 1. Rocketback 2, too. Oh, and crackback 2, of course."

"You are so dead." Pickaxe charged at his snickering brother.

"All right, you two," Strike said with a grin. "Let's run through the playbook."

Strike marveled at Boom, who seemed to get more out of her Ultrabot suit with each play. In just a few hours, she had proven herself to be an offensive battlefield weapon, and she was even better on defense. Manning up against Rock, it was all Rock could do to make any positive gain against her. She tackled him for losses on several sweeps and darts, even hiding in a field pit once, leaping out to surprise tackle him.

"Nice hits," Pickaxe said to Boom as practice ended and they got out of their Ultrabot suits. "You sent Rock flying so many times. Just think of what you could have done against my little bro here. You would have crushed him into moon dust."

For once, Nugget didn't send a snappy comeback his brother's way, his excitement bubbling over. "We're going all the way, Strike," he said. "We got ourselves a game changer." He stepped out of his leg panels and went over to Boom. "This is our year to raise that Ultrabowl trophy, now that we have a new star rocketback."

"There's just one thing," Strike said. He cleared his throat. "Boom is . . . she's from . . ." Taking a deep breath, he bit his lip. "She's a Dark Sider."

Pickaxe's chuckles died out as he studied Strike's somber face. He pushed Nugget protectively behind him, putting up his fists. "You seriously a Dark Sider? You got dark face paint on or something?"

Boom raised her hands, her eyes narrowing with laser focus. "I am displeased with your doubt. I call upon my Dark Side voodoo to curse you." She howled, making Pickaxe flinch.

After Boom rolled her eyes, Nugget broke into peals of laughter. "You should have seen your face. You thought she was going to curse you."

"I'll curse *you*," Pickaxe mumbled. "Strike. You gotta be insane. We can't have a Dark Sider on the team."

"She may be a Dark Sider," Strike said. "But Boom smacked you down. Big-time. What other choice do we have?"

"Great," Boom said. "So I'm your last choice, am I?"

"That's not what I meant," Strike said. He kicked himself inside for being such a moron. "You're great. Without you, we don't stand a chance. You'll get used to Pickaxe. He's solid. Loyal. Great teammate, once he gets to trust you."

Pickaxe shook his head. "Trust a Dark Sider? Never gonna happen. Come on, Strike. We're already the butt of the league after last year's Ultrabowl. I can barely take all the taunting."

Strike squeezed his eyes shut. The horrible memory of TNT throwing the game haunted him every night, TNT letting himself be smothered by Neutron defenders to end the game.

"Guys from Cryptomare Colony came in last week, delivering tunneling equipment," Pickaxe said. "Do you know how much crap Nugget and I caught from them? We got crap from Molemen fans. From *Molemen* fans. The Molemen would be a better team if they put empty Ultrabot suits on the field. We're the biggest joke in the entire league. What are people going to say when they find out we have a frakkin' Dark Sider on the team?"

"What did people say about having an eight-year-old on an Ultraball team?" Strike asked, pointing to Nugget. "What did people say when I skipped over three solid recruits to take you? And did you forget about when the *SmashMouth Radio Blitz* guys started calling you Axepicker?"

The nickname—a play on words, as in someone "picking their axe"—had almost broken Pickaxe. He stared at the ground, scowling at the memory.

"Berzerkatron and the Mad Mongol rode you hard," Strike said. "You nearly crumbled. But I stood by you. We all did. Fireball Five forever. I don't care what anyone outside this arena thinks. Only one thing matters: finally winning the Ultrabowl."

Pickaxe lifted his eyes at Boom, studying her. "She's awful thin. My aunt Keiko looks stronger than her, and Auntie ain't doing so hot. You think she can make it through an entire Ultraball season?"

"I know she can," Strike said. "Look at your little brother's stick arms. And you know how good he is."

"Hey, I got muscles," Nugget said. "Check out the gun show, baby." He raised a tiny bicep and pumped it.

"When are you going to start flexing?" Boom asked.

Rock howled with a salvo of gunfire laughter, scribbling away into his notebook. Even Pickaxe had to turn away to suppress a smile.

Nugget strained even harder, turning red. "Gun. Show. Baby!"

"Quit that before you pass out," Strike said. "Look, Pickaxe. Boom has what it takes to be a rocketback[1]. She can take us all the way to our first Ultrabowl victory. All of us raising that trophy, together. That's the only thing that matters."

Pickaxe slumped over and groaned, but Nugget cautiously walked over to Boom. After a long moment studying her, he raised a hand for a high five. "Welcome to the team," he said.

She slapped his palm. "Thanks. You're going to open up holes for me?"

"Oh yeah," Nugget said. "I'm the best crackback[2] in the entire league. Just ask Tombstone. And Rattler. And Meltdown. I've put them all down so hard they've left butt-shaped craters on the field. You watch any of my film yet?"

"Not yet," Boom said. "I have a lot of catching up to do. I'll need help."

"I'll help," Nugget and Rock said at the same time. They turned away from each other, stealing looks at Boom with awkward grins.

"Whoa, whoa, whoa," Pickaxe said. "Don't you guys understand? Dark Siders hate the UMC. Bunch of frakkin' traitors. Deserters. She's probably a spy."

Boom's eyes narrowed. Her hands slowly squeezed into fists, her knuckles cracking. "I'm no spy," she said.

"Then why are you really here?" Pickaxe said. "First

Dark Sider ever to return? Has to be more behind it than just playing Ultraball."

"I'm here to win an Ultrabowl."

"How did you even sneak into Taiko Colony?" Pickaxe said. "How many Dark Siders did you bring with you?" He shook his head. "She's probably planning on overthrowing the UMC. Or worse."

Boom folded her arms across her chest, glowering at Pickaxe. "I give you my word. This is no Dark Side plot. It's just me, and a few friends to look out for me. So no more questions."

"No more questions?" Pickaxe said. "Why? What the frak are you hiding?"

"Dark Siders respect everyone's privacy. That's why Dark Siders want nothing to do with the frakkin' UMC, always prying into everyone's business. How can you even bear to live in this police state?"

"It's not a police state," Strike said. He looked over to Rock. "What's a police state?"

"Remember what those guys said last night?" Boom asked. "The Blackguard is watching you. That's the very definition of a police state."

"She's right," Rock said. He glanced around before lowering his voice. "The UMC keeps close surveillance on everyone, in the name of public safety. And the rumors of the horrible things the Blackguard has done . . . I can sympathize with the Dark Siders' wish for something better."

"That's exactly right," Boom said. "Rock gets it. So no more questions. It should be enough that I'm going to help you win the Ultrabowl."

Pickaxe turned to Strike. "This is ridiculous. How is anyone supposed to trust someone we know nothing about? The Blackguard might even throw her in prison. We'd have to forfeit with just four players. Our fans are gonna riot."

Strike paused, letting Pickaxe's words sink in. Could Zuna pay off the Blackguard to arrest Boom? Or would they do it on their own, anyway? At the very least, there would be a ton of questions from reporters, insisting on answers. And would fans boycott the Miners? Even with the moon's Ultraball mania, the Taiko Miners lost a little money every year. If they started bleeding U-dollars, the Underground Ultraball League might even take away the franchise and move it to a richer colony.

He turned to the one person who could figure out these complicated issues. "Rock. What do you think?"

Rock stared at Boom in silence, his face tense with concentration.

"Fine," Boom said. "I'm leaving if you idiots can't see—"

"That your skills are already on par with Tombstone or Fang," Rock said. "That you might even become better than Chain Reaction by the end of the season. That although you have a menacing exterior, it's driven by your laser-like focus on victory. But above and beyond everything else, that you represent our one and only chance to win the Ultrabowl."

"Menacing?" She narrowed her eyes at Rock and laughed. "I like that."

Rock's forehead crinkled. "It wasn't meant to be a compliment."

"You are so weird," she said. "But a good kind of weird."

Strike let Rock's words sink in. As usual, his right-hand man was right. Winning an Ultrabowl title for his Miners was the only thing that mattered. "Okay. Boom's our new rocketback 1. Everyone in."

Everyone placed their hands atop Strike's. Pickaxe hesitated, but he finally joined.

"We start now," Strike said. "And we don't stop until we win the Ultrabowl. Miners together?"

"Miners forever," everyone said in unison.

"Until our fans boo us off the field," Pickaxe muttered under his breath.

Cryptomare Molemen

QB	Grinder
RB1	Dirtbag
RB2	Vacuum
CB1	Drill Bit
CB2	Junker

Farajah Flamethrowers

QB	Supernova
RB1	Afterburner
RB2	Firestorm
CB1	Asbestos
CB2	Inferno

Kamar Explorers

QB	Shootout
RB1	Tombstone
RB2	Lasso
CB1	Gunner
CB2	Scout

North Pole Neutrons

QB	Fusion
RB1	Chain Reaction
RB2	Meltdown
CB1	Radioactive
CB2	Ion Storm

Saladin Shock

QB	White Lightning
RB1	High Voltage
RB2	Live Wire
CB1	Electrocution
CB2	Discharge

Taiko Miners

QB	Strike
RB1	Boom
RB2	Rock
CB1	Pickaxe
CB2	Nugget

Tranquility Beatdown

QB	Destroyer
RB1	Uppercut
RB2	Hammer Fist
CB1	Chokehold
CB2	Takedown

Yangju Venom

QB	Serpent
RB1	Fang
RB2	Viper
CB1	Rattler
CB2	Toxin

GAME 1 VS. THE YANGJU VENOM

Strike rubbed his eyes as he kicked off his sheets. He looked across the room at Rock, who was sitting even more rigidly than usual on the grubby sofa. "You okay?" Strike asked.

"Do you need your six fifteen slot?" Rock said. He crossed his legs, rocking back and forth. "I may need to run outside and take my chances."

"Go ahead. I can wait." Everything on the moon had to be recycled or reused, especially fluids. If you couldn't bribe your way out of it, the penalty for peeing outside of a recycling unit was a day in Han-Shu Prison.

Rock jumped up and raced to the door. "Thanks. My detailed analysis is on the table." He yanked open the door and sprinted down the hallway toward the waste collection room. Even though it was early, the sounds of sports talk radio trickled in from the hallway, so much of it still speculating about Boom.

Getting to his feet, Strike made his way through the small room packed with their few pieces of furniture. On their table were two sheets of paper, every square centimeter covered by miniature script. Strike grumbled as he squinted to read Rock's notes. Rock had uncovered all sorts of important things about the Neutrons' new defensive scheme, which *SmashMouth Radio Blitz* had nicknamed "Radioactive Waste."

Strike looked up when Rock came back. "Nice work," Strike said. "The only thing you missed is how many times Fusion takes a dump every day."

"I could make a guess. On average, I poop 1.2 times a day—"

"Never mind. Let's get ready. Big day ahead of us." He tossed a hardtack bar to Rock and gnawed on another one as he scanned through the second page of Rock's notes. "You find anything else on Boom? Or the Dark Siders in general?"

"Just historical records. The first wave of colonists left for the Dark Side one hundred six years ago, and there have been six more mass departures. But it's still a mystery as to exactly where any of them went, or how they survived. I can't even find anything about the Federation of Free

Territories that Boom mentioned. As for Boom . . ." Rock bit his lip. "I don't like spying on her. That's exactly what the Dark Siders hate."

"It's not spying. I just don't want to be in the dark. After what happened last year—"

A knock came at the door. Strike answered it. A group of five men with wavy black hair stood in the hallway, all in blue jumpsuits with Strike's number 8 decal stitched on. Behind them was Nadya from across the hall, wearing both Strike's number 8 decal as well as Rock's number 5.

"Mornin', Strike," the lead man said. "Ready for your escort?"

Strike groaned. It was Jamal, who lived a few doors down. He was always grilling Strike for information. "You sure this is necessary?"

"You guys have targets on your backs, especially now that you got a Dark Sider on the team. We need to make sure Raiden Zuna doesn't pull anything on the pride and joy of Taiko Colony." He scanned the ceiling and walls. "He might even be spying on you right now."

All the bodyguard stuff seemed unnecessary, but it was easier to just go along. Strike wolfed down the rest of his hardtack bar, the dry crumbles scratching his throat. He grabbed his bag. "I just have to wait for Rock's bathroom slot and then we can go."

"You can have mine," Jamal said. He leaned in. "You guys are going to kick the Venom's butt today, aren't you?

I got ten U-bucks on the Miners winning by more than twenty-eight points."

"Come on, Jamal," Nadya said. "You promised you'd leave him alone."

"Sorry," Jamal said. He leaned in to Strike. "But you'll crush them, won't you? By more than twenty-eight points?"

Strike turned away with a sigh. Every season, people pumped him for information. People bet their meager savings on anything and everything, even things as ridiculous as if there would be a repeat of the blackout during last year's Ultrabowl.

Another guy nudged Rock. "I drafted you for my fantasy team. Get an interception, okay?"

"Me?" Rock said. "You drafted *me*? Why? Did you have the last pick in your draft?"

"Well, yeah. But—"

"Look," Strike said. "I appreciate you guys coming along to protect us and all. But the only thing I can tell you is that the Miners are going to do our best to destroy the Venom today."

"But you'll destroy them by more than twenty-eight points, right?" Jamal asked.

"Seriously, shut up," Nadya said. She punched Jamal in the shoulder.

After Strike's pit stop in the waste collection room, the five men escorted them out the apartment building. It was weird to have a posse of bodyguards, people looking out for him. One of Strike's last memories of his parents bubbled up: his mom hugging him tightly as he cried out of fear and hunger, his beaten-up father racing in the door with a handful of stolen hardtack bars, telling them that they needed to hide. Bitter tears burned at Strike's eyes as he stomped the image back down into its dark corner.

Despite it being so early in the artificial morning that the roof lights were still dimmed throughout the massive cavern housing Taiko Colony, the streets were dotted with fans in blue jumpsuits. They clapped and cheered when Strike and Rock emerged. Strike waved to a group of kids he had known from the Tao Children's Home, who were now either working in the mines or begging on the streets. He pushed through the escort to say hi, but Nadya held him back. "Sorry, Strike. We can't take any chances. You never know who might be in Zuna's pocket."

Strike sighed but nodded.

The circle of people escorted them toward Taiko Colony's main airlock leading to the massive Tunnel Ring connecting the United Moon Colonies together. Along the way, adults and kids in mining gear turned out to root for the hometown heroes. "Win it all, Strike," one guy yelled. "You gotta keep Zuna out of Taiko Colony."

Strike's chest tightened. *Why does everyone have to put this on my shoulders?* he thought. *Governor Katana made the bet, not me.*

At the tram station outside Taiko Colony's airlock door, another group of five burly men in blue jumpsuits approached. They broke ranks, allowing Pickaxe and Nugget to emerge. "Strike!" Nugget said. He ran up and whispered, "That was so cool."

Strike mussed Nugget's hair. The boy's enthusiasm brought him back to the early days of his career, when the excitement of playing Ultraball was the only reason he couldn't sleep.

Boom was by herself, leaning on a tram marked with the shiny black-and-chrome Underground Ultraball League logo. She gave them all a short nod.

"Where's your escort?" Strike asked. "If any of us needs protection, it's you."

"I can take care of myself," Boom said. "And I told you, I got friends looking out for me." She glanced at Rock, and her stony glare melted for the briefest moment before hardening again. "Let's get going."

The Miners loaded up onto the Ultraball tram, outfitted to the max by the Underground Ultraball League. Fans waved at them from the station, with Jamal, Nadya, and the rest of the escort watching the crowd for any signs of Raiden Zuna's people. The tram shuddered as it lurched into motion, picking up speed along the Tunnel Ring. The *LunarSports Reports* pregame show played on a huge wall monitor. Rock had muted the sound, but Boom's picture was front and center. Ever since Strike had made the announcement about Boom joining the Miners, the speculation about her and the Dark Siders had continued nonstop.

As before every game, Rock presented his findings about the team they would face, giving a detailed overview about the Yangju Venom. By the time they arrived at Yangju Arena and unloaded their Ultrabot suits, Strike's head swam with information. "That's good for now," he said. "It's almost game time."

Rock flipped a page in his notebook. "But don't you want to hear about Serpent's tendencies to throw short against an atomic blitz if she's behind an invisibility zone?"

"Just remind me when it comes up. Bring it in, everyone." The Miners gathered around Strike inside the locker room. "We have a great game plan. Play loose and have fun. Let's start the season right by kicking some Venom butt."

Boom got to her feet. "They die out on the field today." She bounded down the corridor.

Everyone turned to stare at Strike. Boom's grim words felt off, but he shrugged, waving everyone ahead to follow her.

The Miners jogged out through a giant tunnel, entering Yangju Arena to heavy booing from the crowd decked out in the brown jumpsuits of Yangju Colony, some even holding up "DARK SIDER GO HOME" signs. People everywhere were glued to their phones, bouncing back and forth between *LunarSports Reports'* coverage and the actual game. There were some who even held up multiple phones.

Anger surged through Strike as the displays of riches slapped him in the face. Before Earthfall, everyone on the moon had been treated equally: every single person issued a standard package of essentials, including phone, watch monitor, and radio. But after that apocalyptic day, the moon's economy went berserk. People in colonies that produced less valuable resources had been forced to hock everything, just to buy hardtack bars and water. Yangju Colony, home of all the moon's livestock, was one of the lucky ones—kids in Yangju still had a shot at finishing high school, maybe even going on to Copernicus College. In the meantime, kids in Taiko Colony had no choice but to head for the mines or beg in the streets just to survive. Strike stored up his wrath over the unfairness of it all, preparing to unleash a storm of raw fury against the Yangju Venom.

Scanning the field, Strike focused on the five invisibility zones—twenty-meter circles projecting up blinding lights to overwhelm both human eyes and Ultrabot visual sensors. They made for a strong home-field advantage, players virtually disappearing inside. The Yangju Venom weren't a very good team, but they always used the invisibility zones in clever ways.

The Miners locked into their blue Ultrabot suits and lined up to receive the first kickoff of the 2352 Ultraball season. "Miners, let's go," Strike said. He stood close to one sideline, while Boom stood by the other. The remaining three Miners lined up ten meters in front of them, ready to form a wedge and block.

The head ref pushed a button on his chest plate armor, and a piercing whistle echoed throughout the stadium.

The five players in brown Ultrabot suits jogged forward, accelerating into a sprint. With a great swing, the Venom kicker slammed his foot into the ball, sending it soaring nearly fifty meters into the air.

Strike focused on the ball, arcing high, straight down the center of the field. He shifted over, never taking his eyes off it.

"Got it," Boom yelled over the helmet comm.

"I got it," Strike said. "Clear out."

"You clear out. I called it."

The ball headed directly toward one of the invisibility zones. It would cross through the giant cylinder of blazing light before dropping into catchable range. Edging around the perimeter of the invisibility zone, Strike ignored the warning lights flashing on his heads-up display and trusted his eyes. He focused on the Ultraball, ready to catch it in his gut like he had done a hundred times before. With some luck, he'd break a few tackles and be off to the races.

As he jogged sideways, he crunched into something: Boom.

"Move it," she yelled. "It's on my side of the field."

"I said, I got it." Strike shoved Boom to give himself space to make the catch. In that split second of inattention, he lost sight of the steel ball as it arced down into the invisibility zone, disappearing into the dazzling cylinder of light. He tensed to catch it, but it blipped out of the back edge of the invisibility zone sooner than he expected. It pinged off his chest plate before he could engage his glove electromagnets to lock on.

"Fumble!" the announcer yelled. The crowd let out an earsplitting roar as Strike scrambled for the ball.

Players from both teams came racing in. Strike chased the Ultraball as it bounced with erratic caroms off the turf, scooping it up near the back of their end zone. Spinning away from a Venom defender who had squirted through the blocking wedge in the confusion, Strike charged forward.

Another Venom defender raced in at an angle, getting a hand on Strike, but Boom threw herself at him, smashing the guy off his feet. Boom sprinted up the middle of the field, where the other Miners were in chaos, trying to block the Venom defenders. "Shield three," she yelled.

The Miners shifted to the right to form a wedge for Strike. With Rock at the front and Boom protecting Strike's side, the Miners charged up the field. A Venom player sprinted in like a cannonball, but Boom crunched into him. Strike stiff-armed another Venom defender and threw him to the ground. Crossing the fifty-meter line, Strike accelerated, the goal line in sight.

"Incoming," Boom said into the helmet comm.

Strike glanced over his shoulder at another defender closing the angle. He braced for impact as the Venom player charged in like a runaway mine car.

"Ground it!" Boom yelled.

Just as the defender launched himself high, Strike remembered Boom's signal. Throwing himself to the turf, he slid low, kicking up a trail of dust. The defender sailed above him, and Strike pushed his body down, just avoiding the defender's magnetized gloves.

Strike popped back into a full sprint, heading toward an invisibility zone. A Venom defender charged at him. Strike neared the edge of the invisibility zone just as the defender dove at him, flying in like a missile. But with a sudden stop, Strike leapt straight up in a twisting backflip, the defender sailing underneath him. Strike landed and bounced into the invisibility zone, with two other Miners trailing close behind.

Venom defenders raced in to cut Strike off at the other side of invisibility zone. Serpent, the Venom's QB, blasted full speed into Strike just as he emerged. She drove him sideways before leaping with him in her grasp, body-slamming him to the turf.

A gasp went up through the crowd.

Serpent jerked her head up, her gaze darting around the stadium. Then she pounded the black number 5 on the chest plate beneath her.

She had tackled Rock, not Strike.

By the time the defenders realized that Strike had been waiting inside the invisibility zone, playing possum as he pushed Rock out in his place, Strike had already snuck out the rear of the blinding spotlight and raced across the goal line for the score. He roared and spiked the ball.

A cannon sounded, and the scoreboard flashed "TOUCHDOWN: MINERS." On its feet, the small Miners section dressed in blue screamed and hollered. The rest of the stadium, filled with Venom fans, booed.

Pickaxe, Nugget, and Rock ran in to chest-bump Strike. *Perfect way to start the season*, he thought.

Boom jogged in. "What was that?"

"That's exactly what I was going to ask you," Strike said. "I told you I had it."

"I waved you off," Boom said. "The ball was on my side of the field."

"We're up 7–0. Let's just get ready for the next play, okay?"

Boom walked away, grumbling.

As the refs set up for the Miners' kickoff, Rock nudged Strike and pointed to the scoreboard, where a replay flashed. The Ultraball fell into the invisibility zone as

Strike and Boom bunched together, boxing each other out. Strike winced as he spotted where they were: clearly on Boom's side of the field.

"She was right," Rock said.

Strike let out a deep breath. What a jerk he had been—not only had he hijacked Boom's runback, but he hadn't said thanks for her big block, or for calling the ducking play for him. He had made a nice deception play inside the invisibility zone, but the Miners weren't up 7–0 because of Strike.

They were up because of Boom.

Strike chewed on his lip as he approached Boom. "Uh . . . hey."

Her visor flicked to clear, her eyes blazing with fire.

Strike hid behind his reflective visor, hot shame rising through his face.

Boom stared him down. "You gotta stop trying to take over games all by yourself. You lost three straight Ultrabowls that way. Do you want to frakkin' win this one or not?"

Strike froze, shocked by the harshness of Boom's words. But she was right. In the past, he had always put the Miners on his back, the team's fortune living and dying with their quarterback. If his Miners were going to have any shot at winning the Ultrabowl, Strike had to let his new rocketback 1 do her job.

MINERS ROLL IN SEASON OPENER BEHIND ROOKIE

By Vikram Cho, Senior Staff Reporter

The 2352 Ultraball season opened with a bang, with the Taiko Miners steamrolling the Yangju Venom, 84–35. The bloodbath at Yangju Colony saw Strike throw seven TDs and pass for 548 meters. On defense, he had three interceptions, four sacks, and seven batted-down passes.

But the real story was the Miners' rookie rocketback 1, Boom. Never in the history of the league has a new player made such a huge splash, catching six touchdowns and rushing for two more, setting a new rookie rocketback record with an astounding 521 total meters gained. She made one of her touchdown catches in double coverage, nabbing Strike's bullet pass nearly twenty-five meters in the air, before dropping into a swarm of Venom defenders inside an invisibility zone, kicking, punching, and thrashing her way out before muscling into the end zone for the score. She was even a force on defense, with two interceptions and three sacks.

Boom's play was astounding, but it's the off-field intrigue that still holds everyone's attention. The first Dark Sider ever to return to the United Moon Colonies, Boom has refused to give interviews or take part in press conferences. The only statement she's released: "I just want to win an Ultrabowl. Leave the other Dark Siders alone. They don't want anything to do with the United Moon Colonies." But Boom has done nothing to quiet the rumors circulating throughout the UMC, allowing the mystique and fears surrounding the Dark Siders to run rampant.

When asked about the Dark Siders and the potential threat they pose, Yao Al-Farouk, a professor of history at Copernicus College, said, "I highly doubt the Dark Siders are any danger to us. It is true that little is known about them, but they are a fiercely private people. Every wave of Dark Side colonists has left in protest over various UMC policies they considered a violation of their civil rights. A colleague of mine went with the most recent mass exodus ten years ago, when martial law was declared right after Earthfall. I haven't heard from him since."

Kaylen Lin, Captain of the Blackguard, had a different answer to the question. "The Dark Siders are a serious threat. Everyone knows that a government must sometimes take strict measures to keep society in order. I don't care how great an Ultraball player Boom is. She will be kept under close watch at all times."

No one even knows why the Dark Siders wear

white jumpsuits. Professor Al-Farouk speculated that it's the Dark Siders' way of displaying their separation from the UMC, renouncing the centuries-old tradition of each colony adopting a distinctive jumpsuit color. Others have guessed that it helps the Dark Siders move stealthily, without being detected. Boom has refused to fill in any of these gaps, leaving herself shrouded in secrecy.

What is known, though, is that Boom can play Ultraball. Many analysts predicted that the Miners would fall apart without TNT, their old rocketback 1, who some say threw Ultrabowl IX. But in many ways, the Miners have never looked better. As the Miners-Venom game progressed, bookies scrambled to adjust their betting lines. The Neutrons are still heavily favored to win the Ultrabowl, the oddsmakers giving them a 64 percent chance. But the betting line on the Miners has now ballooned all the way from 13 percent to 21 percent.

In the other morning game, the North Pole Neutrons beat down the Tranquility Beatdown in commanding fashion, 105–70. The Beatdown, the only other team besides the Neutrons and the Miners to make the playoffs three years in a row, held their own in the first half but then got stuffed the rest of the way by the Neutrons' "Radioactive Waste" defense. The Neutrons' star rocketback, Chain Reaction, made the Beatdown pay for several mistakes, intercepting five passes, returning two the other way for pick-sevens. He also had seven sacks, all unassisted.

On offense, Chain Reaction scored a total of eleven TDs, catching six, rushing for three, and returning two kickoffs all the way. With a total of 657 meters gained, Chain Reaction came close to breaking his own single-game record. "I am unstoppable," he said after the game. "I guarantee a fourth straight Neutrons title."

The Neutrons' star rocketback 1 looked every bit like the MVP he's been the past three seasons, and more. The oddsmakers have set their betting lines astoundingly high for the MVP race, giving Chain Reaction a 78 percent chance of winning his fourth MVP title in a row.

With the Miners and the Neutrons scoring fast and often, the race has begun for the all-important season tiebreaker: total points scored. The Neutrons have come out strong, leading the Miners by twenty-one points now.

But who knows if the total points tiebreaker will even be relevant this year? The way both teams played this morning, everything might come down to the regular season game every fan is eagerly awaiting: the week-five matchup between these two powerhouses.

TNT

STRIKE, ROCK, PICKAXE, and Nugget emerged from the boys' locker room to a horde of screaming people. Hanging around with loyal Miners fans was one of Strike's favorite parts of playing Ultraball. With a big smile, Strike pointed at a girl holding out a pen, motioning for her miniature rock shaped like an Ultraball—the most common souvenir.

"Where's Boom?" the girl said.

"Uh, dunno." Strike looked around, their star rocketback nowhere in sight.

"Oh." The kid's chest deflated.

Strike took the ball and started to sign his name over the laces in his traditional giant style, but the kid stopped him. "Leave room for Boom to sign, okay?"

Strike raised an eyebrow. "You want me to make my autograph smaller? How about I just sign the tip of the ball?"

"Yeah, that'd be great!"

Pulling his lips into a tight smile, Strike signed his name in the tiniest print he could manage. "Like that?"

"Thanks." She took the ball back. "Let's go find Boom," she said to a friend.

"I guess you were right," Strike said, nudging Rock. "Having a Dark Sider on the team isn't that big of a deal to the fans."

"Just as long as she wins us games," Rock said. "And she will."

"I still don't trust her," Pickaxe said. "Why is she being so secretive about the Dark Side? Something feels weird."

"Dark Siders value their right to privacy over everything," Rock said. "They believe there is never a reason to spy on people." He shot a glance toward the ceiling. "I think they have a good point. It is kind of creepy that the Blackguard might be watching us at any time."

"Only creepy if you have something to hide," Pickaxe said. "Right, Strike?"

Before Boom showed up, Strike hadn't thought much about the UMC's constant surveillance. It was just the way things were. But now, a cold shiver ran down his spine. "Let's just sign autographs, okay?" he said.

Strike turned away from his teammates, watching as a

group of fans left in search for Boom. Jealousy itched at him. For three years, his number 8 Miners decal had been stitched onto hundreds of jumpsuits of all colors, seen all over every one of the moon's twenty-one colonies. The only other decal that had sold more was Chain Reaction's number 2, in the bright red of the North Pole Neutrons. Now Boom might pass them both—her blue number 3 decal was going to go gangbusters. It had been a crazy preseason, with hordes of reporters constantly pressuring the Miners' new rocketback with all sorts of questions, but this single game might silence them all.

A voice whispered from Strike's side, "Hey."

Nausea rose into Strike's chest. The boy had his filthy blue jumpsuit hood pulled down over his face, but Strike would recognize that voice anywhere. It had been months since Strike had seen TNT. His thin face had gone even bonier, his cheeks sunken, his bloodshot eyes outlined by dark folds of skin. His tangled black hair was patchy, as if he had been yanking it out. It looked as if TNT hadn't slept since Ultrabowl IX, eight months ago.

His hands trembling, rising as they squeezed into fists, Strike turned and walked off.

"Strike!" TNT bounded toward Strike and grabbed his shoulder.

"Get away from me before I kill you," Strike hissed. He wrestled away and stormed into a maintenance tunnel at the side of the stadium.

TNT chased after him. "Strike. Please, just listen to me. It's really important."

Halfway down the tunnel, Strike slowed, closing his eyes tight. He couldn't bear to look at his former best friend, the traitor to the Fireball Five. "You got a lot of nerve, showing your face."

"I'm so, so, so sorry, Strike." TNT laced his hands together and dropped to his knees, pleading. "I can't change what I did. But you have to know how sorry I am."

"Doesn't do me a lot of good, does it?" Strike held up a fist. "You see an Ultrabowl ring?"

"No." TNT lowered his gaze to the ground. "But I've spent the past eight months trying to figure out a way to make it up to you. And I think I finally have."

"Impossible. Now get out of here before I—"

"Raiden Zuna is going to buy off a Miner."

Strike's eyes went wide, but they quickly narrowed. "How do you know? And why should I listen to anything you ever say again?"

TNT turned away. "I don't blame you if you never forgive me. I won't ever forgive me. But I'm doing everything I can to make it up to you. I won't stop until I make things right."

"You can't ever make up for what you did. How could you stab me in the back like that? Zuna paid you off to throw last year's Ultrabowl, didn't he?"

"I..." TNT wrung his hands together, his face crinkling

up, tears pooling in his eyes. "I can't say anything. I promised." TNT shot a glance over his shoulder and motioned Strike close. "I've been trailing Zuna for weeks. I followed him all the way to North Pole Colony. He's planning on buying off a Miner. I'm sure of it."

"You followed Zuna? His goons didn't pick you up?" North Pole Colony, where most of the moon's energy was produced, was the richest of the United Moon Colonies. A kid from Taiko Colony would stick out like a solar flare.

"I went in with a bunch of Guoming Colony junkers," TNT said. "Stole one of their pink jumpsuits and blended right in."

"You could have gotten yourself killed. What if he recognized you?"

"Wouldn't have mattered. My life is worth nothing." He looked down at his feet.

Dammit, Strike thought. The least TNT could do was to let Strike hate him properly.

"It took me ages, hanging around his headquarters, pretending like I was cleaning," TNT said. "But I finally overheard him say something. That he was off to tap his next prospect."

"So? All teams look at prospects."

TNT took a deep breath. "Last year, Zuna called me his prospect. You know, like a prospector? As in, a Miner. He's going to buy someone off. It has to be your new rocketback."

Strike studied TNT's face. He sure did look sincere. For all the years they had been inseparable, Strike knew TNT better than he knew himself. He so badly wanted things to go back to the way they used to be, the two of them playing pranks on their Fireball Five teammates, staying up all night drawing up trick plays, dreaming big plans for the future. "So it was Zuna? How much did he pay you to throw the Ultrabowl? To stab me in the back?"

TNT squeezed his eyes tight. A tortured groan came from somewhere deep inside. "I really can't say anything. I swore I wouldn't." He slammed a fist into his thigh, moaning in despair.

Turning, Strike shook his head and walked away.

"Remember the day we met?" TNT called out. "Shinjuku Park?"

Strike slowed, his feet shuffling along the airtight tunnel surface. "'Course I remember." He'd never forget the day four years ago that had turned around his life, flipping his path from one breaking his back down in the mines to one of Ultraball stardom.

"Some of those kids wanted to jump you," TNT said. "Two of them still blamed your mom for the Fireball Blast. Who stuck up for you? Said you could play football with us?"

Strike paused. He shrugged.

"Ever since the first time I had you over, my mom thought of you like a second son. Sometimes I think she liked you better than me. I bet if there had only been one slot open at that Miners tryout, she would have made sure you got it instead of me."

"That's not true. Well . . ." Strike had to admit, it probably was true. TNT's mom worked for the Underground Ultraball League back then, and had gotten all of them tryouts. But she had put Strike's name at the very top of the list. He squeezed his eyes tight as the memories of TNT's mom, taking him in like a son, came flooding back.

"I gave you a chance when no one else would," TNT said. "Now you gotta do the same for me."

Strike stood in place for a long time. He shook his head, and then walked down the long tunnel. The pain of last year's Ultrabowl was just too great.

"Please, Strike," TNT said. "Miners together. Fireball Fire forever."

At the end of the tunnel, Strike slowed and then stopped. He turned and spoke over his shoulder. "Get me hard proof. And then I might listen."

RESULTS, WEEK 1

Miners	**84**
Venom	35

Neutrons	**105**
Beatdown	70

Shock	**63**
Molemen	14

Flamethrowers	**70**
Explorers	63

STANDINGS, WEEK 1

	Wins	Losses	Total Points
Neutrons	1	0	105
Miners	1	0	84
Flamethrowers	1	0	70
Shock	1	0	63
Beatdown	0	1	70
Explorers	0	1	63
Venom	0	1	35
Molemen	0	1	14

8

NUCLEAR WASTE

MONDAYS WERE OFF days for the Miners. It was a good thing that Rock had gone to the library in Copernicus Colony—Strike needed some space to think, and their tiny apartment often got cramped with Rock there. Strike paced in a tight circle for hours, mulling over and dissecting TNT's words. There had been nothing but sincerity and truth in his former best friend's eyes. A big part of Strike wanted to believe TNT. To make things right.

But that would mean Boom was plotting to stab him in the back.

What do I really know about Boom, anyway? Strike thought. Although most of the sports talk chatter had switched from Boom's background to her incredible playing, the rumors surrounding the first Dark Sider to ever return to the United Moon Colonies hadn't died out. It would be so much easier to fully trust her if she would just answer some of the most basic questions. Against his better judgment, Strike couldn't help wondering if TNT was onto something.

Later that night, Strike and Rock headed to Taiko Commons for the weekly Nuclear Poker game. They had skipped the card game during the preseason to focus on Ultraball, but Strike needed the distraction now. If there was anything that could take Strike's mind off TNT, it was the high-stakes risk and strategy of the best card game ever. With Strike's ability to fake people out and Rock's brains, they had become one of the best pairs in Taiko Colony. If only there had been jobs that paid people to play Nuclear Poker, the two of them would be set in their post-Ultraball days, whether they won an Ultrabowl or not.

"How many hardtack bars do we have?" Strike asked. In dirt-poor Taiko Colony, hardtack bars were the true currency, not U-dollars.

"Twelve," Rock said, patting the bag tightly strapped to his side. "Are you sure we shouldn't leave at least a few at home, just in case? Next distribution drop won't be for another four days."

"I have a good feeling about tonight. We could double

our stash. That's almost enough to trade for some real food. Fresh food." His stomach grumbled as he thought about the time at the Tao Children's Home when one of his roommates had stolen some baked potatoes from Frigoris Colony, where all the moon's crops were grown in the precious stockpile of soil. It had cost Strike fourteen hardtack bars to get one of those potatoes, but it was worth it. Memories of the warm, flaky deliciousness made him drool. "That computer brain of yours better be in tip-top shape. And work really hard to keep your poker face on."

"I've been improving my bluffing skills," Rock said. "Watch this." He stared at Strike, his face blank.

"Great," Strike said. "Just keep that same face if we hit a nuclear straight."

"A nuclear straight?" His breath quickening, Rock's eyebrows rose high.

"Great poker face."

"Darn it," Rock mumbled. He jotted into his notebook, shaking his head.

It was still early, but Taiko Commons was already packed. Most of the people were glued to a giant monitor mounted high on a wall, the only TV left in all of Taiko Colony. *LunarSports Reports* blared on it, the color commentators shouting in debate about who would finish last in the league, the Molemen or the Venom. At the top of the screen was the ever-present Ultraball standings chart, listing out wins, losses, and total points scored.

During Ultraball season, the standings chart was front and center on every monitor, screen, phone, and scoreboard, from airlocks to schools to factories to Tunnel Ring trams.

Most people wore blue Taiko Colony jumpsuits, but there were people in other colors milling around, Nuclear Poker fanatics traveling for any game available. Strike did a lap around the room, giving high fives. Even Governor Katana was there, waving to Strike. The governor didn't say a thing, but the look on his face conveyed the weight on his shoulders.

"Hey, Strike," came a voice from a corner of the room. "Great season opener."

Strike grinned when he spotted Torch, relieved to have an excuse to escape from Governor Katana. He headed over to where Torch was hanging out with other dust-covered miners. "You watch the game here?" Strike asked.

"Yeah. You wouldn't believe how crowded it was. I could barely move."

Strike nodded. When he and Rock were living at the Tao Children's Home, Sunday afternoons at Taiko Commons were crowded, and that was before Taiko Colony even had an Ultraball team. "You see anything we can improve on?"

"You're asking me?"

It was still unreal, Strike's boyhood hero so unsure of himself, nothing like the legendary QB of old. The teenager in front of him had been broken by all the talk about the Torch's Curse, so many Flamethrowers fans blaming him for four years of bad luck. "Absolutely," Strike said. "I need all the help I can get. Did you watch the Neutrons' game, too?"

"Oh yeah. That Radioactive Waste defense is insane." Torch shrugged. "If you're serious, I do have some thoughts."

"Shoot." Strike braced himself for a repeat of the commentary Berzerkatron and the Mad Mongol had been spouting off that morning, about Rock's play being too mechanical and predictable.

But to his surprise, Torch went to a different subject completely. "Boom is good. Really good." He paused. "You trust her one hundred percent? There's nothing to all those rumors about some Dark Sider plot? She just wants to win the Ultrabowl, yeah?"

There were so many unanswered questions surrounding Boom. But Strike's only choice was to trust her. Without Boom, the Miners had no chance. "Yeah," he said.

"Then you should use her more," Torch said.

"More? She caught six touchdowns."

"I bet she can do a lot more. Have you tried her on rocketback options?"

"A couple times, in practices. She has a good arm."

"What do you think about dual QB sets?" Torch said. "Dragon and I never used them, because he was too nervous to pull them out during games. But I think you and Boom could make them work. Save them for a big game, and you'd shock the league."

Strike hesitated. He was the quarterback of the Miners, the one directing every play. Ever since he became the coach and general manager of the Miners two years ago, he ran the entire show—along with major support from Rock.

"I think if we had used those dual QB sets, we could have won that Ultrabowl," Torch said. "The Beatdown couldn't have blitzed both me and Dragon." He squeezed a fist tight. "If I had more time, I wouldn't have thrown that frakkin' interception. I'm sure of it."

Strike forced himself to nod. Torch was right. No one had ever tried something like this, because good QBs didn't come around very often. An Ultraball team was lucky to find one workable QB, and here the Miners were, maybe with two.

"And Strike?" Torch said. "There's something else."

"Um. Okay." Strike braced himself to hear about Rock's mechanical play.

"Even playing against a weak defense, you got the bum rush too often." Torch shook his head. "I know you're loyal to Pickaxe. He's been a solid crackback. Fireball Five and all. But Rattler, a crackback past her prime, blew by him twice yesterday. What's going to happen once Pickaxe faces the Neutrons' Radioactive Waste defense? Did you see how many sacks Chain Reaction had yesterday? He loves to atomic blitz from the blind side. That's Pickaxe's side."

Strike tried to ignore the issue that had been bugging him all preseason. Pickaxe had been a rock-solid and trustworthy blocker for three years now, but it seemed like he might be slipping. Maybe it was the pressure, or the Ultrabot suit getting tighter around Pickaxe's growing body. Whatever the case, Pickaxe had made some mistakes against one of the worst defenses in the league.

"Hey, I didn't mean to piss you off," Torch said. "I was just trying to—"

"No, you have a good point. It's just that Pickaxe and me, we go a long way back. Fireball Five forever."

Rock tapped his shoulder before he could think about it more. "Nuclear Poker is starting," Rock said.

"Thanks, man," Strike said to Torch. "Keep your eyes open. If it's okay with you, I'd like to meet up once in a while to get your thoughts and advice. I think you could help us out a ton."

"Really?" Torch beamed. "Yeah, that'd be great." He hesitated. "Hey. You couldn't put me on payroll, could you? Probably not, but I have to ask. Things are tight, what with my kid sister not strong enough to work in the mines yet."

Strike looked toward Rock, who shook his head. As the general manager of the Taiko Miners, Strike was used to getting asked for handouts. But there was nothing to go around. It was all Rock could do to keep the team from bleeding U-dollars every year. "Tell you what. If we win the Ultrabowl, we'll probably make a bunch more money through souvenir sales and stuff. We'll talk then, okay?"

"Thanks, Strike. If I could help the Miners win an Ultrabowl, that'd be awesome. Maybe it'd force people to finally stop saying that I cursed the Flamethrowers."

"Give me all the ideas you got. I'm going to need them." Strike studied him. "You play Nuclear Poker?"

Torch nodded. "I don't have a partner, though. None of the guys play."

That wasn't a surprise to Strike. After a long day down in the mines, most people just wanted to kick up their feet and unwind. Nuclear Poker was an intense card game, and at Taiko Commons it was always high-stakes, with dozens of hardtack bars and even U-dollars riding on the line. "Come along and watch. Occasionally I need a stand-in when Rock is doing research or obsessing over game film or cataloging his jokes."

"Cataloging his jokes?"

Rock took out his little notebook and gleefully started to explain his system, but Strike held up a hand. "Don't ask, unless you have ten hours to kill," he said.

Strike pulled open a door to a tiny room packed full of blocky tables and gray-brick seats. Pairs from all over the moon were huddled together, discussing strategy. Strike almost felt sorry for all these suckers.

"Well, well," came a voice. "Prepare to lose."

Strike's eyes narrowed as he caught sight of two bright red jumpsuits in a corner of the room: Chain Reaction and Fusion, the Neutrons' rocketback 1 and quarterback. "What are you doing here?"

"Delivering a message," Chain Reaction said. "Mr. Zuna says he's giving you one last chance to take his deal. He'll set you up for life."

"Zuna is scared he's going to lose, after seeing what Boom can do?"

"Mr. Zuna isn't scared of anything," Chain Reaction said. "Come on, Strike. When the Miners become the North Pole Fusion next year, I'm going to need a quarterback to put the ball into my hands. It should be you. I watched your game yesterday. You're even better than last year, and that's saying a lot. Take the deal, and you'll be sitting pretty with the rest of us. Mr. Zuna makes sure Neutrons are very well taken care of." He pulled a foil-wrapped lump out of his pocket.

"Is that . . ." Strike's eyes widened. "Where did you get a baked potato?"

Chain Reaction laughed. "We all got big raises this year. We eat real food once a month now. Mr. Zuna set up a regular shipment from Frigoris Colony for us—potatoes, mushrooms, carrots, corn, whatever new crop experiments they're working on. Some of the stuff is incredible." He held the potato out, unwrapping a corner. "Want a sniff?"

All the sound sucked out of the room as people crowded in. Strike could barely hold himself back, the fragrant aroma pulling him in like a magnet. "You better get out of here before you get jumped."

"Like anyone would dare," Chain Reaction said. "Anyone who even touches me answers to Mr. Zuna and his Meltdown Gun. Who wants to get hauled to Han-Shu Prison? Or nuked?"

Everyone backed away. People turned as if they hadn't been listening, but plenty of eyes still trained on the steaming baked potato.

"Don't you see, Strike?" Chain Reaction said. He pointed to his head, his dark skin cracked and covered with sores, clumps of his hair missing. "I know I look like hell. But I don't care. People respect me. Fear me. I live large. I am bigger than God. That's what it means to be a Neutron." He lifted the potato to his nose and took a long whiff. "Mr. Zuna will even let you take a few friends with you to live in North Pole Colony."

Strike was about to tell off Chain Reaction, but he stole a glance at Rock and paused. Years ago at the Tao Children's Home, Strike had sworn that no matter what happened, he would always protect Rock. Taking Zuna's offer meant setting up Rock for life. Pickaxe and Nugget, too. Winning the Ultrabowl would achieve the same thing: all of them landing cushy jobs at one of the sports broadcasting companies or even better. But nothing could compete with the lifestyle Raiden Zuna could provide.

He turned to Torch, standing in the back corner of the room. The older boy's words came back to Strike: *Think about life after Ultraball more than I did.*

Torch chewed on his lip and gave Strike a shrug, as if to say that he'd understand if Strike took the deal.

"I won't lie," Strike said to Chain Reaction. "It would be awesome to throw to you. That twisting midair one-handed spin grab you made yesterday, even after Hammer Fist and Uppercut both smashed giant boulders into you? Incredible."

"Oh, I'm going to top that for sure," Chain Reaction said. "Wait until you see what I have planned against the Flamethrowers this Sunday. What I'm going to do off the launching ramps is going to blow your mind. And my new slingshot zone moves? I'm going to wait for the Ultrabowl to break those out. Winning the Ultrabowl in Neutron Stadium, as a North Pole Neutron—you'd be the king of the moon. King of the universe." He stuck his hand out. "So you're in? Neutron Nation?"

Strike's hand moved toward Chain Reaction as if it had a mind of its own. But he jerked it back and shook his head. "We'll see you in our week 5 matchup."

Chain Reaction hocked something up and spit it on the ground. "You're a whole lot dumber than I thought. Now you're going down with the rest of this frakkin' scum."

Strike clenched his teeth, furious with himself for considering the deal even for a split second. "Get out of here."

"I heard there was a lousy Nuclear Poker game here. Lots of chumps pretending they can play." Chain Reaction moved in, chest to chest with Strike. "I hope you two are better at Nuclear Poker than you are at Ultraball. Fusion and I are going to clean your clocks."

"Why are you even here?" Strike said. "Go play in your fancy North Pole game."

"You scared to play us?"

"Just don't want to deal with the cleanup."

"Cleanup? What cleanup?"

"For when you smack the pants . . . for when we crap . . ." Strike pointed at Rock.

Rock paged through his notebook. "The cleanup, when you crap your pants after we put the smackdown on you."

Laughter broke out all around the room, and Chain Reaction scowled. "Okay, you frakkin' fools. Nuclear Poker. If you go all in and win, you get this potato."

"We don't have enough hardtack bars to match that," Rock said.

"We don't want your piece-of-turd hardtack bars. Neutrons get all the hardtack bars we can eat."

Strike turned to Fusion, who had backed his way into a corner of the room, doing his best not to be noticed. "Why do you even hang around this guy?"

Fusion's baby-faced cheeks pinched up as he shrugged. "He is the greatest rocketback to ever play the game."

Chain Reaction pushed a finger into Strike's chest. "I talk the talk, and I walk the walk. Three MVP titles. Three Ultrabowl rings." He held up a fist in Strike's face, the brilliant platinum and diamonds glimmering. "That fourth ring is going to look good on my pinkie." He shoved Strike, knocking him off his feet.

Strike charged, but Rock grabbed him around the waist, holding him back. "Don't let him get under your skin," Rock said. "You can't afford to get injured."

Strike swore under his breath. "All right, you asked for it," he said. "Nuclear Poker. Someone get the cards."

"But we don't have anything to put up against his potato," Rock said.

"There is something you can wager," Chain Reaction said. "I want a full diagram of one of your trick plays."

There was a long pause before Strike exploded. "Is this the secret to your Radioactive Waste defense? You fix games?"

Chain Reaction leaned in and whispered, "If anyone would know about that, it'd be your pal TNT." A sneer crept onto his face before Strike lunged at him. Rock and others in blue jumpsuits wrapped Strike up before he could throw a punch.

"Temper, temper," Chain Reaction said. "You Taiko morons are so jumpy. How about this? You lose, you throw all your hardtack bars into a waste collection recycler. We flush them. And then you moon your fans in your home opener. Deal?"

Strike couldn't take his eyes off the potato Chain Reaction was waving in his face. But even more than the potato, Strike wanted—no, *needed*—to wipe the smile off Chain Reaction's scraggly face. "Deal."

Rock pulled Strike away, pleading as he tugged on Strike's jumpsuit sleeve. "All our hardtack bars. We'll starve if we lose them all. We can't do this."

"We have to," Strike hissed. He jabbed a finger at a table and sat down, Rock taking a seat opposite him. Chain Reaction and Fusion sat in the other two spots.

Strike motioned to the guy in charge of Taiko Commons, who brought over one of the ten decks of cards, well-worn after years of use. As he took his seat at the corner of the table, he shrank under the gaze of everyone in the room. He shuffled the cards, nearly showering them across the table once in his nervousness, before dealing out two facedown cards to each person.

Strike turned up the corners of his cards, stealing a peek at them. The queen of spades and the two of hearts. Not bad, but not great, either. He glanced across the table at Rock, whose frown told the entire story.

The dealer burned ten cards, turning them faceup into a discard pile. Then he flopped three cards into the center of the table:

Jack of spades.

Nine of spades.

Nine of clubs.

Suddenly, Rock's face lit up, his eyebrows going high. It immediately told Strike that between the two of them, they might be onto a spade flush. Maybe even an atomic flush. But with Rock's terrible poker face, the Neutrons knew exactly what they had, too.

Chain Reaction put his head near the table surface, stealing a peek at the two facedown cards in front of him. "Raise you ten hardtack bars," he said.

"Ten?" Strike said, trying not to let his alarm show. Were the Neutrons onto something even better? Maybe their own spade flush? Or a nuclear straight?

The betting quickly escalated as the dealer placed live cards into the center of the table, in between burning more and more cards faceup into the discard pile. When the last live card went down, Strike studied Rock, who was nearly jumping up and down in his seat in excitement. They had won. It was a lock.

As the final round of betting began, Strike grinned. "We're all in," he said.

Given Rock's complete lack of a poker face, Strike expected Chain Reaction to fold. But to his surprise, Chain Reaction slammed a fist into the table. "We call," he said.

What a moron, Strike thought. With a flourish, he flipped

over his cards, and Rock followed. Exactly as Strike had thought: between the two of them, the Miners had an atomic flush. "That potato is going to taste awesome," he said.

"Not so fast." A wicked grin smeared across Chain Reaction's face. He flipped over his two cards and burst into maniacal laughter. "Nuclear straight. You lose."

"What?" Rock shouted. He leapt to his feet, gaping at the cards in front of Chain Reaction and Fusion.

"The North Pole Neutrons win again," Chain Reaction said. "I can't wait to see you moon all your fans. Now let's go toss all your hardtack bars."

"This is impossible," Rock mumbled in disbelief. "It's. Not. Possible."

Chain Reaction grabbed all the cards and shoved them into a pile. "Let's go flush those hardtack bars. Man, I'm going to enjoy this."

"Rock," Strike said, his voice pleading. Rock was never wrong when it came to facts and numbers. "What happened?"

"I counted all the cards. I was one hundred percent sure. We should have won." Rock bent over, holding his stomach. His face going sickly green, he looked like he was about to heave. "We won't eat for days. We'll starve. We should never have agreed to this."

"Wait." Torch stepped forward. He pushed Chain Reaction. "Pull up your sleeves."

"I'll pretend you didn't touch me, you frakkin' turd eater," Chain Reaction said. "Even an idiot like you has to know that Mr. Zuna would have a meltdown if somebody laid a hand on his star rocketback 1. You hear me? A *meltdown*."

Torch took a step back, his hands held up. He retreated, but he made his way around the table and whispered to Strike, "Count the cards."

Strike reached for the pile, but Chain Reaction slapped his hand. With a quick swipe, Chain Reaction flung the cards across the room in a shower of red and black. "No one disrespects a North Pole Neutron," he said. "We're outta here. Come on, Fusion." He yanked his quarterback up by the arm and stormed toward the door.

A furious rage boiled inside Strike, and he shot up to chase the Neutrons. But Rock caught hold of him as the card room exploded in chaos. "Don't," Rock said.

Strike tugged away, but he realized that Rock was right. This might even be part of some Neutron scheme. It wouldn't be a surprise if Chain Reaction had a bunch of Blackguard cops waiting outside to gang up on Strike, maybe even break his arm "in self-defense."

The guy in charge of Taiko Commons elbowed everyone out of his way, gathering up the cards and counting them. "I am so dead. I'll lose my job if even one card is missing." He paused as he sorted them. "Huh. There's an extra king of spades. Did one of the other decks get shuffled in?"

"I knew it," Torch said. "Chain Reaction must have had cards up his sleeve. That lousy cheat." He turned to Strike. "Be careful out there. Neutrons don't play by the rules."

"Dang," Strike said. "We owe you, big-time. We would have lost all our hardtack bars if it hadn't been for you." He cocked his head. "Can you come to our game this Sunday?"

Torch shoved his hands in his pockets. His face twisted into a mix of shame and anger. "You know I can't afford a ticket. Not even a nosebleed seat."

"No, that's not what I meant," Strike said. "Torch. We can't pay you. But I want you to sit in the front row of the stands. I sure could use your eyes. I bet you still read defenses better than anyone else on the moon."

"You want me in the stands? How are you going to get me a front-row ticket?"

"It won't be just any front-row ticket. I want you watching from our coach's box." Each team had a single bench reserved for a coach, but since Strike was the Miners' player-coach, he had always given that seat away to a random fan. Strike knew that he had finally found the perfect use for that seat.

Torch stood in shock for a long time. "You're not afraid I'm going to curse the Miners, just like I did the Flamethrowers?"

Strike shook his head. "No such thing as curses. I want

you on our side. I *need* you on our side."

Finally, Torch's grin grew from ear to ear. "Okay, then. I'll be there. You're really serious?"

"Absolutely. Welcome to the team, Coach." Strike shook his hand.

People came in from everywhere, swarming Torch, high-fiving the newest member of the Taiko Miners.

Strike thought back to TNT's dire warning about Zuna paying off Boom. If there was any truth to that, Strike now had the sharpest pair of eyes on the moon watching out for him.

QUESTIONS AND ANSWERS

THE NEXT MORNING, Boom was waiting for Strike and Rock outside the main airlock connecting Taiko Colony to Taiko Arena. Strike slowed as he caught sight of her, TNT's warning still bouncing around his head. *Why does she guard her privacy so fiercely?* Strike thought. *What is she hiding?* Not that Strike trusted TNT one bit anymore, but there had to be a serious reason for him to risk his neck by showing up at an Ultraball game. If any Miners fan had recognized TNT, he would have been beaten into a pulp. Maybe even killed.

Before Strike could say hi, Boom spoke. "What do you think about adding in some out-of-suit workouts?"

"Out of our suits?" Strike said. "Why? We need all the time inside our suits we can get."

"If we could all improve our reflexes and quickness, we might perform better. Ultrabot suits respond to the wearer's slightest muscle movements. Remember Serpent's flying clothesline in the second quarter? If you had ducked a tenth of a second quicker, you would have avoided the tackle and broken for a touchdown. And think what you could do if your crackbacks could change directions quicker to keep you better protected." She cleared her throat. "One crackback in particular."

There it was again: the issue Torch had brought up, the same one that Berzerkatron and the Mad Mongol had been debating that morning on the *SmashMouth Radio Blitz*. Berzerkatron had even started calling Pickaxe "Axepicker" again. Years ago, that nickname had badly shaken Pickaxe. Maybe Boom's idea would help, but it could also mess with Pickaxe's head even further if he thought he was being singled out. Strike turned to Rock. "What do you think?" he asked.

"Boom has a point," Rock said. "Ultrabot suits respond to the smallest of movements. Even microseconds could translate into tremendous improvements."

"Got an idea for something else that could help, too," Boom said. "We're going to work on your improvisation, Rock."

"Oh no," Rock said, his hands wringing together. "Oh no, oh no. A pointless effort. My strengths lie in my ability to repeat known patterns with great accuracy."

Boom raised an eyebrow. "Defenses love known patterns."

"That's why we have so many plays in our playbook. Defenses cannot possibly anticipate which of the forty-six plays we might run, not to mention the audibled variants. Strike always knows exactly where I'll be."

"You remember every one of those plays?" Boom asked Strike.

"Yes," Strike said in a huff.

"And all the variants?"

He shrugged. "Mostly. Pretty much."

Boom stared him down.

"Okay, I forget sometimes," Strike said.

Boom kept staring.

"Fine, a lot of times," Strike said. "We have a ton of plays, okay?"

"Let's spend some time reviewing the playbook, then," Rock said. "With careful study, you should have no problem recalling even the extra seventeen plays we deleted two years ago."

"You really think that's the best use of practice time?" Boom asked. "And is Strike really capable of that?"

"Hey, wait just a second," Strike said. "Are you calling me dumb? I admit, I screw up a lot of things, but I'm not as dumb as I look. I mean, I'm not as smart as I am dumb . . ." He sighed. "I am dumb."

"You're not dumb," Rock said. He held up his notebook

to Strike with a big grin. "You got that one right. 'You're not as dumb as you look' is funny, because although it seems like a compliment on the surface, there's actually an underlying insult." He ripped out a rat-a-tat laugh.

Strike was still trying to figure out Rock's explanation when Pickaxe and Nugget approached. "Why are you all hanging around outside?" Pickaxe asked. "Let's suit up. I got some big hits to put on my dingleberry bro."

Strike gave Boom a sidelong glance and made his decision. "We're going to do something different today," he said. "We're not going in just yet."

"Why? Let's start hitting."

"Ultraball is more than just hitting," Boom said. "We're going to work on agility."

"Agility?" Pickaxe snorted. "What a waste. The Ultrabot suits give us all the agility we need."

"I think it's a good idea," Strike said.

"I agree one hundred percent," Rock said.

All was quiet for a moment before Pickaxe exploded. "Is this about those two blocks I missed? Why the frak is Berzerkatron riding me so hard? Every crackback is going to miss a block once in a while."

"Not Chokehold," Nugget said. "Or Radioactive. Asbestos did miss one in the regular season game against the Neutrons last year, but since then—"

"Shut up," Pickaxe said. "So I missed two blocks. Big deal. We still rolled the Venom, big-time. I'm no Axepicker."

"Hey, I'm not making any accusations or anything," Strike said. "But we need to do everything we can to prepare. What happens when we play the Beatdown three weeks from now? And the Neutrons in week 5? A single missed block could mean the difference between a win and a loss."

"Why are you all ganging up on me?" Pickaxe shouted. "I wasn't the only one who didn't have a perfect game. What was Rock doing the last play of the first half, way out on the left, all by himself?"

"That was the play call," Rock said. "Strike must have audibled at the last moment." He mulled things over. "Or perhaps he forgot the play. Frak."

"No one's ganging up on you, Pickaxe," Strike said. "Just come on, let's try this out." He pointed to Boom. "Lead on."

She jogged toward the airlock connecting Taiko Arena to Taiko Colony. "Follow me. Whoever can one-up me becomes the leader." She burst into a sprint and leapt for a gray-brick ledge on top of the airlock. She swung around, launching herself high, then curling into a perfect forward roll.

"Whoa," Nugget said.

Strike took off, jumping for the ledge and nearly missing it. He flung himself like Boom. Although he didn't get as high, a rush of adrenaline surged through him. Doing crazy physical feats was the norm in an Ultrabot suit.

Doing them on your own was totally different—even better, in a way.

"This is dumb," Pickaxe said. "Anyone can do that." He took off after Strike and leapt for the ledge. But as he heaved himself off it, his hand slipped. With a scream, he flew off at an angle, thudding to the ground on his back.

Nugget sprinted to copy Boom, his eyes locked onto the ledge. He jumped high and grabbed it, using his momentum to swing himself into a high arc. Landing and rolling close to Strike, he grinned at his brother. "You're right. Anyone could do it."

"Not bad," Boom said. "But not as high or as far. Come on."

"Wait," Strike said. Boom had just handed him the perfect way to dig up more information about her. Genius ideas came to Strike so infrequently that he had to stop and admire it. "We'll add a twist. The leader gets to ask anyone a question, and it must be answered."

"No," Boom said. "I'm not doing that."

"I'm the coach and general manager of this team, and I say that's what we're doing," Strike said. "It'll be good for us to get to know each other better."

She shook her head. "This is exactly why Dark Siders stay far away from the United Moon Colonies. You have zero respect for people's privacy. I'm not answering any of your stupid questions."

Strike almost backed down, but the word "stupid"

made him bristle. "You don't want to answer any stupid questions? Then you better keep the lead."

Boom glared at him. "Fine. I just won, so I get to ask a question." She turned to Rock. "Why do you write so much stuff in that notebook? I mean, who catalogs jokes?"

Rock's face turned a shade of red even brighter than the jumpsuits of North Pole Colony. He looked at Strike, his eyes pleading.

"Hold on," Strike said. He kicked himself inside for thinking that any idea of his could be genius. "That first one didn't count."

"Sure it did," Pickaxe said. "Dang, I always wanted to know about this. I mean, do you really write down details about all of your farts?"

"Don't be ridiculous," Rock said. "I only keep track of my poops."

Strike stepped in front of his rocketback 2. "Look, it didn't count, and that's final. Rock gets a pass on that one. He doesn't have to answer."

"I thought you said any question must be answered," Boom said. "Or does that only apply to frakkin' Dark Siders?"

Strike stammered, but Rock stopped him. "I'll answer," he said. "Working together as a team means knowing and understanding each other." He pulled the little notebook out of his back pocket. He hefted it in his hand, his lips pressed tightly together.

A long moment passed, long enough that everyone looked at each other in an uncomfortable silence.

"This is the only thing I have left of my father," Rock finally said. "He gave it to me when I turned five, so I would stop scribbling in his notebook." He bit his lower lip, his jaw trembling. He stopped and started, finally forcing out his words. "That was three days before he died. In the Fireball Blast."

Everyone fell quiet. Strike hated himself. Memories of those soul-crushing days after the Fireball Blast clawed their way into his head. Dark, evil daggers pressed into his brain. It had to be just as bad or even worse for Rock. Strike squeezed his eyes tight, forcing himself to push and stomp and punch every one of those memories back down into his dungeon of nightmares.

Boom took a cautious step toward Rock. A lump slowly choked down her throat. "Oh jeez," she said. "I didn't mean to—"

"It's okay. I should have told you all about this a long time ago." Rock turned pages until he reached the very first one, with a note signed by his father. He displayed it with fierce pride. "My father was a great engineer. The best on the moon. He obsessively recorded anything and everything. He used the data to make Taiko Colony a better place. His analysis of satellite information allowed him to locate the Hokkaizen ice field just underneath Taiko Colony. Without it, Taiko would be in a serious water crisis by now. And the colony would never have been able to solve its post-Earthfall carbon dioxide level fluctuation without my father's observations. I must carry on his work. I must record everything I can. Without data, there are no answers."

The arena went quiet as everyone looked at each other. At the ground. Anywhere but at Rock.

Finally, Boom approached and awkwardly patted him on the shoulder. "I didn't mean to put you on the spot." She took a deep breath. "My name is Malala Al-Bashir. My mom was a tunneler from Cryptomare Colony. My dad was an electrical engineer from Saladin Colony. They both left for the Dark Side in the mass exodus after Earthfall. They were taken in with open arms, lots of Dark Siders helping them make a new home for themselves in one of the caverns that make up the Federation of Free Territories. They had me, and then . . ." She turned away from everyone, her fists shaking. "I don't want to talk about this anymore."

Strike glanced guiltily at the others, wishing he had never opened his mouth. He was such an idiot. "Hey, Boom—"

"This is exactly why I value privacy," she said. "No more of this frakkin' touchy-feely crap. We got work to do." She raced off, toward the heart of Taiko Colony.

The Miners followed Boom down Main Street, winding their way toward Taiko Square. She bounded along, the others barely keeping up as she executed crazier and crazier stunts. Most people were already at work, but the sick and the elderly and the people caring for their kids came out to watch the spectacle. Boom slid all the way under a green delivery rover from New Beijing Colony at a full run, and Strike had to tell her all about his most embarrassing moment, when he peed in his jumpsuit during his first day at the Tao Children's Home. She leapt for a high window ledge before doing twenty straight pull-ups, and Strike had to tell her about his secret crush on Hammer Fist, the Beatdown's rocketback 2.

Even though Boom was putting up a highlight reel of athletic prowess, Strike was sure he was going to beat her. But every time he got close, that was her cue to up her game.

Then they ran down the same alley that Strike and Rock had chased Boom into the first day they had met. From the back of the dead-end alley, Boom spun around and took off at full speed. After zigzagging between the two close-set walls, kicking off higher and higher, Boom leapt to slap the bottom of a windowsill before dropping back down.

Strike sprinted and jumped to follow her, kicking off one wall and then the other. His final burst propelled him high enough that he caught the windowsill with one hand. With a desperate grunt, he held on tight, his shoulder burning. One finger popped off, but he bore down and somehow managed to work his other hand up. Gripping on strong, he did ten pull-ups before turning to grin at Boom.

She studied him as he landed, a poof of dust kicking up under his feet. "Okay, not bad. You going to pump me for information now? Demand that I spill everything about me and the Dark Side? What is it with you United Moon Colony people, so frakkin' interested in everyone else's business?"

Strike's not-so-secret plan to get Boom to tell all her secrets now seemed even dumber. Teammates weren't supposed to grill each other—they were supposed to trust each other. Why was he listening to TNT, anyway? "I'm giving my question to Rock," he said. "It's only fair, because you got to ask him one—"

"Do you have a boyfriend on the Dark Side?" Rock said.

"What?" Boom said. "Eww, no. You could have asked me anything in the world, and that's what you want to know?" She shook her head at all the snickers coming from the others, but a tiny smile creased her face. "Just lead on, Strike, will you?"

As he searched for new feats to try, Strike ran the Miners in a circuit through the gray-brick buildings in the heart of Taiko Colony, past Taiko Elementary, the Tao Children's Home, Shinjuku Park, and dozens of apartment towers. His chest heaving, Strike ran past the machinery complex containing the oxygen recycler and the waste control systems, the entire facility surrounded by a high chain-link fence. He was keeping ahead of Boom, but her footsteps pounded right behind him.

Workers on a break were standing on top of the oxygen recycler, eating hardtack bars in front of a big radio as they listened to Berzerkatron and the Mad Mongol. One caught sight of the Miners and waved to them in a frenzy of excitement. A crowd gathered by the fence, the workers abuzz as they pointed at the hometown heroes. They excitedly held out the decals on their jumpsuits, many of them sporting both Strike's number 8 and Boom's number 3, and a few having all five Miners decals.

Suddenly, Nugget tore away from the pack. Racing toward the fence surrounding the oxygen recycler, he yelled to a guy standing on top of the giant apparatus. "Miners are going all the way this year. High five!" He bounded up a large rock and launched himself upward, crashing into the fence. Clinging to the chain links as they rattled back and forth, he crawled up toward the workers atop the oxygen recycler before slapping his hand through the metal wire. "Come on, Miners, get up here!"

The other Miners turned to look at Strike. He couldn't help but grin at the little boy's enthusiasm. He raced toward the fence and vaulted off the rock, slamming into the fence and scrambling up next to Nugget to high-five the adults covered in sweat and grime. Pickaxe followed behind, and then Rock, the four of them clinging to the fence and yelling at the tops of their lungs, whipping the workers into a frenzy. The cheers heightened from the growing crowd, a chant of "Mi-ners, Mi-ners, Mi-ners!" starting, people slamming their hands against the chain-link fence in a metallic drumbeat.

"I don't care what Berzerkatron or the Mad Mongol say," one of the workers yelled. "Miners are going to win the Ultrabowl!"

Strike was breathing hard, and his legs, arms, and back were burning. He hadn't been this exhausted in a long time. But as he looked at his teammates, hanging on to the chain-link fence and roaring with pride, he realized that their futures were not his burden alone. They were all in this together.

Except that there were only four Miners hanging from the fence. Boom stood back by one of the boulders, hands on her knees, catching her breath.

"Come on," Strike said, waving her up. "Miners together."

Boom nodded, looking up briefly before dropping her head. She planted her back foot and raced into a sprint, flying up the boulder and leaping high. She smacked into the fence next to Rock, sending it shaking.

Strike kept his eyes forward, holding out a hand for fans to high-five. He stole a glance at Boom. By telling them something incredibly painful about her past, she had given Strike even more reason to trust her. But something bothered him. Boom was in way better shape than the rest of them. She didn't need to catch her breath.

Why had she paused for so long?

10

GAME 2 VS. THE CRYPTOMARE MOLEMEN

SUNDAY MORNING, THE Miners headed down the Tunnel Ring to Cryptomare Stadium on an Ultraball league tram. Cryptomare Colony was the next stop after North Pole Colony, but the two couldn't have been more different. North Pole Colony was the cushiest and most extravagant place on the moon, while Cryptomare Colony was the center of the moon's tunnel-digging industry, filled with no-nonsense engineers and urban planners. It hadn't fallen on hard times as badly as Taiko Colony, but it was close.

As terrible a team as the Cryptomare Molemen were, the fans were still diehards. The tram station and the airlock entrance to Cryptomare Arena were jam-packed with rabid fans in gray jumpsuits, most of them displaying Grinder's number 6 decal or Dirtbag's number 2. Hardly anyone had phones, but a lot of people carried cheap radios, all tuned to the *SmashMouth Radio Blitz*. Genghis Brawn, a former league MVP and Ultrabowl champion with the Tranquility Beatdown, was doing color commentary, belting out his pregame analysis in his trademark raspy growl.

After unloading all their gear and suiting up, the Miners waited on one side of the playing field for the announcer to finish his pregame routine. Strike looked around the deep cavern, scanning for any new features and details the Molemen had added since last season. The people of Cryptomare Colony sure knew how to dig and tunnel. The arena walls were so smooth, fused to a glossy shine. Every detail was done with so much care. A gigantic Molemen logo—a tunneling machine with ten sets of gnarly drill teeth spinning in front—was etched into the stadium's ceiling. The tunneling device looked not only alive, but like it was hunting for prey. And the maze of tunnels built under the turf was staggering. Most of it was covered with clear impactanium so fans could see the action, but it was the visiting team's guess as to where any new secret passageways might be.

After the coin flip, the Miners lined up to kick off, the five Molemen in their gray Ultrabot suits lined up to receive. The crowd was roaring and chanting, but Strike could hear his teammates over helmet comm. "Miners ready?" he said.

"We smash their teeth in," Boom replied. "No mercy."

And she showed the Molemen none. As Strike kicked off to start the game, Boom raced like a runaway tram, beating everyone else down the field in a blur of blue. She juked out a blocker and smashed Grinder a split second after he caught the ball, launching him backward off his feet. It was all he could do to hold on to the ball as they tumbled toward his end zone, Boom launching a furious assault of punches at his chest plate. They rolled to a stop near the goal line, Grinder frantically clawing with one hand to stay out of his own end zone. Miners rushed in from one side and Molemen from the other, in a gigantic shoving match. It was all the Molemen could do to smother their own quarterback to the turf to prevent a Miners touchdown.

Refs ran in, clearing the pile to spot the ball. The stands went silent, the home team pinned to their own two-meter line, lucky to not be down 7–0 already. Even the field announcer paused before saying, "What. A. Hit. That Boom is a killer. I know Grinder is in an Ultrabot suit and all, but I would not want to be him. First down and a long, long, long ways to go."

The Miners gathered together by the ten-meter line. "Awesome hit," Strike said.

"Just getting started," Boom replied.

Near the back of the end zone, the Molemen crouched down together, Grinder jabbing wildly in Boom's direction. They broke the huddle, the five Molemen approaching the line of scrimmage.

Grinder paused as he neared the ball. Boom had dropped into a three-point stance right in front of him, with Nugget shoulder to shoulder. Boom's right glove was twitching, as if she couldn't wait to launch a barrage of punches into Grinder's face. She flipped her helmet visor to clear. Her nostrils flared, her eyes like that of a wild animal. She cracked a boot into the turf, making Grinder jump.

Swiveling around and motioning to his teammates in a panic, Grinder dropped into a shotgun formation, all the way at the back of his own end zone. He motioned to his crackback 1, Drill Bit, to set up as his center, right over the ball. His gaze still locked on Boom, Grinder took a step back. Then another. Then another. He stomped a tentative foot.

At the same moment Drill Bit long-snapped the ball between his legs, Boom leapt up and kicked off Nugget's shoulder, hurdling over Drill Bit. She shot in at Grinder a second after he pulled the ball in and tried to scramble. He juked hard and gave her a spin move, but she read it perfectly. Accelerating, she speared him in the chest. As she drove into him, she lifted him off his feet and whirled him around into a dizzying tornado. She let go, rocketing

Grinder backward. He slammed into the protective impactanium back wall of the arena before dropping to the turf.

The ball bobbling in his grasp, Grinder scrambled toward a hole in terror and dove into the underground maze, running scared. Boom leapt in after him, racing in hot pursuit. Even though it was Grinder's home field, Boom somehow managed to gain on him with each turn. But as they raced through a long straightaway, Grinder took a hard right under a slab of opaque turf and then suddenly disappeared. "Where'd he go?" Boom yelled over helmet comm.

Torch's voice came on as he screamed through his headset on the sideline. "Boom, go left and cover the exit by the fifteen-meter line! Strike, take the one by the twenty-five-meter line, center of the field. Everyone else, choose a Moleman and stick with them wherever they go."

Mobilized, the Miners raced into position. Shortly afterward, Grinder sprang out of the exit at the center of the twenty-five-meter line, but Strike locked onto his legs and whipsawed him into the ground. He picked Grinder up and whirled him around just as Boom had done, spinning faster and faster. As other Molemen rushed in to help, Strike let go of Grinder, firing him all the way back through his own end zone for a second time. With a thunderous crunch, he smashed helmet-first into the back protective barrier.

The Ultraball popped loose.

Players from both teams scrambled in pursuit as the ball pinged around, knocking off chest plates and gloves. It tumbled into a gaping entrance to the underground maze, and Boom dove for it, plummeting in. Drill Bit and Junker dropped down to chase her, but Boom had already recovered the fumble and was off and running, zigging and zagging through the tunnels. Junker gained ground on her, leaping for one of her ankles, but she high-stepped out of his grasp. Spotting a hole leading back to the surface near the five-meter line, she burst out and leapt for the end zone. Stretching out at maximum extension, she slammed the ball to the turf for a touchdown.

Grinder, still splayed out by the clear impactanium barrier Strike had thrown him into, flipped his visor to clear. His face in a red rage, he screamed bloody murder at his teammates. "You frak-face morons!" he shouted. "You have to protect me!" He got up and stormed off the field, calling for their one and only time-out of the game.

Strike wondered if Grinder was mad enough to click right out of his Ultrabot suit. Strike understood the frustration that came with broken plays, but Grinder seemed to have snapped.

The bloodbath continued through the first half and accelerated into the second, the Miners pounding the Molemen into submission. Strike ran for five TDs. Boom scored seven of her own, three of them on defense. Even

Rock got in on the action with a twisty TD run, racing through the underground maze as Torch helped him navigate the secret passageways. The Torch came up huge all game, helping Strike direct the action. There was something about having an Ultraball legend in his coach's box that made Strike think the Miners might be destined to go all the way.

When the final whistle blew, Strike looked up into the stands, feeling bad for the fans in gray jumpsuits trudging to the airlock exits, having shelled out their meager savings just to see their beloved home team crushed into dust yet again.

After a short autograph-signing session, the five Miners plus Torch rode a league tram through the Tunnel Ring back to Taiko Colony, their Ultrabot suits lined up along one wall. Pickaxe and Nugget wrestled and roughhoused on the floor, with Rock serving as a makeshift referee. Nugget's nose was jammed into Pickaxe's armpit. "What did you say?" Pickaxe asked. "You're mumbling. Speak up."

Nugget slapped at his brother's arm, his punches nothing more than slaps. Twisting away, he gasped for breath, his face dark red and dripping with sweat. He turned to Rock. "Shoving my face into his armpit is illegal. It smells like someone took a dump in there and then smooshed some foot cheese in for good measure. Why didn't you stop him?"

Rock pulled out his notebook, writing like mad as he fired out his rat-a-tat laugh. "Because it was funny. Not nearly as funny as a fart in the face, but still funny."

"Maybe there's hope for you after all," Strike said.

"Knock it off," Boom said from a corner of the tram. "We have work to do. Let's go over game film so we're ready to practice when we get back to Taiko Arena."

Everyone went silent, the Miners turning toward Strike. "We're going to practice?" Nugget said. "Why?"

Boom stared at Nugget in silence, her eyes burning like coals.

Nugget shrank down. "What I meant to say was, more practice sounds like a lot of fun."

"This isn't about fun," Boom said. "It's about winning the Ultrabowl. Nugget, you missed a block in the second half and Strike almost got sacked because of it. Pickaxe, you got faked out twice defending inside slants. Let's figure out how to fix that."

"Geez, cut us some slack," Pickaxe said. "We won big today, didn't we? And we rolled the Venom last week. We lit them on fire."

Rock flipped through his notebook. "Venom is not flammable," he muttered.

"Look." Boom pointed to a TV screen on the tram wall, broadcasting Ultraball highlights on *LunarSports Reports*. The Neutron's QB, Fusion, threw a pass through a slingshot zone to Chain Reaction, who superjumped off Ion Storm's back to snag the metallic blur of a ball that blasted into him like a missile. The brash rocketback had outleapt two Flamethrower defenders to make the catch—and then twisted midair to throw a lateral to the Neutrons' crackback 1, Radioactive, who was wide open on the other side of the field. "That was just one of the Neutrons' sixteen touchdowns on the day," Boom said. "Sixteen. The Neutrons crushed the Flamethrowers."

"Who cares if they beat up on a cursed team?" Pickaxe said. He shot a look at Torch.

Even though Torch was half a meter taller than Pickaxe and a whole lot stronger, he shrank down into his seat. He stared at his feet, flipping his black hair so it covered his eyes.

"Come on, man," Strike said. "Be cool. There is no such thing as the Torch's Curse."

"The Flamethrowers are a lot better than a lot of people think," Boom said. "They have a real shot at the playoffs this year. Might even beat us if we're not careful."

"No chance," Pickaxe said. "We're going to run roughshod over the Flamethrowers."

"Maybe so," Boom said. "But we have to practice even harder to keep up with the Neutrons." She reached up and tapped the top of the screen, at the ever-present Ultraball standings board. The Neutrons and Miners were the only two undefeated teams, but the Neutrons had already scored forty-two more points over the course of just two games.

Nugget stared at Strike with pleading eyes. "Do we really have to go practice right now?"

"What about going to our aunt Keiko's to play Nuclear Poker?" Pickaxe said. He crossed his arms and glared at Boom. "That's what the Miners have done after every game, for four straight years now. We're not practicing right after a game. That's just plain old stupid."

"We have to catch up to the Neutrons' scoring pace," Boom said. "And don't forget, they played two strong teams, while we played two of the worst." She slammed a fist into the side of the tram, making everyone jump. "We have to do better. We will do better."

Strike watched the Neutrons' highlights streaming on *LunarSports Reports*. Chain Reaction juked his defenders with electric moves. He and Meltdown shot themselves through slingshot zones together, exploding apart at rocket speeds to baffle the Flamethrowers. Fusion threw full-field bullets so hard that the ball didn't even arc. He bounced his passes off protective barriers with uncanny precision. And the Neutrons' defense sacked the Flamethrowers' quarterback nine times. It was like the Neutrons were playing a bunch of amateurs, running circles around a Farajah Flamethrowers team that had won their season opener in surprising fashion. After week 1, the Flamethrowers had looked like they might actually break the Torch's Curse—until they had been punched in the mouth by the North Pole Neutrons.

The tram chugged along in silence, only the clacking of the wheels along the tunnel tracks breaking the quiet. "Strike," Pickaxe said. "We can't keep up this pace all season long."

Boom bristled, her hands curling into fists. "You're a coward if you're afraid of practice."

"We need to rest," Pickaxe said.

"We can rest after the Ultrabowl. We can rest after we're dead."

"I agree with Boom," Rock said. "She makes good points. Although I hope the time for death is not too close at hand."

Boom's forehead wrinkled up, but she grinned at Rock. "This is one strange kid, but we should all be more like him. He's not afraid to work."

"I like you, too. I mean, I like to work. I mean . . ." He yanked out his notebook, mumbling as he wiped at the sweat beading up on his forehead.

"We can't break tradition," Pickaxe said. "We have to go over to Aunt Keiko's place like always. She's doing worse than ever. Even with Nugget and me giving her all our Ultraball money, she can't barely get by. Seeing us all is the only bright spot in her miserable existence. So what's it going to be, Strike? You gonna listen to Boom, or the Fireball Five?"

"Let me remind you, I agree with Boom," Rock said.

"Traitor," Pickaxe said. "What ever happened to standing with your teammates? You're choosing your girlfriend over us, your family?"

"Girlfriend?" Rock's eyes darted around the tram in panic. "I'm not her boyfriend. We're just friends. Right? We are friends, right?"

Boom rolled her eyes. She shot Rock a quick nod before focusing her scowl back onto Pickaxe. "Make your call, Strike," she said.

Strike bristled at all the bickering, and even more at Boom for having started it. The Miners were his clan. The Fireball Five had always been so tight, even closer than blood relatives. Why couldn't everyone just get along like in the past?

Unsure of what to do, Strike turned to the teenager who had shoved himself into a corner of the tram, out of the way. "Torch. What do you think?"

"I don't want to take sides. But . . ." Torch shrugged. "Boom has a point. The Neutrons have smashed up two good teams now. I thought the Flamethrowers might actually break the Torch's Curse, until I saw how badly the Neutrons smacked them down. We have to accelerate our scoring if we're going to catch the Neutrons in the season tiebreaker."

Strike nodded. He didn't want to make Pickaxe any madder than he already was, but Torch—and Boom and

Rock—had good points. "Yeah," he said. "If we lose the Ultrabowl, and there was a single thing we could have done . . ." He clenched his jaw, thinking yet again about what Torch's life would be like if he had just won an Ultrabowl. The sad, broken teenager in the tram might even have been Governor Torch of Farajah Colony. "We'll watch game film today when we get back. But we practice first thing tomorrow morning. We won't stop until night."

"A full day of practice?" Pickaxe said, his eyes going wide. "That's insane."

"That's going to kill us," Nugget said.

"You can't let a Dark Sider and a washed-up old QB tell you what to do," Pickaxe said. "You're the coach and general manager, not any of them."

Disgust smeared across Boom's face. "Strike knows that an Ultrabowl title doesn't just fall into your lap. You have to work for it."

Pickaxe got up out of his seat and stood toe-to-toe with her. "I'm tired of all your yapping. I work. I work hard. And you don't tell me what to do. You got that? Why don't you just go back to the Dark Side, where you came from?"

Strike jumped up, pushing Pickaxe back. "Everybody calm down. We're the Miners. Miners together, Miners forever, remember? No more arguing. We'll take a break tonight, and then go at it with a full day tomorrow. Pickaxe, you good with that?"

"Fine," Pickaxe grumbled.

"Nugget?"

"You know I'm with you one hundred percent," Nugget said. He sighed, slumping with exhaustion.

Strike chucked Nugget's shoulder. "I know you're tired and you want to goof off. How about this? We'll take it easy until we get back home. That's another hour. Plenty of time"—he nodded at Pickaxe and Rock—"for a dog pile."

"Now we're talking," Nugget said. "Who are we going to dog-pile—"

Strike, Pickaxe, and Rock dove onto Nugget. Squished to the ground, he groaned. "You guys suck."

At the top of the pile, Strike bounced up and down on top of the others, making everyone cry out and laugh.

Everyone but Boom.

RESULTS AND STANDINGS, AFTER WEEK 2

RESULTS, WEEK 2

Miners	**91**
Molemen	21

Neutrons	**112**
Flamethrowers	77

Explorers	**91**
Venom	49

Beatdown	**98**
Shock	35

STANDINGS, WEEK 2

	Wins	**Losses**	**Total Points**
Neutrons	2	0	217
Miners	2	0	175
Beatdown	1	1	168
Explorers	1	1	154
Flamethrowers	1	1	147
Shock	1	1	98
Venom	0	2	84
Molemen	0	2	35

BOOM'S BEATDOWN

PICKAXE AND NUGGET were already on the field when Strike and Rock arrived at Taiko Arena the next morning. "Where's Boom?" Strike asked. She had been the first player at practice every single day.

"Dunno," Pickaxe said, stifling a yawn. "She better get here soon though, or I'm going back to sleep." He scanned the airlock entrances to Taiko Arena, but there was no sign of Boom. "Where does she get off, calling an extra practice—a full-day one—and not even showing up? If she were here, I'd give her a piece of my mind. I don't care that she's a girl. I'd kick her ass."

"Why don't you say that to my face?" screamed a high-pitched voice.

Pickaxe ducked into a crouch, his hands covering his head. He cracked an eye open when Nugget busted up with laughter.

"You thought I was Boom," Nugget said, barely able to breathe through his giggles. "You almost pooped your pants."

"I knew it was you, you little butt booger," Pickaxe muttered. He glanced around before getting up. "And now you are going to die."

"All right, all right," Strike said. "Let's get warmed up while we wait for Boom."

Nugget continued to snicker, but he flinched when Pickaxe fake-punched at him. With a screech, Nugget reached up to his neck and rubbed it, cringing as he massaged out a knot. "We aren't really going to practice all day, are we?"

"Yes, we are," Strike said.

"Are you sure this is smart?" Pickaxe said. "A major injury during a game means we get disqualified. Isn't that right, Rock?"

"Well, not exactly," Rock said. "It's only clicking out of your Ultrabot suit on the field that disqualifies the team. And Ultrabot suits make it nearly impossible for their wearer to be injured. Nothing less than a nuclear explosion would hurt someone inside an Ultrabot suit."

Strike squeezed his eyes tight. All the arguing and these big decisions were making his head throb. The days of the Fireball Five playing loose and easy seemed like a lifetime ago.

A figure emerged from one of the tunnels leading into Taiko Arena. Her blue hood pulled down low over her face, Boom bounded in with choppy steps.

Strike froze at the sight of what looked like a bruise on her face. "Are you okay?"

"Fine." Boom slowed down, trying to disguise her awkward stride, but something was wrong.

Strike bounded over and bent down to stare at Boom's right leg. Boom was keeping it stiff as a board, not bending her knee. And although her jumpsuit hood was pulled down, she couldn't hide the deep purple-and-yellow splotch on her cheek. "What happened?" Strike asked. He reached toward her, but she slapped his hand away.

"Nothing," she said. "I fell down the stairs at my apartment building. Stop asking questions. Let's start practice."

Something's fishy, Strike thought. People didn't get hurt like that falling down stairs. But as Strike and Rock prodded Boom with further questions, her grunts and snarls made it clear that she didn't want to discuss it more.

Boom winced while getting into her Ultrabot suit. During the warm-up laps, she lagged Strike, her Ultrabot suit mirroring her limp. But by the last lap, she kept up with everyone, and at the ending one-hundred-meter dash, she just barely lost to Strike in their usual flat-out sprint.

"Got you today," Strike said. "Finally edged you out."

Pickaxe flipped his visor to clear. "What's the matter, Boom?" he asked. "You need a break?"

"No," Boom said.

Hours went by as the Miners practiced their formations and plays over and over. Boom never showed signs of stopping, even complaining when Strike called an end to practice after eight hours. After they had clicked out of their suits, the Miners tossed around a football made from compacted trash as they headed toward the arena exit. "I'm going to sleep for a week," Nugget said. "I've never been this tired."

Boom nodded and trudged away. "See you tomorrow. Got another hard day of practice ahead of us."

Strike reared back and fired a pass at her, Boom snagging it. "Wanna go over to the Tao Home with me and Rock?" he asked. "We're going to hang out with some of the kids there. Maybe even play some schoolyard football with them."

"Can't," Boom said. "Gotta go train."

"Come on, just hang out for a while," Strike said. "You know, team spirit and all. It'd be awesome for the kids, too. Playing football with you would be the highlight of their year."

"Strike brings up an excellent point," Rock said. "Time together off the field builds better communication on the field. It also can build friendships, of which I have few."

He slowly pulled his notebook from his back pocket. "If you wanted, I could show you all the details of how I categorize jokes. Over eighty-one percent of everything I've recorded is actually funny."

"I . . ." Boom bit her lip and turned away. "Sorry, Rock. I am curious about everything in that little book of yours. And I will go to the Tao Home with you one day. I promise. I know how much that place means to you guys. But not today."

"You have to stop training and practicing sometime," Pickaxe said.

"You don't understand how badly I need to make Raiden Zuna suffer, do you?" Boom said.

Pickaxe protested, but Strike held up a hand. "It's okay," Strike said. "Just go. See you tomorrow morning at seven."

Boom studied Strike for a long moment and walked off. "I'll be here at six." She left the airlock exit and disappeared.

Pickaxe waited until the door jerked closed and then exploded. "You can't let her talk to us like chumps. And don't you find it strange that she disappears into thin air after every practice? She's hiding something. Maybe all the sports talk people have stopped asking questions about her and the Dark Side, but we can't afford to. We have to know what she's up to. We have to follow her."

"What?" Nugget said. "No way. We can't spy on one of

our own teammates. Auntie Keiko would be furious with us if she ever found out we did something as low as that. I'll tell her; I swear I will."

"No, you won't," Pickaxe said. "Aunt Keiko has enough to worry about. So you better shut your trap."

Rock looked at Strike, who had gone quiet. "You can't actually be considering this," Rock said. "Don't do it. We must respect her privacy. It's of utmost importance to her. Following her could mess everything up."

Strike chewed his lip. He rarely went against anything Rock suggested, especially when he was this adamant. But Boom was definitely hiding something.

If she was mixed up with Raiden Zuna, Strike needed to find out about it.

CAST NO SHADOWS

THEIR HOODS PULLED low over their grime-streaked faces, Strike and Pickaxe walked down a side street, staying in the shadows behind Boom. She blended into the crowds, wearing the same thing as all the people returning home from work in the mines: a filthy jumpsuit with layers of gray moon dust caked on. Most everyone in Taiko Colony would usually recognize the famous Miners, especially considering how many people carried radios tuned to broadcasts from *LunarSports Reports*, *SmashMouth Radio Blitz*, or the *Touchdown Zone*. But with all the crud they had scrubbed all over their faces, and their hoods pulled down low, Strike and Pickaxe passed for any of the grubby dropout kids in the streets, too weak to work in the mines, forced to beg for hardtack bars just to stay alive.

In a way, it was good that it was just Strike and Pickaxe on this mission, Rock and Nugget staying behind after refusing to spy on Boom. It was easy for two people to blend into the crowd. "Where did she go?" Strike asked.

Pickaxe jabbed him with an elbow. "There."

Strike caught a glimpse of Boom turning the corner onto another dim street. They raced over, hiding behind the edge of a tall building. A cluster of run-down apartments, this neighborhood was one of the worst in all of Taiko Colony. The lighting grid mounted to the roof of the massive underground cavern barely lit the streets here, eerie shadows thrown across the ramshackle structures. Strike moved in tiny shuffling steps, making sure to keep low to the ground.

After they nearly lost her three times, she finally arrived at a giant apartment building with a flight of stairs leading up to the main entrance. Hardly anyone was around. They waited behind a recycling dumpster as Boom bounced up and opened the door.

"Go!" Strike hissed. There had to be dozens of individual apartments inside, so they had to move quickly to follow her. Strike raced toward the front staircase behind Pickaxe. With one giant leap, Pickaxe bounded up the full flight and raced toward the main door.

Strike was right behind Pickaxe when he caught a blur of movement. "Look out!" he yelled.

But it was too late. Someone sprang out of the door, launching a karate kick at Pickaxe's chest. He flew backward, spinning head over heels.

Strike leapt in, ready to fight. But when he saw the person's face, he put down his fists. "Boom?"

Bouncing on her toes in a fighting stance, Boom stepped into the hazy light. "Why did you follow me?"

Strike gulped. "You knew we were following you?"

Boom pushed up her sleeves. "Because you don't trust me? We're never going to win the Ultrabowl if we don't trust each other, on and off the field—"

"I heard something about you," Strike blurted.

"Yeah?" Boom said. "That I'm in Zuna's pocket? That he paid me to throw games?"

Strike's eyes widened. "How did you know?"

"After getting stabbed in the back like you did last year, you'd be a fool if you didn't worry about the same thing happening again. And you may be a lot of things, Strike, but you're no fool." She looked toward a flickering lighting panel mounted to the cavern's ceiling, her eyes narrowing. "I bet TNT is behind this, isn't he? He thinks I turned traitor, just like he did."

Strike exchanged surprised glances with Pickaxe. *How could she possibly know so much?* Strike thought. The only people he had told about TNT were Rock and Pickaxe. Not even Nugget knew, the crackback being too young to understand these kinds of things. It was like Boom had ghostly Dark Side powers, pulling bits of information straight out of his mind. "Yeah," Strike said. "That's exactly right."

Pickaxe rolled up onto his elbows with a groan. "How come you wouldn't say anything about what happened to your face?"

"Who beat you up?" Strike asked. "How am I supposed to trust you if you don't trust me?"

Boom touched the dark purple bruise on her face. Her stony gaze melted away. She sighed and sat down on the top step, motioning for Strike to sit next to her. "Two of Zuna's goons jumped me," she said.

"What do you mean, jumped you?" Strike asked.

"I mean, two guys came out of an alley on my way to practice this morning. Two on one—that's Zuna's idea of a fair fight. They told me to take payoffs to throw games, or they'd break my legs."

Strike's throat went dry as a hardtack bar. "What did you do?"

"What choice did I have?"

Strike slumped, putting his head in his hands. It was happening all over again. Last year it was TNT; this year it was—

"We had to break their legs," Boom said.

"You did what?" Pickaxe said.

"You took on two of Zuna's thugs?" Strike asked. "And who's 'we'?"

"Some of my Dark Sider friends. How do you think I was onto you two so easily?"

Strike looked around the nearly deserted area. "Where are they?"

"You'll never see them. In blue jumpsuits we stole for them, they blend right in. But they're around. And Dark Siders have built all sorts of secret tunnels all over the moon. We use them when we need to."

"Is that how you originally got into Taiko Colony?" Pickaxe asked.

Boom shrugged. "How many times do I have to tell you to respect my frakkin' privacy?"

"Zuna's got a lot of power," Strike said. "And a lot of money. He's going to come after you."

"No, he's not," Boom said. "We told those guys that anything I get, Chain Reaction's going to get it twice as bad. Even if they do manage to break one of my arms, Chain Reaction is going to find himself with two broken arms."

"But you couldn't do anything to Chain Reaction," Strike said. "All the Neutrons are living large in North Pole Colony. Probably protected by Blackguards."

"Secret tunnels. And Dark Siders cast no shadows. So Zuna now knows he can't do a thing to me. He knows that without Chain Reaction, his Neutrons are dead meat."

Strike's head was even more jumbled than usual. Not just one Dark Sider showing up out of nowhere, but a couple? Popping out of tunnels, wherever they pleased? "I want to believe you," he said. "But look what happened last year with TNT."

"There's a big frakkin' difference between me and TNT," Boom said. "Without the Ultrabot suit on, TNT is just a scared little turd eater. I'm not scared of anything."

"Even death?" Pickaxe said. "If what you say is true, Zuna's goons are seriously going to try to kill you now."

"I'm not afraid of Zuna. Or death."

"But Raiden Zuna—"

"Raiden Zuna is coming after the Dark Side. His alliance has already tried to seize one of our ice mines. They killed ten people, including . . ." Her nostrils flared, her breathing quickening. "Including my parents. I must make him pay. Even if it costs me everything, I will make Zuna pay."

Boom's words covered Strike in a toxic haze. For years, Strike had sought vengeance on whoever or whatever caused the Fireball Blast that took his parents' lives. No wonder Boom was so focused on beating down Raiden Zuna. "Why didn't you tell me this earlier? And how do you know it's Zuna that killed your parents?"

"Their charred faces . . ." Her eyes lost their focus, her voice going hollow. "My parents were found in an ice mine cavern, with eight others. Oxygen levels were normal, no signs of a struggle. But everyone's bodies were all burned, skin peeling off everywhere. There's only one weapon on the entire moon that could have done that: the Meltdown Gun."

Strike and Pickaxe looked at each other, unsure of what to say. Strike had known that Zuna was one of the most crooked of the moon's Colony Governors. He had paid off TNT to throw last year's Ultrabowl, after all.

But maybe Zuna was even shadier than Strike had thought.

"Are you and your friends doing this on your own?" Strike asked. "Or is it a Dark Side plot, like Berzerkatron says?"

"Just us," Boom said. She shook her head in disgust. "The government sealed off the tunnel Zuna came in through, plus a whole lot more. The Federation of Free Territories doesn't want anything to do with the United Moon Colonies. They'd never send people over to this side, especially when doing so could start some kind of war. So it's up to me and my friends to stop Zuna. To destroy the Meltdown Gun."

They sat quietly for a minute. Everything Boom said was making sense. But the way TNT had plunged a knife into Strike's back last year would never be forgotten. "Swear to me that you haven't taken money from Raiden Zuna," Strike said.

Her deep brown eyes filled with determination, she put a hand to her heart. "On my parents' souls, I swear that I'm going to destroy his Meltdown Gun."

Strike nodded. There was no doubting Boom anymore. No matter what happened from here on out, he would trust his star rocketback without question. She had a raw thirst for vengeance. "Miners together?" Strike said, sticking out his hand.

"Who are you going to listen to if TNT makes accusations about me again?" Boom asked.

"You. I swear it on my parents' souls. Come on. Miners together?"

She studied Strike's hand and shook it. "Miners forever."

"See you tomorrow morning," Strike said. "We have a game plan to put together. The Explorers are looking really strong."

"We're going to crush the Explorers into dust." Boom headed into her apartment building and closed the door.

Strike and Pickaxe started down the road. Pickaxe kept stealing glances over his shoulder, peering into alleys and dark corners. A couple of blocks away, he nudged Strike and whispered, "Dark Siders just popping up whenever she needs them? Breaking the legs of two hired goons? That story is crazy."

Strike nodded. "It is hard to believe, but—"

"And what was all that about Zuna killing people? He's a Colony Governor. Colony Governors don't kill people. I don't know what she's up to, but we can't trust her."

"Yes, we can. We have to. All those stories do sound

weird, but she is giving her all to help us win the Ultrabowl. I believe her."

"What about TNT insisting that there's a traitor on the team?" Pickaxe said. "He risked his life to find that out. He has to be right."

Strike scuffed his feet along the dusty road. A notion struck him:

What if TNT is right . . . but only partially right?

Dark inklings swirled around Strike's head, slowly gelling into a story that might finally make sense of everything. He tried to push the sinister notion away. But it kept on tugging, willing him to listen. It was the only explanation that made sense if both Boom and TNT were to be believed.

What if someone else in his Miners family—someone in the original Fireball Five—was planning on stabbing him in the back?

He shook his head and swore at that nightmarish thought, squashing it back down into its pit of despair.

13

GAME 3 VS. THE KAMAR EXPLORERS

THE MINERS CRANKED up to a new level in preparation to play the Kamar Explorers in their home opener at Taiko Arena. Practices pushed everyone to their max, starting with full calisthenics during the mornings while wearing weight jackets filled with rocks, followed by eight intense in-suit sessions with only short water and hardtack breaks in between. Film watching and review went to five nights a week, each person being quizzed for hours by Boom and Strike on what they saw. Deafening artificial noise was screeched into the helmet comm so everyone would read hand signals and body language better. Pickaxe complained bitterly about the aches and pains and all the practice time, but by the morning of their home opener, all five Miners were playing together like never before.

In the Taiko Arena locker room, Pickaxe and Nugget stretched while Boom and Rock sat on a bench together. Over the past week, the two of them studying Rock's notebook had become a common sight. She pointed at a tattered page. "Shouldn't this one be categorized under 'One-liners,' not 'Humor Based on Exaggeration'?"

"That was my first thought, too," Rock said. "But I can only place each joke into one spot, so I have to make a judgment call. This one was particularly tough, since it's actually two lines. And not very funny."

"No doubt." Boom read out of the notebook. "'Yo momma's so stupid, she got hit by a delivery rover. One that was parked.' That doesn't even make sense."

"Yes, it does," Strike said. "It's parked. Who gets hit by a parked rover?"

"Exactly my point," Rock and Boom said in unison. Rock peeked at Boom out of the corner of his eye. He cautiously held out a fist to her. A huge grin came to his face when she bumped it.

"Let's get ready for the game," Strike said. "And it was funny."

Everyone gathered around Strike. "This team is not the Molemen or the Venom," he said. "The Explorers are the real deal. Our first real challenge of the season. If we give them even the slightest opening, they're going to punch our helmets off. So let's go out there and score a couple TDs right off the bat. We have a lot of points to score if we're going to catch up to the Neutrons. Score early. Score often."

The four Miners nodded, placing their hands on top of Strike's. "Rip out their frakkin' throats," Boom said. "No mercy."

Rapidly becoming a Miners pregame tradition, Boom's ominous words didn't have the raw energy and noise of TNT's rock-'em-sock-'em cheers from years past, but they had a similar effect. A chill ran up Strike's spine. "Line it up," he said as the announcer's pregame routine started on the overhead speakers in the corners of the locker room. "Get ready to make our fans proud." He got behind the rest of his team, rubbing his neck. It was aching more than ever after Boom's extra-hard workouts during the week, but Strike was getting used to it. And his muscles were starting to feel bigger. Stronger. Faster. Strike liked it.

The announcer finished calling out the other team's lineup, his voice echoing through the tunnel leading into the locker rooms. "And now, the home team, the runner-up in each of the three past Ultrabowls, the pride and joy of Taiko Colony, I give you . . . the Taiko Miners!"

The crowd roared, sending a surge of pride through Strike's chest. Pickaxe got called first, running into a shower of cheers from the home crowd. Nugget followed behind his brother. Rock bounded out next.

The announcer called Boom's name. But Strike put a hand on her shoulder, holding her back.

"What are you doing?" Boom said.

"We're going together, you and me," Strike said. "If that's okay with you."

Boom nodded and fist-bumped Strike. They ran out together to an eruption of noise, a wall of sound penetrating through their Ultrabot suits. Strike marveled at the crowd, Governor Katana front and center at the fifty-meter line, leading everyone in cheers, screaming at the top of his lungs. It made Strike think about all the fan letters he had gotten over the years telling him how important the Miners were, how they gave people a glimpse of sunshine in a lifetime of darkness and misery.

After winning the coin toss, the Miners elected to kick off. Strike lined up behind the teed-up ball on the goal line and raised a hand. Studying the Explorers' lineup, he scowled. "They're in a modified I-formation," he said into his helmet comm. "Cover three package."

As the Miners moved into position, Boom nudged Strike. She pointed to the sidelines, where Torch was waving in a complicated set of hand signals. "Cover red two two?" Boom said. "Smart call. The Explorers might try a full-field lateral."

Strike looked over to the coach's box and gave Torch a thumbs-up. For more than a week now, he had been attending practices and film sessions after work, racing over to Taiko Arena to join the Miners after his shift at the mines ended. Torch's body might have outgrown the Ultrabot suit, but his head was still in the game.

"Okay, everyone," Strike said. "Cover red two two." He charged forward, booting the ball high. Soaring through the dusty air of Taiko Arena, the ball arced and dropped to the corner of the end zone. It went over the receiver's head and hit the back wall, bouncing off. The Explorer grabbed it and set up behind his wedge of blockers.

"It's the reverse pitch," Strike said. "I'll take out the lead man." He widened his path, circling toward the Explorer with the ball.

The ball carrier charged right at him in a collision course. When he was only ten meters away, he pitched it back to the man behind him, who swept the other way.

"Boom, your side!" Strike said just before the Explorer smashed into him, driving him to the ground.

"Double-teamed," Boom yelled back. "Rock, get in there."

Strike turned to see two Explorers wrestling with Boom. He swore under his breath. Even with Boom's phenomenal skills inside an Ultrabot suit, not even she could tear away from a full-on double-team. "Pickaxe, cover the lateral!"

"Got it!" Pickaxe said.

The runner slowed and looked across the field. Just as his wedge collapsed and Rock rushed at him, he swiveled to change direction, stepping on the edge of a trapdoor field pit, plummeting down in surprise. But just before he disappeared, he lobbed the steel ball wildly across the field.

Pickaxe sprinted in. He chugged along, closing the gap. It was going to be close. Either Pickaxe would bat the ball away, or the Explorers would have an easy touchdown.

"Go!" Strike yelled.

Spurred on by his QB, Pickaxe launched himself into the air, soaring. His left arm fully outstretched, he caught the nose of the Ultraball as he passed, sending it wobbling high and out of everyone's reach. His arms windmilling as he tried to regain his balance, Pickaxe fell back to the turf, slamming awkwardly onto his side.

A whistle blew, and a ref dressed in armor plating jogged to the sideline where a pile of players had fallen on the ball. "Explorers' ball, first down," the ref announced over the arena's speaker system. The crowd erupted in a cheer, calling out Pickaxe's name in a hypnotic chant.

"Nice work," Strike said as he jogged toward Pickaxe, who was still on the ground. "You saved that touchdown."

But Pickaxe didn't reply. Writhing on the ground, he groaned. He clutched his right shoulder.

Nugget came over. "Nice play, fart face." He offered his brother a hand.

Letting out a moan of agony, Pickaxe shook his head. "I'm hurt. Bad."

Dread seeped into Strike's bones as the rest of the Miners approached. "What's going on?" Boom asked.

"Crap," Strike said when Pickaxe changed his visor to clear, a pained grimace on his face. Standing up, he waved his teammates over. "He's hurt." He flipped his own visor to clear and bent down. "How bad is it?"

Pickaxe's eyes were squeezed together tight, a flood of tears running down his face.

Strike's head swam with disbelief. The impactanium Ultrabot suits made it nearly impossible to get hurt. No one in the nine-year history of the Underground Ultraball League had ever gotten hurt on the field. A team could call up a sub for the following week, but one of the core principles of the Underground Ultraball League was that all five people had to be on the field for every single down.

No exceptions.

Bending down low, Boom inspected Pickaxe's Ultrabot suit. "Maybe you twisted something? But even that's not really possible."

"I have to take my suit off," Pickaxe said, moaning in pain. "My arm is on fire."

He went to unlatch his chest plate, but Rock stopped him. "If you get out of your suit, we'll lose this game. You can't leave your suit until halftime."

"You can play through it, right?" Strike asked.

Pickaxe shook his head. "No way. I have to unclick."

Strike hovered over Pickaxe while keeping an eye on

the play clock, ticking down. He turned to a ref and put his hands together in the shape of a T. He hated to use their one and only time-out, but it had to be done.

"Where does it hurt?" Boom asked.

Pickaxe pointed to his shoulder, wincing. "It's from all the extra practice. You did this to me. Boom broke my arm."

Boom took hold of Pickaxe's gloved hand. "Brace yourself. This is going to hurt. A lot."

Strike jumped in to stop her, but Boom held up her free hand. "Trust me," she said.

Unsure of what to do, Strike looked to Rock, who nodded.

"Okay, Boom," Strike said. "Do it."

Boom rolled Pickaxe over onto his stomach. She placed her foot onto Pickaxe's back and jerked up his arm, wrenching it far behind him.

Pickaxe shrieked, pounding the turf with his left glove. "Get off me! You're gonna tear my arm out!" He continued to wail, but his cries slowly died out. Soon, he quieted to whimpers.

"Better?" Boom asked. She carefully lowered his arm.

"I guess," Pickaxe said. "What did you do? Dark Side voodoo?"

Boom offered a hand and pulled Pickaxe up. "You had a cramp. I stretched out your shoulder muscles until it went away. Get up."

"A cramp?" Strike said. "You've never had a muscle cramp before?"

"We almost forfeited the game because of your owie," Boom muttered.

Pickaxe tentatively prodded at his shoulder. "It was the worst pain I've ever had. It's Boom's fault."

"It's my fault I worked you so hard that you could actually make that play?" Boom said.

"Everyone line it up," Strike said. "Our time-out is almost over." He scanned the Explorers' offense, setting up for what looked like a trick play.

"That wouldn't have happened to me if Boom hadn't worked us so hard," Pickaxe said. "It's her fault we almost had to forfeit. Not mine."

"Get your head out of your butt and back into the game!" Strike yelled. "They're changing the play!" As the Explorers shifted from slingshot V formation to a deep shotgun, Strike ran over to yank Pickaxe to his new position.

Shootout, the Explorers' quarterback, took full advantage of the Miners' confusion, quick-hiking the ball. The rocketback Pickaxe was supposed to jam at the line ran right around him, untouched, streaking toward the end zone. Shootout heaved a bullet to the wide-open Lasso, no Miner within five meters of him. It was the easiest touchdown the Explorers had ever scored.

And it was all Pickaxe's fault.

Explorers fans in the crowd started in with a jeering "Axe-picker, Axe-picker" chant. Strike knew he needed to go over and tell Pickaxe to shake it off, to not let the nickname get to him. But in that moment, it was all he could do to not explode at his crackback 1.

RESULTS, WEEK 3

Miners	**91**
Explorers	63
Beatdown	**105**
Molemen	14
Neutrons	**84**
Venom	28
Flamethrowers	**105**
Shock	42

STANDINGS, WEEK 3

	Wins	**Losses**	**Total Points**
Neutrons	3	0	301
Miners	3	0	266
Beatdown	2	1	273
Flamethrowers	2	1	252
Explorers	1	2	217
Shock	1	2	140
Venom	0	3	112
Molemen	0	3	49

THE DEEP PROSPECT

THANKFULLY, THAT WAS Pickaxe's only big mistake of the game, the crackback playing solidly after Strike begrudgingly pulled him aside to give him a pep talk. After the 91–63 victory, the Miners walked out of the locker room to a crowd of people waiting for autographs. Strike shrugged at Boom, who groaned at having to go through it all. "We have to do what we have to do," Strike said. "The fans helped win this game for us."

"Fine," Boom said, taking an Ultraball-shaped rock from a fan and signing it. "Let's get this over with." Even with her sour attitude, fans swarmed her, the star of the game. Not only had she scored six touchdowns, but she had five sacks and twenty-one solo tackles.

An eager fan pushed against Boom. "Hey, Boom! Can you sign my chest?" He handed her a permanent pen and lifted his shirt to expose his rib cage poking out under dark brown skin.

An evil grin came to Boom's face. "Sure, I can sign it." She let out a low laugh.

"Boom," Strike said. "No dirty jokes."

She stopped, her eyes shooting toward Strike. "Aw. But—"

"Just sign your name, okay?"

"Fine." Boom autographed the boy's chest so hard he squealed. Tossing the pen back to him, she yelled out, "Anyone else?"

"C'mon, Boom," Strike said. "You have to treat our fans better—"

But to Strike's surprise, the boy lifted his arms and roared to his friends. Groupies charged toward Boom with their pens, swarming the wide-eyed rocketback.

Strike laughed, elbowing a fan who had sidled up next to him. "Serves her right, huh?" Strike said.

"Here," the boy said, sticking out his hand.

Strike started to sign it, but paused. "What is this?"

The kid's hand had "Explorers vs. Molemen, 77–14" scrawled on it. He pulled it back and ran off.

Strike stole a glance around. "Hey, Rock. I'll be back in a bit."

"Where are you going?"

"Just gotta take care of something." Strike made his way through the crowds and into the locker room. He crept out through the security exit, pulling his hood down low over his face. Nodding to a guard at the door, he stepped out and turned down a maintenance tunnel that followed along the perimeter of Taiko Arena and then cut inward, under the stadium. He slid behind a big stone and slithered through a hole. The tunnel angled up and curved around.

"You came," a voice said.

"Been almost four years since we used this place," Strike said. TNT's ashy face appeared as Strike made his way into the secret cave TNT introduced him to, where they had gone every day after school to watch the empty strip-mining crater being transformed into Taiko Arena. Through peepholes bored into the stadium walls underneath the bleachers, TNT and Strike had watched the exhibition game between the Explorers and the Molemen that opened the new Taiko Arena. Even with the two teams just playing for fun, that first live game had blown Strike's mind, the raw speed and power of Ultraball players making them seem like superheroes.

"You're in deep trouble," TNT said. "Boom is in Zuna's pocket."

"You better have proof."

"I do. Just listen, okay?"

Strike looked down at the ground, kicking at trash he

and TNT had left behind years ago. "I'm listening."

"I swear to you on my father's grave. I heard Raiden Zuna buy off a Miner."

Strike studied TNT's face, desperate and pleading. "What exactly did you hear?"

"He set up a meeting with his 'deep prospect.' And then he sent out a big guy, carrying a briefcase full of money."

"How do you know it was money?"

"Why else would you handcuff a briefcase to your wrist?"

It was just like the rumors Strike had heard: Raiden Zuna's people moved money around in locked briefcases. Strike's stomach churned as memories of last year's Ultrabowl swirled through his head. Was Zuna setting him up again, this time to take an even bigger fall? "Do you have a recording of him saying he was delivering the money to Boom? Or pictures?"

TNT bit his lip. "You know I don't have a phone or a camera."

"How am I supposed to believe you if you don't have any real proof? And are you absolutely sure the traitor is—"

"There's more. A lot more. Zuna. If he becomes governor of Taiko Colony . . ." TNT held his breath for a long, tense moment. "He's going to destroy it. His alliance is planning on blast fracking and explosion mining to collect all the ice deposits far underneath. The entire cavern will collapse."

Strike blinked hard, stunned into silence. Then he grabbed TNT's filthy jumpsuit, violently shaking him. "Shut up. Just shut up. That's insane. No one would do that. Not even Zuna is that crazy."

But a cold shiver ran up Strike's back. With each passing second, it sounded less and less crazy. Cratering an entire colony to harvest the priceless ice deposits far underneath . . .

That was exactly what Boom had said Zuna was doing on the Dark Side.

"You know I'm right, Strike," TNT said. "All that ice has to be worth millions of U-dollars. You have to stop Zuna from becoming governor of Taiko Colony. The Miners must win the Ultrabowl. You have to do something about Boom before she stabs you in the back."

"Wait," Strike said, shaking his head. "No. This can't be right. Who did you get this information from?"

"I overheard one of his bodyguards. He said that—" TNT flinched at the sound of rapidly approaching footsteps.

Strike swiveled around. "Rock?"

Rock glared at TNT. His usually stoic demeanor had been replaced with the look of a rabid animal leaping in for the kill. "I appreciate what you've done for Strike and me in the past. I really do. Without your mother's help, we would never have gotten a chance to try out for the Miners, nor would we have gotten practice time in Ultrabot suits before those tryouts. But if you ever again accuse Boom of being a traitor, there's going to be trouble. She's an incredible teammate and a very good friend. I will defend her honor with fists to your face."

TNT scrabbled past Rock, the bony boy covering his head with his hands as he scrambled away. "I'll get more proof, Strike," he said. "I swear, I will." He shoved his way through the tunnel opening and disappeared.

"You made a promise to Boom, on your parents' souls," Rock said, still breathing hard, his eyes wild. "You cannot go back on that. TNT is poisoning your mind."

"You overheard him?" Strike said.

Rock nodded. "He thinks he's helping, but he's only making more trouble."

"But what about what he said? Zuna is going to destroy Taiko Colony."

"Ridiculous. The Council of Governors would never allow something like that to happen. Even if Zuna does become governor of Taiko Colony, he'd still only control two of the twenty-one votes."

"What about that alliance of his?"

"He'd need fourteen votes to control the Council of Governors. How could he possibly convince so many governors to go along with such a criminal plan?" Rock looked over his shoulder to where TNT had disappeared.

"Maybe TNT is delusional. Dust poisoning would have that effect. Or more likely, Zuna is feeding him stories designed to mess with your head."

Rock made sense. Could Zuna be setting TNT up, feeding him fake calls, sending out henchmen on made-up payoff missions? Maybe Strike was being played like a fool.

It wouldn't be the first time.

"Listen to me," Rock said. "Boom is not a traitor. I've never been more sure about anything in my life."

Strike nodded. "You're right." He held out a fist for Rock to tap. "Thanks for looking out for me."

But as they walked back along the path to the stadium, Strike thought about TNT catching touchdown after touchdown after touchdown, knowing exactly what route his best friend was going to run without even calling a play. They had been the tightest quarterback-and-rocketback pair there had ever been, even tighter than Fusion and Chain Reaction, or Torch and Dragon. Even after TNT's betrayal, Strike still felt the threads of their unbreakable connection. TNT had dedicated the rest of his life to making things right. And he made a ton of sense about Zuna aiming to plunder the ice deposits deep underneath Taiko Colony.

There was one explanation that would allow Strike to believe Rock, Boom, and TNT. The fiendish thought clawed again at the back of Strike's brain, hissing, screeching, demanding that it be heard:

Another one of your Fireball Five brothers is going to stab you in the back.

Now that the very future of Taiko Colony was in jeopardy, Strike no longer had a choice in the matter. He opened the door and let the nightmare in.

THE
SMASHMOUTH
RADIO BLITZ

"And we're back! This is Genghis Brawn of the SmashMouth Radio Blitz, bringing you the most smashmouth Ultraball play-by-play on the moon. Folks, can you believe the Tranquility Beatdown? The Miners are still clinging to the lead, 70–63, but my old team has been punching the Miners in the face during the second half. Destroyer is poised to lead the Beatdown to the tying score and send the game into overtime. I haven't seen such a stellar performance from a Beatdown quarterback, well, since I put the team on my back and rammed us to an Ultrabowl VI victory. Today, Destroyer is playing with that same heart and fire.

"It's fourth down. The teams break their huddles. Destroyer and his wrecking crew stride forward, their royal purple Ultrabot suits gleaming under the spotlights of Taiko Arena. The hometown Taiko Colony crowd is on its feet, stomping and roaring in waves of blue. The Beatdown set up in shotgun formation. Destroyer jogs toward a long field trench. He drops in and disappears! Chokehold is over the ball, ready to hike it. But to who?

"Chokehold looks up to the scoreboard, waiting. The Beatdown are stalling, allowing the last thirty seconds to tick down. Over in the Miners coach's box, Torch is frantically signaling to Strike. Torch has been making *great adjustments the entire game. The play clock is now at fifteen. Ten. Five. Destroyer comes rocketing out of the far end of the deep trench! Chokehold hikes it high into the air, and it pings right into Destroyer's hands as he's vaulting skyward!*

"But Nugget is right on it. He's going to superjump off Pickaxe's back and intercept Destroyer. Nugget slips off Pickaxe's shoulders! Yet another mistake by the Axepicker. Nugget is flying toward Destroyer, but he's off course. Destroyer soars by Nugget with a meter to spare. Strike launches himself up on an intercept course.

"But Destroyer is twisting in midair! He throws a lateral across the field! Hammer Fist is wide open! The pass rockets into Hammer Fist, blasting her clear off her feet, crunching into the impactanium barrier. She pops back up and takes off running. Only Boom has a shot at stopping her now. But Boom is changing her angle. She's letting Hammer Fist have the corner, untouched! Hammer Fist is going to score!

"No! The turf collapses underneath Hammer Fist. Boom let Hammer Fist take the sideline—right into a camouflaged pit. Boom dives in after Hammer Fist, plummeting out of sight. Other players race in. Boom rockets out of the pit! She's got the ball. Boom has the ball! She front-flips over a Beatdown defender, landing on her feet and sprinting the other way.

"Uppercut is in hot pursuit of Boom. Uppercut has the angle. They cross the fifty-meter line. The forty. The

thirty. Uppercut launches himself at Boom. She ducks, catching his outstretched glove with her free hand. She whips him over her head, flinging him like a meteor into the impactanium barrier. She sprints across the goal line. Touchdown, Miners! The game is over! Unbelievable. If that's not number one on LunarSports' Top Ten tonight, I will shove a hardtack bar up my nose.

"Miners 77, Beatdown 63. The Miners race in to join their star rocketback. Everyone except Strike, that is. He's up in Pickaxe's grill, chewing out his crackback 1 in a firestorm of fury, and for good reason—the Axepicker's moronic third-down offsides penalty kept the Beatdown in the game. And what the frak happened with his botched launch of Nugget on fourth down? Good thing Boom saved the game. Saved Pickaxe's axe.

"The Miners remain undefeated on the season. I'm heading down to the postgame press conference now. Can't wait to hear what Strike has to say about his star rocketback saving the day. Or his crackback 1 nearly costing the Miners the game. The Miners cannot afford to let Axepicker pick his axe like that next week against the North Pole Neutrons.

"What a game, folks, what a game. This is Genghis Brawn of the SmashMouth Radio Blitz, bringing you the most smashmouth Ultraball play-by-play on the moon. Stay tuned for more."

RESULTS AND STANDINGS, AFTER WEEK 4

RESULTS, WEEK 4

Miners	**77**
Beatdown	63
Neutrons	**91**
Explorers	63
Flamethrowers	**112**
Molemen	21
Shock	**42**
Venom	35

STANDINGS, WEEK 4

	Wins	Losses	Total Points
Neutrons	4	0	392
Miners	4	0	343
Flamethrowers	3	1	364
Beatdown	2	2	336
Shock	2	2	182
Explorers	1	3	280
Venom	0	4	147
Molemen	0	4	70

15

THE JUNK HOLE

A FEW DAYS before the Neutrons game, Strike sat on the edge of the old quarry connected to Taiko Colony. The giant sloping pit had once been a source of raw materials, moon rock scraped out by the bucketful to be pressed and fused into gray bricks. But after Earthfall, the quarry had been transformed into a storage spot for what little junk couldn't be reused or recycled. Things had been different before Earthfall, all this trash ejected straight toward the sun. But now that there were no more regular Earth-to-moon supply runs, everything had to be saved, in case someone could figure out how to someday use it. The pit was halfway full at this point, and it was getting fuller every year. Strike picked up a rock and heaved it into the abyss, watching as it smacked into something goopy.

This place was so nasty that even the Blackguard didn't bother to monitor it. But that was what made it Strike's refuge. It was where he came when he needed to think.

And right now, he needed to think more than ever.

When Strike was still living at the orphanage, this junk hole had been his and TNT's private hangout. No one had any reason to go there except to dump anything the Guoming Colony waste processing factory wouldn't take. The rotting smell kept people away, but the stink was a small price to pay for the peace and quiet of one of the few uncrowded places on the moon. Strike had even grown to like the overpowering stench, the odor reminding him of better times. Sometimes he and TNT had stayed there for hours, digging through trash, challenging each other to rock-throwing contests, or making up stories about their futures as Ultraball players. This was where they had come right after finding out about Taiko Colony getting an Ultraball team.

That day four years ago was burned into Strike's head. He had stood on the welcome mat to TNT's apartment, peeking inside. Bright throw rugs covered the floors. The smell of something delicious wafted through the air. It was a real home, a real family, neither of which Strike would ever have again. Not after the Fireball Blast.

"What are you waiting for?" TNT asked from inside. "Come in already, you butt-wipe."

"Wei-wei," said a woman. "Is that any way to treat a guest?"

"Mom," TNT said, his voice dripping with embarrassment. "I told you, don't call me Wei-wei anymore. It's TNT. And Strike *is* a butt-wipe." He yanked Strike inside.

Strike stopped in front of a picture of TNT at the mass funeral for the Fireball Blast victims. Memories leached their way out of dark places in the shadows of his mind: People crying. A monk saying how these miners gave their lives for Taiko Colony. Adults offering their condolences. But so many people blaming Strike's mother for the fifty-six deaths.

Just as he turned to run, TNT's mom appeared with a tray of hardtack bars. But there was something different about them. The delicious smell . . . Strike froze in place. His eyes were telling him that these were just hardtack bars, but his nose was screaming for him to step closer.

"So nice to meet you," TNT's mom said.

"You too, Mrs. TNT," Strike said.

"Mrs. TNT? Most of my little Wei-wei's friends call me Mrs. Tsai."

"Mom!"

"I'm sorry. It's hard for me to think of you as anything but my baby." She put down the plate and returned to the kitchenette. "Eat."

TNT took a bar and handed one to Strike. "Awesome,

huh? For special occasions, she adds some kind of spice she stashed right after Earthfall."

Strike tried to answer, but he was too busy wolfing down the hardtack bar. Instead of the usual bitterness, it was sweet and spicy and mouthwatering. He let out a contented sigh as he licked his fingers to get the last specks.

TNT leaned in. "You better not tell anyone that she calls me her baby. I'd have to kill you."

"Don't worry. I won't say a thing. Little Wei-wei."

"You are so dead." TNT shook his head and smiled. "Just you wait until you hear my mom's news. She said it's big. Really big. Come on."

TNT's mom worked for the Underground Ultraball League. If she had any news about the rumors of an expansion team, Strike had to find out. He followed TNT into the kitchenette.

Mrs. Tsai bent down in front of a hot plate, her hands wrapped in strips of cloth as she inspected two hardtack bars. Something choked in Strike's throat, a memory of him as a little kid burning himself on a hot plate, and his mom squeezing him hard as he wailed and cried.

But before he could run, Mrs. Tsai smiled. "The good news is that Ultraball is coming to Taiko Colony," she said.

TNT whooped. He raised his hand and high-fived Strike. "Can you get us into games?"

"I can do you one better. The league is going to hold open tryouts for the team."

Strike whipped around to TNT, staring at him in astonishment. "You mean we could actually be real live Ultraball stars?" TNT said. "This is incredible."

"Not so fast," Mrs. Tsai said. "The bad news is there are already hundreds of kids wanting to try out. I don't know how the news leaked. The league is limiting tryouts to just fifty slots. It's going to be a lottery system. The odds aren't good."

TNT thumped his head down against the counter.

Strike's disappointment sank all the way down to his toes. Why did he ever hold on to hope? In just three months, he'd turn ten, aging out of the jam-packed Tao Home to make room for other orphans, and go work in the mines.

"Don't you two want to hear the good news?" Mrs. Tsai said.

TNT looked at her in confusion. "But you already told us the good news."

"The other good news." She cracked a mischievous smile, her eyes twinkling. "How would you like to try out for the Taiko Miners?"

"What?" TNT asked. "Seriously. This better not be another one of your jokes."

She threw an arm around TNT and laughed. "I'm sorry. I couldn't help myself." She pulled tickets out of her pocket. "I called in every last favor to secure tryouts for you. I might even be able to sneak you in and get you some time inside Ultrabot suits before then."

TNT rushed his mom, tackling her so hard she almost toppled her over. He smothered her with hugs before freezing and stealing a glimpse at Strike. He released his mom, trying to act cool. "Thanks, Mom. You're the best. Even with your terrible jokes."

"Well, I thought it was funny." She smiled and winked at Strike.

"Come on," TNT said. "Let's get to the junk hole. We have a lot of planning to do. We're gonna take the Miners all the way to an Ultrabowl title. I already thought of an awesome slogan: Miners together, Miners forever. You and me, Strike. Blood brothers, on and off the field."

Strike grinned from ear to ear.

Footsteps snapped Strike out of his trance. Rock was approaching along with Torch, who had his little sister in tow. Torch picked her up after she started coughing, carrying her the rest of the way, nestled in his arms.

"So this is the dump," Torch said. "People all the way over in Farajah Colony talk about the stink. It's even worse than everyone said." He peered over the edge. "Sure is a ton of trash down there. You think there's anything valuable?"

"Nah," Strike said. "TNT and me, we scoured the

place years ago. Two dumb kids, convinced we would find buried treasure."

"How can you take the smell?" Torch covered up his nose with the front of his jumpsuit.

"It's not so bad," Strike said. "Kind of brings me back."

"Man, you musta had one strange childhood," Torch said.

Strike shook his head, his face pinching up. "You have no idea."

After an uncomfortable silence, Torch cleared his throat. "Hey, hope you don't mind me coming to your private spot here. Rock said he had a guess as to where you might be."

"No problem. What's up?"

"Is it cool with you if I miss practice for the next few nights?"

"Yeah, of course," Strike said. He stole a glance at the little girl, her dark face splotchy and sickly-looking, her chest heaving with spasms. "Is she okay?"

Torch shrugged. "She's been like this for two weeks now. It's been getting worse. I gotta take her over to Salaam Colony."

"The hospital?" Strike exchanged a nervous glance with Rock, his heart sinking for Torch. Salaam Colony was the medical center of the moon and the site of its lone hospital. But only the rich could afford to go there. People in Taiko Colony soldiered through pretty much any sickness or injury, no matter how serious. "I really wish we could pay you a salary, Torch. You've been so valuable to the team. To me."

"I totally understand. But, if you don't mind, there is something I wanted to ask."

"Anything."

"My sister is such a huge fan of yours." He brought the ashen little girl forward. A black number 8—Strike's number—was hand-drawn on her chest. "Could you give her an autograph? I bet that would make her feel a lot better."

Strike gaped in horror at the girl barely filling out her tiny jumpsuit. She looked like she would break in two if you breathed on her wrong. How could Strike possibly make her feel better? Plenty of kids didn't make it in Taiko Colony.

He caught sight of Rock, raising his eyebrows and jerking his head toward the little girl.

As always, Rock had the right answer. Strike couldn't give the girl medical treatment, but he could give her hope. He gently tousled her hair. "Be strong, okay? Fight. Get better."

"You're my favorite player ever," Jasmine said. Her head rolled from side to side, her eyes half-closed in her fevered state. "Can I have your Ultrabowl ring when you win?"

"Jasmine!" Torch said. "You can't ask that. Sorry, Strike."

"No, that's okay." Strike smiled at her. "You know

what? It's yours. It's the least I can do, given that I can't afford to pay your brother for all the coaching he's given us. I owe him, big-time. You can even come up for the awards ceremony."

Torch's eyes went wide. "You'd give her your Ultrabowl ring?"

"The ring itself means nothing." Strike was a little surprised to hear those words come out of his mouth, but really, it was only a piece of jewelry. What really mattered was delivering an Ultrabowl title to his Miners family, setting up him and his teammates for life.

Torch wiped his cheek with the back of his hand. "Thanks, Strike. I don't know what I've done to deserve a friend like you."

His sister pressed her face into Torch's arm, but she peeped out over his shoulder as they left, giving him a delirious smile.

"So," Strike said. "You find out anything new?"

Rock picked up a pebble and chucked it into the hole. "I hate spying on Boom. It makes me feel like I'm no better than the Blackguard."

"I'm not singling out Boom. I need to know as much as I can about her, the Dark Siders, Zuna, everything. What did you turn up?"

"I found out more about the Dark Siders." Rock pulled out his notebook, staring at it with intense concentration. "And Zuna."

"How?"

"It wasn't easy. I had to book computer time at Copernicus College under a fake name. Then I used combinatorial guessing to figure out passwords for classified United Moon Colonies documents. Then—"

"What did you find?"

Rock frowned as he flipped a page. "There's good news. And there's bad news."

"What's the good news?"

"It's very likely that Raiden Zuna has been explosion mining and blast fracking across the Dark Side. The seismic data is all there. And there's more: ten bodies were found at the site of one incident, the blackened corpses exhibiting high radiation levels. Only the Meltdown Gun could have done that."

Strike recoiled. "That's the good news?"

"Yes, because it matches everything Boom has told us. She has every reason to get revenge on Raiden Zuna. It disproves everything TNT said about Zuna paying off Boom. She would never work with him, not in a million years. I'd bet any amount of money that Boom will find a way to destroy his Meltdown Gun. Maybe even steal it."

"There's no way she could steal it. Zuna is a Colony Governor."

"Remember how easily she stole that Blackguard's security badge when we first met her? She'll find a way."

Strike picked up another stone and hucked it into the

junk pit. "Okay. So TNT is definitely wrong about Boom. What's the bad news?"

"TNT might not have been all wrong. If Zuna becomes governor of Taiko Colony . . ." Rock took a deep breath. "He might actually be able to destroy it."

Strike's eyes went huge. His lungs seized, unable to draw in a breath. His throat strangled as he waited for Rock to say that this was some sort of sick joke.

But Rock kept staring down at his notebook.

"You said he couldn't do that," Strike said. "He needs fourteen of the twenty-one votes to control the Council of Governors. North Pole Colony and Taiko Colony, that's only two."

"I'm not positive about any of this," Rock said. "But he's formed all sorts of partnerships with many other colonies. None of them is formalized. Some seem to be just handshake agreements. I don't know how solid they are, or how deep they go. I can't be sure of how many votes his alliance might be able to control." He swallowed a lump lodged in his throat. "But it's possible that it's thirteen. Taiko Colony's vote might be the fourteenth and final vote he needs."

Strike's eyes went wild. He grabbed the front of Rock's jumpsuit, desperately shaking him. "No," he said. "Don't. You can't put all this on me. It's too much pressure. It's not fair."

"I'm just speculating about some of it," Rock said,

struggling in a panic to free himself. "Maybe I'm wrong."

But Rock was rarely wrong.

Strike let Rock go. He dropped his head into his hands. His body trembled as he fought to hold back the storm of tears, the frustration and despair threatening to tear him apart.

"Strike?" Rock asked. "Are you okay? Maybe we should head back. Do more planning for the Neutrons game. We have to win this one."

"Gimme a moment, okay?"

Rock wavered. But he nodded and left.

Strike stared into the gaping quarry, his head spinning as he tried to make sense of everything. *Why does all of this have to be on me? All I ever wanted to do is win an Ultrabowl for my Miners.*

Strike had come to the junk hole to mull over the stomach-churning thought that he had been trying so hard to ignore. But facts were facts. Pickaxe had nearly cost the Miners a forfeit against the Explorers, for getting out of his Ultrabot suit on the field. He had almost cost the Miners another game with his offsides penalty and botched plays against the Beatdown.

The idea of Pickaxe being in Zuna's pocket was insane. Ever since the first day Strike had signed on with the Miners, Pickaxe and Nugget had been his loyal teammates. They had all been brought together by the fact that all of them had lost someone to the Fireball

Blast. But they had grown into something so much more. The Fireball Five had been through so many wars and battles together. There hadn't been a single day where they didn't at least see each other. They could almost read each other's minds. Every one of them would die for Strike, and he'd do the same. Fireball Five forever.

But that's what Strike had thought about TNT.

Strike couldn't imagine that it was true. But now with the fate of an entire colony on the line, he had to face the horrible possibility that Pickaxe's mistakes on the field might not be mistakes at all. Pickaxe and Nugget had been struggling to support their aunt Keiko for years now. Maybe Pickaxe was finally up against the wall.

Desperate enough to take a payoff from Raiden Zuna.

His stomach churning, Strike put his head between his knees. He stared down into the junk hole, his entire world decaying, rotting into trash.

16

GAME 5 VS. THE NORTH POLE NEUTRONS

THE NEUTRONS VS. the Miners—the rematch of Ultrabowl IX the entire moon had been waiting for all season. A victory would put the Miners in charge of their own destiny, with the inside track to a first-place finish and home-field advantage in the semifinals.

A loss would allow several hungry teams to claw their way to within striking distance of the Miners.

What with the Miners' increasing practice schedule, Strike had never conked out at bedtime so quickly in his life. But he never slept more than a few hours in a row, constantly waking up in a cold sweat. No matter how wrong and gut-wrenching it felt, Strike owed it to himself—to all of Taiko Colony—to figure out if Pickaxe had really taken a payoff from Raiden Zuna.

The morning of the big game finally arrived. Five thousand fans in red jumpsuits booed as the Miners entered the massive cavern that housed Neutron Stadium. Giant Neutrons flags were raised at the four corners of the field, the Meltdown Gun logos blasting out their streams of nuclear radiation. There was barely any blue in the crowd—no one was stupid enough to come into Neutron territory with Taiko blue on, unless they wanted a trip to Salaam Hospital. Neutron posses roamed the stands, waiting to beat the living daylights out of anyone who even looked like a Miners fan.

Neutron Stadium was state-of-the-art. The best locker rooms, the best field surface, the best stands and food, the best everything the moon had to offer. The enormous space was lit by dozens of blinding ceiling spotlights, the air perfectly clear and clean. The stadium was connected to North Pole Colony's top-of-the-line oxygen and water recyclers, and two nuclear reactors providing uninterrupted power. If something catastrophic happened on the moon, Neutron Stadium would be the perfect place to house refugees. *Not that Zuna would let a single person stay here*, Strike thought.

The Miners waited on their side of the field, and the crowd roared when Raiden Zuna walked from the stands to the middle of the fifty-meter line to do his usual pregame greeting. The crowd went quiet as Zuna raised his hands. "Ladies and gentlemen, welcome to Neutron Stadium." He pointed above the skyboxes, where a spotlight blazed upon three gleaming trophies mounted atop a spire. "Home of the three-time Ultrabowl champions, the North Pole Neutrons!"

The crowd went nuts, the masses of bright red jumpsuits dancing like flames.

Zuna continued. "Neutron Stadium has the honor of hosting the Ultrabowl this year, and with a 4–0 record— soon to be 5–0—there's no stopping us from winning a fourth trophy in a row." He pointed at Strike and grinned as the audience hooted and hollered. "There is no stopping the force of nature that is the North Pole Neutrons. The lights will never go out on Neutron Nation!"

Strike's stomach flip-flopped. This was standard Raiden Zuna and his hyping-up of the crowds before each home game. But never were the stakes as high as they were today. Zuna went on and on about how the Neutrons had crushed all their opponents this year, scoring a league-record 392 points through four games. And doubt ate away at Strike.

Strike startled when someone bumped his shoulder from behind. "Gonna throw up inside your helmet?" someone in a red Ultrabot suit said. The visor flipped to clear, and Chain Reaction's ugly mug came into view, with Fusion standing right behind him. "You should have taken Mr. Zuna's offer when you had a chance. Now you're going down."

"We'll see who's going down," Strike said.

"I hope you try some quarterback sneaks," Chain Reaction said. "I'll slam you into the ground so hard I'll smash you into a pile of rubble." He leaned in with a maniacal grin, lowering his voice. "Just like Taiko Colony, after this season."

The words paralyzed Strike, his limbs frozen in shock. He tried to say something to Chain Reaction, to make sure he hadn't misheard. But there was no mistaking it.

If Zuna took over as governor, he was going to destroy Taiko Colony.

Strike lunged at Chain Reaction, fists flying, screaming at the top of his lungs. Rock and Boom wrapped him up before he could make contact, but Strike launched punches into his teammates' helmets in a furious attempt to break loose and pound Chain Reaction into the turf.

"How much suit power did you just waste, moron?" Chain Reaction said. He sauntered off, laughing. "Come on, Fusion."

Strike stopped struggling against his teammates, swearing at himself. A quick peek at his heads-up display showed that his suit power was already down to 96.2 percent, and the game hadn't even started.

Fusion stole a glance at Chain Reaction and quickly held a fist out to Strike. "Good luck," he said. He leaned in close, so they were nearly touching helmets, and whispered something Strike couldn't make out. His eyes flicked to the other Miners, and then he bounded away.

In his confusion, Strike stared at the back of Fusion's bright red Ultrabot suit. What had he whispered? Why had he shot glances at the other Miners?

Then Fusion's words snapped into place: *Watch your back, Strike.*

If Strike had had any last doubts about TNT's warnings, they melted away. Fusion might have been a rival Neutron, but he was also in the tight fraternity of Ultraball quarterbacks. If things had been different, they might have even been friends.

Strike motioned his Miners to the line to receive the opening kickoff, keeping his visual targeting sensors trained on Pickaxe. He'd be keeping a close eye on his crackback 1. As the refs signaled for the game to begin, Strike gave the hand signals for the upcoming play, glad that Boom had pressed him to practice with unbearable shrieking noises pumped into their helmets. It would serve them well today.

Fusion ran forward and kicked the ball, sending it in a high arc toward Boom. She backpedaled all the way to the corner of the end zone, adjusting to catch it after it bounced off the back wall. Boom turned and accelerated to full speed in just a few steps.

Strike pulled in behind her. His eyes widened at the sight of the Neutrons closing in. They had always been one of the quickest teams in the league, but they had somehow found a fifth gear. Before he knew it, the lead

Neutrons crashed into the Miners' wedge, Pickaxe getting smashed off his feet straight into Nugget, both brothers going down in a heap. Another Neutron took out Rock, pancaking him to the ground.

Just before another Neutron leapt over the mass to tackle Boom, she flipped the ball backward to Strike. With a sharp juke, he moved to circle around, back the other way. When Strike had enough space to maneuver, he could easily evade one, two, and sometimes even three defenders.

But not this time. Two Neutrons homed in on Strike as if they were reading his mind, cutting off his path. A third defender leapt into one of Neutron Stadium's slingshot zones—magnetic accelerators that sent anything metal flying like a rocket—and smashed a clothesline tackle into Strike's neck, whipping him head over heels. Strike's world went into a smeared blur, all his heads-up displays blinking wildly. Crunching to the ground, Strike tried to get to his feet, but the rest of the Neutrons leapt on him, punching to knock out the ball.

The whistle blew to signal that the play was over, but the Neutrons kept wailing away. Clutching the Ultraball with all his might, his glove electromagnets engaged to full power, Strike ground his teeth together. *It's gonna be a dirty game*, he thought.

Boom yanked the Neutrons off and helped Strike to his feet. He heard her yelling something but couldn't make out a single word over the roar of the crowd. Strike looked over to Torch in the coach's box, who signaled in a play. Strike relayed it to the team—a fake QB sneak, Strike slinging a long bomb to Boom after she gave him a block and then launched herself through a slingshot zone. This would hopefully silence the crowd.

Strike stood over the ball, ready to give the snap count. He stomped his right foot, trying to draw the Neutrons offsides with a hard first step, but got no takers. On the second stomp, he tucked in the ball and curled to his right as if he was going to run a QB sneak. Boom gave him a huge block, and then she raced toward a slingshot zone, accelerating through and flying out like a bullet.

But just as Strike cocked the ball to throw it, a Neutron punched in from the blind side and popped the ball loose. Strike scrambled toward it but got smashed to the ground by another Neutron.

Rock and Nugget sprinted alongside two Neutron defenders in a footrace for the loose ball. Rock bashed one of the Neutrons with a forearm, the guy's head snapping back as he flew off his feet. Nugget dove and grabbed the ball, but another Neutron speared him.

The ball flew loose again, skittering backward toward the Miners' end zone. A mass of players raced in, all jumping for it. Punches flew, some players aiming at the ball and some aiming at opponents' helmets.

Strike scrambled to the pileup, a mass of arms and legs

lashing out. With a surge of relief, Strike saw one of his Miners with the ball: Boom. She had come all the way back from her long route to dive on top of the ball. She was smothered to the ground, and the whistle would blow any second to signal the end of the play.

But no whistle came. Strike looked for the refs in impactanium armor, still coming in from the sidelines, as the pileup on top of Boom continued to wail away. Then Chain Reaction came out of nowhere, blasting out of a slingshot zone to explode the pile backward in a mass of flailing limbs. The ball squirted out, bouncing into the Miners' end zone, and Ion Storm grabbed it. She triumphantly held it up to a ref in black armor, who jerked his arms up, signaling touchdown.

Strike raced over, screaming at the ref. "Are you blind? The play was over way before the ball came out! Did you swallow your whistle or are you just a moron?"

The ref glared before pressing a button by his shoulder to make an announcement over the loudspeaker. "Number 8 on the Miners is assessed a yellow-card warning for unsportsmanlike conduct."

Boom raced in front of Strike, going helmet to helmet with him. She flipped her visor to clear and yelled at him, spittle flying from her mouth. He couldn't hear a word she said, but he could read her lips well enough. Strike had just made the dumbest of rookie mistakes—you never yelled at a ref, no matter how bad a call was, especially when you weren't on your home field. With this yellow card, Strike was one more infraction away from getting ejected. And a team without five manned Ultrabot suits on the field had to forfeit.

As the Miners gathered by their own end zone to receive the kickoff, Strike smacked Pickaxe's helmet in frustration. None of his teammates could hear a thing due to the crowd noise, but Strike ripped into Pickaxe anyway. "Your only job on that play was to block your rusher. Get your head into the game and stop playing like an Axepicker!"

Pickaxe's face crumpled. He turned and kicked at the turf.

Boom whirled Strike around, yelling in his face. She beat her helmet three times, the sign for *get your head in the game*, then pointed toward the Neutrons, who were setting up for the kickoff. Boom grabbed Strike's arm and pulled him into place just as the Neutrons kicked off.

The Neutrons continued to crush the Miners in the first half, picking apart the Miners for score after score, running through slingshot zones and even throwing passes through them, accelerating the Ultraball to light speed. With so much more practice time on their home field, the Neutrons kept beating the Miners with a dazzling array of bullet-like passes and trick plays through the slingshot zones.

And more important, on defense, the Neutrons

repeatedly sacked Strike from his blind side—Pickaxe's side. On two of the sacks, it was like the Neutrons had known exactly what play the Miners had called, countering it perfectly.

The Miners went into halftime down by thirty-five points. No team in league history had ever come back from that far behind.

As the Miners got out of their suits and assembled inside the locker room, Strike couldn't even bear to look at Pickaxe through his rage. No one could play so poorly unless it was on purpose. Four times, defenders blew by Pickaxe as if he wasn't there. And on certain plays, it seemed like the Neutrons knew exactly what the Miners were going to do.

Did Pickaxe somehow accidentally telegraph what we were doing? Strike thought. He narrowed his eyes at his crackback 1, whose eyes were glued to the ground, his mohawk flopped over with sweat.

Or was it no accident?

Strike caught sight of Torch sitting in the corner. The former QB's talent for making things up on the fly was legendary. "Gunslinger mode," Strike said through gritted teeth. "I'm gonna wing it."

"What?" Nugget said. "How are Pickaxe and I supposed to block for you if we don't know what the play is?"

Pickaxe put his hands over his head, trembling, not saying a word.

"You'll figure it out," Strike said. "Boom, you good with that?"

She took a deep breath as she thought it over, and then nodded. "The Neutrons are all over some of our plays. It's like they have some pages out of our playbook. But there's no way they can predict crazy."

"Oh no, oh no, oh no," Rock said. "I'm no good at improvising."

"Stay back and block, then," Strike said.

"Won't the Chain Reaction and Meltdown be able to double-team Boom every play?" Rock asked.

Boom nodded. "We need you out there, running routes with me. Even if you're the decoy most of the time, you'll still be a threat."

"Just wing it," Strike said.

"I can't wing anything, much less routes out on the field," Rock said.

Strike grabbed Rock's shoulders in frustration, but before he could say anything, Boom stepped in between them. "Wait," she said. "He's right."

"How hard is it to just run around and get open?" Strike said.

"Very hard, especially in a real game," Boom said. She studied Rock. "How about this? Before every play, you pick a random number from one to forty-six. You run whatever route you're supposed to run on that page of the playbook."

Rock's forehead wrinkled up. "What if it's a QB sneak? Or I'm supposed to block?"

"Then that's what you do."

It took him a moment, but he slowly nodded. "I can do that."

"How is that any different from what I said?" Strike asked. He glanced at the clock. "Never mind. We gotta get going. Everyone gear up."

As the Miners headed for their suits, Boom approached Strike. "I'll get open," she said. "Just throw it high and hard and I'll go get it. Trust me."

A buzzer sounded, echoing through the locker room, and the other Miners hurried to suit up. "Okay," he said. "You and me. We'll win this."

"Not just you and me," she said, throwing a glance to the others. "All of us. Miners together." She put her hand out, and Rock, Nugget, and Pickaxe put theirs on top.

Strike slapped his hand down on top of Pickaxe's. Hard.

After a huge four-and-out stop on defense to start the second half, the Miners got the ball on the Neutrons' forty-meter line. Everyone jogged a few meters back to where the huddle usually would be, but Strike waved them off, pointing to the line of scrimmage for a no-huddle offense. He signaled to Boom, pointing to the sky. *I'm going to throw it up. You go get it.*

She nodded.

The Neutrons swarmed like angry insects, darting back and forth, continually in motion. It was unusual for an offense to go without huddles, but the Neutrons didn't seem fazed. They set up in a run protection scheme, with everyone jammed up at the line. Then, as Strike got over the ball, the Neutrons fell back into a deep pass protection setup.

Strike yanked the ball off the ground, even his teammates not knowing he was going to quick-hike it. As Rock crossed from one side to the other, Boom ran behind him, using Rock to pick off her defender. She took off like a shot, racing toward a slingshot zone.

But Chain Reaction had already adjusted, switching defensive assignments and zeroing in on her. He leapt for her and hit the slingshot zone a split second after she did, grabbing her ankle to lock on. Both of them shot into the sky like a gigantic boomerang, spinning around each other in a whirlwind of red and blue.

On the other side of the field, Strike ducked a tackle. He kicked another defender's legs out from under him. A third Neutron sent himself spearing in, blocking Strike's passing lane. Strike cocked back the ball as if he were going to throw it right at the defender's head, but he swiveled at the last moment and threw an angled pass toward a slingshot zone. It didn't have much zip on it, but it didn't need any. As soon as it entered, it accelerated with a blast of speed, exploding like a bullet out the other side. It hit the clear protective barrier separating the field from the stands with an earsplitting bang and ricocheted high, toward the center of the field.

Forty meters off the ground, Boom and Chain Reaction were locked in a midair dogfight, chokeholding and punching each other as they spun around at a dizzying speed. Strike's visual targeting system hadn't been able to lock onto Boom, but he'd eyeballed the bounce pass well. The Ultraball was speeding right at them. Now the rest was up to her.

And as the Ultraball zoomed in, Boom smashed a kick into Chain Reaction's chest plate, the two players bursting apart in opposite directions. Twisting and contorting, Boom reached out at full extension. Her glove magnetized for the lock, but the ball's unholy speed whipped her into a frenzied spin. She hurtled out of control toward the corner of the end zone. With an echoing crunch, she crashed into the back protective barrier, shooting shock waves through the clear impactanium barrier. She plummeted down toward the end zone in a death spiral, barely holding on to the ball.

Neutrons came rushing in from all directions, leaping up to spear her. But Strike outjumped everyone. He caught one of Boom's boots, and in one smooth motion, whipsawed her down toward the turf with all his might. Before the Neutrons knew what had happened, Boom crashed like a meteor into the end zone for a touchdown.

After landing, Strike raced up to Boom, pounding on her helmet to make sure she was okay. "Incredible grab!" he yelled to her, but even he couldn't hear himself amid the crowd's thunderous booing.

Boom flipped her visor from reflective to clear. She couldn't lock onto Strike, her eyes wandering in circles as if she were trying to get the world to stop spinning. But she lifted a glove and gave him the thumbs-up.

Throughout the second half, Strike continued to scramble around like a madman, not even his teammates sure where he was going. And it worked. The Miners scored on each of their next three possessions, on a frenzied scramble by Strike, a wild cross-field pass to Boom, and a bull run where Strike and Boom hit a slingshot zone together, both of them blasting into the Neutrons' defense like a double-wide cannonball. The Neutrons slowly adjusted, but not before the Miners clawed their way back to make it a game.

By the fourth quarter, the Neutrons started answering every Miners score with a touchdown of their own, momentum swinging from one team to the other and back again. After a huge defensive stop by a blitzing Boom, the Miners got the ball back with five seconds left in the game. The Neutrons were up by a single touchdown, 105–98. The Miners had one last play to tie up the game and send it to overtime. On the Neutrons' side of the field, they were just forty meters away from scoring.

Strike couldn't hear anything over the crowd's roar. The Miners huddled up. Making hand signals at Boom and Rock, Strike hoped they'd understand what he wanted: one of Torch's new plays, the highball bounce. He looked toward the coach's box and gave the signal, hoping Torch would repeat it for any of the Miners who hadn't understood him.

But to Strike's confusion, Torch waved his hands in the air, shaking his head with exaggerated motions. He seemed to be screaming a warning, but Strike couldn't make it out. Had he seen something? Strike considered changing the play to something out of their standard playbook, but the Miners needed something killer.

Strike ran to his players, repeating the hand signals. He pointed at Boom, who would charge into a magnetic slingshot zone and then run up Nugget's back, superjumping so high that she'd slam off the roof, hopefully ricocheting in toward the corner of the end zone. They'd practiced it a few times, but since Taiko Arena didn't have magnetic slingshot zones, this would be the first time they would run it for real at blinding speed.

As Strike was lining up over the ball, Pickaxe flipped his visor to clear and yelled something. Strike squinted, trying to read Pickaxe's lips, but he couldn't make anything out. He glimpsed at the play clock, ticking down to ten seconds. He waved Pickaxe off, pointing at the play clock. Boom and Rock lined up in the backfield.

As soon as everyone got into a three-point stance, Strike hiked it. Charging backward, he prepared to flip it up so Boom could latch onto it as she flew by. Nugget bent over like a ramp, set for Boom to run up his back and shoot into the sky. But to Strike's horror, the Neutrons went full blitz from the blind side, as if they knew exactly what the Miners were up to. One broke through, on course to ram Strike before he could flip the ball to Boom as she passed by.

Strike pulled the ball into his chest and ducked away from the rusher. Boom had already launched herself through the slingshot zone and couldn't stop herself from racing up Nugget's back to go flying over the middle of the field. She went soaring toward the roof, her hands empty.

Bracing for impact as another Neutron charged at him, Strike tucked the ball in as if he was going to take the sack. But just as the Neutron launched himself, Strike spun low, twisting away and scrambling. He looked to the skies for his star RB1 in case he could still whip a pass to her. But Chain Reaction had superjumped, intercepting her as she flew. Locked in struggle, they spun uncontrollably through the air.

Strike pulled the ball in and ran. Only Ion Storm separated him from the end zone, but there wasn't enough room for Strike to put a big juke on her. Even if the defender didn't make the tackle straight-on, she'd slow Strike enough that the other Neutrons would pile into him.

Then Strike spotted a flash of blue in the back corner of the end zone. Waving his arms, Pickaxe was open. Strike had no choice but to jump high into the air, gunning a bullet over Ion Storm's outstretched arms. A split second later, Ion Storm smashed into Strike, crushing him backward.

Twisting to see the play, Strike punched his arm into the air when Pickaxe leapt at full extension, the ball snapping into his glove electromagnets. As Pickaxe fell backward, he looked down to touch a foot into the end zone. But just before he could, a Neutron defender crunched into his legs, sending him whipping head over heels.

The ball popped out of Pickaxe's magnetized gloves. It fell to the turf. Incomplete.

A cannon fired. "Receiver did not have control over the ball," a ref announced over the loudspeakers. "The game is over."

A crazed roar went through the crowd. The scoreboard blazed in bright red:

NEUTRONS WIN, 105–98!

RESULTS, WEEK 5

Neutrons	**105**
Miners	98

Beatdown	**98**
Flamethrowers	91

Explorers	**84**
Shock	28

Venom	**49**
Molemen	35

STANDINGS, WEEK 5

	Wins	**Losses**	**Total Points**
Neutrons **X**	5	0	497
Miners	4	1	441
Flamethrowers	3	2	455
Beatdown	3	2	434
Explorers	2	3	364
Shock	2	3	210
Venom	1	4	196
Molemen	0	5	105

X= *clinched playoff spot*

MEETING AT THE MINES

THE NEUTRONS WERE now solidly leading the race for the number one seed in the playoffs. It was still theoretically possible for the Miners to get that all-important top spot, but the Neutrons would have to lose at least one of their next two games. That wasn't going to happen. So the Miners would be facing an uphill battle during the playoffs, having to play in Neutron Stadium at least once.

That was *if* the Miners made the playoffs. Not since his rookie year had Strike been concerned about that. The Miners currently had a one-game lead over the Flamethrowers and the Beatdown, but both of those teams had been high-scoring offensive machines all season. If the Miners lost their upcoming game against the Flamethrowers, they'd be in big trouble.

Strike peeked over to Rock's cot early the next morning. Quiet snores came from under the sheet, a regular rise and fall of Rock's chest. Strike eased out of bed and crept toward the door. He hated sneaking around, but Rock was so convinced that there was nothing behind TNT's words. He wouldn't understand what Strike had to do.

Strike peered out the door, relieved. The corridor was empty, most everyone already having gone down to the mines. After facing so many questions, hard stares, and desperate looks upon arriving home last night after the defeat, he couldn't bear any more. Someone had even accused him of throwing the game.

Pulling his hood over his head as low as it would go, Strike made his way through the nearly empty streets, going out of his way to avoid any people milling about. He sped up when a young girl shouted his name, and thankfully her mother yanked her back before she could approach. "Leave him alone," the mother said. "He has enough to worry about."

Strike felt the familiar knot in his stomach and broke into a jog, heading down the street toward the mines. He wound around to the outskirts of town and finally arrived at the airlock separating the mines from the main cavern of Taiko Colony. A dark-haired woman stood by the doorway: Nadya, Strike's across-the-hall neighbor.

She motioned to Strike. "Where have you been? Section fourteen needs a shaft crawler right away. Get down there, right now."

"It's me, Strike." He pulled back his hood. "Is Torch around?"

Nadya squinted at him. "Strike? What are you doing here?" She kneeled to look Strike in the eyes. "I'm so sorry about the game yesterday. What happened on that last play? You had the Neutrons' backs to the wall. I thought Pickaxe was going to score for sure."

"I thought so, too. I was hoping Torch could help me figure it out."

Nadya checked her clipboard. "Taj Tariq . . . he's in section six today. He has extra quotas to make up for, but I can spare him for five minutes." She pushed a button and the airlock opened, the door squealing. "Get Tariq, down in section six."

A lanky man appeared, his eyes widening at the sight of Strike. "Big game coming up," he said. "The Flamethrowers are looking really good. They might even break the Torch's Curse." He leaned in. "The spread is 17.5 points. Think you'll beat them by more than that?"

"Go get Tariq already," Nadya said.

"Come on, Strike, be a pal," the man said. "I really need this. Gimme something I can use to bet on. I got two kids to take care of."

"Uh." Strike winced. "I really can't say."

The guy's forehead wrinkled. "You can't say? Or you won't say?"

"Stop bothering Strike and go get Tariq," Nadya said. She turned the guy around and shoved her foot into his rear, sending him stumbling away. Shaking her head, she closed the airlock door. "Sorry about that. You wouldn't believe all the bets people are making. Some morons even pooled their money and put down a hundred u-bucks on a blackout happening during the Ultrabowl. The idiots think they're going to strike it rich."

Betting really is the moon's national pastime, Strike thought.

"Is there anything I can do to help?" Nadya asked. "It's not fair that you have so much pressure on you. It's more than anyone should have to bear."

Nadya's kind words should have made Strike feel better, but he felt sicker than ever. "Thanks," he said. "But I think only Torch can help me."

Footsteps approached and the airlock door slid back. Torch stepped through, covered from head to toe in a layer of fine gray powder. He pulled back his hood and shook out his hair in a cloud of dust.

Strike stepped back as Torch went into a coughing fit, his chest heaving. As the spasms died away, Strike counted his lucky stars that he had been able to avoid that life.

"Hey," Torch said. He brushed a layer of grit from his

eyes. "What are you doing here?"

"I need someone to bounce something off of."

"Not Rock?"

Strike shook his head. "Usually, yes. But not about this. Can we talk?" He eyed Nadya. Strike trusted her more than almost anyone on the moon, but the stakes were huge. "You mind if I talk to Torch in private?"

"Whatever you need, Strike," Nadya said. "But keep it short, okay? Tariq has a ton of work to do." She narrowed her eyes at Torch. "No cutting out early again tonight. I'm watching you."

"Yeah, yeah." Torch gave Nadya the evil eye as he pulled Strike off the path. They sat down on a big boulder. "What's up?"

The only person Strike had told about Fusion's whispered message was Rock. But Rock kept stubbornly insisting that there was no traitor. Strike had to talk to someone else he trusted—someone else who would face up to the truth.

Torch's eyes went wide as he took in everything. He interrupted when Strike brought up Fusion's warning. "Are you absolutely sure that's what Fusion said? You're positive?"

"I'm one hundred percent sure. Zuna's paid someone off to stab me in the back. Just like last year."

Strike expected Torch to tell him how crazy that was, how he should forget all of this and just play. But Torch sat quietly on the boulder, staring off into the distance. "Did you hear the rumor Berzerkatron and the Mad Mongol were talking about this morning?"

"No," Strike said. "What rumor?"

Torch paused. "Someone saw a guy in a blue jumpsuit. Riding the trams late last night."

"So?"

"He was spotted next to a big guy. In a red jumpsuit. With a briefcase. Had to be one of Zuna's guys."

Strike's eyes widened. "Pickaxe stormed out last night after the game. Didn't even stick around to sign autographs. It has to be him."

"Pickaxe?" Torch slumped over. "Pickaxe." He shook his head, squeezing his eyes shut tight. "He did almost cost you the Explorers game by clicking out of his suit. And his play the past two games . . ."

"Exactly," Strike said. "Finally, someone sees what I do. The evidence all points to him. This thing about the tram is the nail in the coffin."

Torch gulped. "You seriously think Pickaxe is a traitor?"

"Who else?" Strike asked. "Nugget, Rock, and Boom were with me. Nugget insisted on us looking for his brother, but we never found him. Because he was on his way to North Pole Colony to take a payoff." He paused, thinking about Pickaxe's aunt Keiko, who had always been so kind to him. Pickaxe and Nugget were the only people supporting her, barely keeping her alive. But they couldn't help much on their meager Miners' salary. Sympathy briefly welled up inside Strike before he swept it aside.

"So what are you going to do?" Torch asked.

A stabbing pain pierced Strike's gut. What was once the Fireball Five would lose another of its members. His world would collapse even further. But too much was at stake. "I have to cut him. I need your help picking someone off my backup list."

Torch snapped around, the blood draining out of his face. "No. You can't do that. Don't." He shook his head, his lips pressed into a tight line. "Who are you going to get as a replacement? Good crackbacks are hard to come by. And how are you going to work in a new person without risking this next game?"

"I don't know. But I don't have any choice. I've already waited way too long. It's cost us, big-time."

"Hold up, hold up," Torch said. "Just hold the frak up." His brow wrinkled as he concentrated. "No. No! You can't cut him. Think about what that would do to Nugget. He'd quit."

Frak, Strike thought. He smacked the side of his head. *I'm such a moron. Why didn't I think of that?* Cutting Pickaxe would take Nugget down as well, the brothers always sticking together. There was no way the Miners could survive losing both crackbacks at once. "But what are we going to do about the upcoming game?" he asked. "The Flamethrowers might actually beat us if I get chased all around the field like last week. We cannot lose this one."

Torch chewed at a fingernail. "You know what? We could adjust the playbook. Nothing huge. But we could bring Nugget to the blind side once in a while. Even set up Rock to help out. Secretly. So Pickaxe doesn't realize that we're giving him backup."

"But that doesn't solve the bigger problem. I have to cut him sooner or later."

"Maybe. I don't know. But one thing is for sure: making a huge move like that right now is suicide. I'll help you figure out a plan. Just promise me you won't do anything until we can come up with a solid plan. And don't say anything to Pickaxe just yet. Trust me on that."

Strike nodded, relieved he had the greatest mind in Ultraball on his side. "Okay. Can you meet up tonight to help me figure it out?"

"Can't tonight. I have to go see my sister."

Strike bit his lip. "How's she doing?"

A radiant glow came to Torch's face. "She's getting a lot better. Thanks, man. For saying what you said back at the junk hole. She talks about it every time I see her."

"Wow. Really? I mean, glad I could help." It was hard to believe that someone who had looked that bad could have recovered. But maybe hope was even more powerful than Strike had thought.

Torch turned away, choking down a lump in his throat. "Jasmine is everything to me. I'd do anything for her. She's the only family I have left."

"You got other family," Strike said. "You got us. You're a Miner. Miners forever. Miners together." He held out a fist. "Tomorrow night? Help me plan things out?"

Torch looked at Strike, a tear running down his cheek. He gave Strike a melancholy smile and bumped his fist.

"Thanks," Strike said. "Don't know what I'd do without you."

"Don't thank me until you raise that Ultrabowl trophy," Torch said. "Right now, let's just make sure we do what it takes to beat the Flamethrowers."

FLAMETHROWERS BREAK
THE CURSE
By Vikram Cho, Senior Staff Reporter

After losing a heartbreaker to the Neutrons in week five, the Taiko Miners kept sliding in week six, stunned by the Farajah Flamethrowers, 77–70.

With the surprising victory, the Flamethrowers have now guaranteed themselves their first winning season in four years, officially breaking the Torch's Curse. Farajah Colony was in near riot, fans staying out all night to celebrate their team's victory. Three people were arrested and taken to Han-Shu Prison for burning Torch's yellow number 7 decal, with dozens of others defacing number 7 decals as the party continued all night.

The Miners' first losing streak in over a year has put them in a three-way tie for second place, with the Flamethrowers and the Tranquility Beatdown. And the young and hungry Kamar Explorers are only a single game behind at 3–3. The Explorers looked rough earlier in the season, but they've now won two in a row and have momentum on their side.

The Taiko Miners are now in a precarious position. With only one more game left in the Ultraball regular season, missing the playoffs for the first time in the history of the franchise is a real possibility.

Pieces of the Miners' offense looked sharp against the Flamethrowers, with Boom continuing to play like a superstar rocketback, scoring five TDs on two runs of thirty-nine and sixty-six meters, plus three fifty-plus-meter catches after skyrocketing up off Farajah Arena's launching ramps. Strike also had five TDs on a mixture of QB whips, slingshot Vs, and a delayed superjump off Boom's back that fooled the entire Flamethrowers defense. Strike's mighty leap was measured at over sixty meters high, yet another record broken by the talented QB.

The Miners' blocking, on the other hand, crumbled even further from their weak performance in their week-five loss to the Neutrons. The Miners' crackbacks allowed a team-record eight sacks and six deflected passes, two of which were returned by Afterburner for pick-seven touchdowns. The blind-side hits were particularly devastating, leading to two fumbles, one at the Flamethrowers one-meter line. At times, Pickaxe looked confused, seeming to let his blind-side rusher race by without even a block. The Miners attempted to adjust by shifting blocking assignments, but nothing could stop the Flamethrowers relentless pass rush.

During the postgame press conference, Pickaxe

said, "Those sacks weren't my fault. They were double-teaming me all day. Not even Radioactive or Chokehold could take a two-man blitz all by himself."

When asked about his fight with Strike right after the game ended, both players needing to be restrained by their teammates, Pickaxe got up and stormed out, whacking his microphone off the table. And when three reporters followed Pickaxe out, asking him about the rumors that he had secretly been on a late-night tram to North Pole Colony, he threw a punch, flooring one of the reporters, before running off.

Aside from the rumors and stories surrounding Pickaxe, the more important question remains: What has become of the Miners' lead crackback? Pickaxe seemed baffled by the Flamethrowers' overwhelming array of blitzes and stunts. Whether it's the pressure rattling the Miners' crackback 1, everyone calling him "Axepicker," brilliant defensive game plans from both the Neutrons and the Flamethrowers, or something else, the Miners must find a way to fix the glaring weakness in their lineup.

The final week of the season pits the Miners against the 2–4 Saladin Shock. If the Miners win, they make the playoffs. If they lose, they'll need some help from other teams if they are to squeak in.

But even if the Miners do make the playoffs, they are in serious danger of falling into the deadly fourth seed. In the nine-year history of the Underground Ultraball League, no fourth seed has ever gone on to win the Ultrabowl. And this year, the fourth seed will have to travel to North Pole Colony to play a semifinals game against the undefeated Neutrons.

The oddsmakers are currently giving the Neutrons an 84 percent chance of taking the title, making them heavy favorites to win it all.

RESULTS, WEEK 6

Flamethrowers	**77**
Miners	70
Neutrons	**91**
Shock	28
Beatdown	**98**
Venom	35
Explorers	**98**
Molemen	35

STANDINGS, WEEK 6

	Wins	**Losses**	**Total Points**
Neutrons **XY**	6	0	588
Beatdown	4	2	532
Flamethrowers	4	2	532
Miners	4	2	511
Explorers	3	3	462
Shock	2	4	238
Venom	1	5	231
Molemen	0	6	140

X=*clinched playoff spot*   **Y**=*clinched #1 seed*

18

THE TRAITOR

OVER HIS ULTRABALL career, Strike had lost some games. There had even been times when the Miners had lost two in a row. But it had never been anywhere near as bad as this. Strike had even tried to go to the weekly Nuclear Poker game to take his mind off the problems, but that had been a huge mistake. Fans were frantic. *SmashMouth Radio Blitz* had been brutal, Berzerkatron and the Mad Mongol calling for Axepicker's head on a platter. They had even started a campaign to get Strike to step down as general manager.

Strike sprawled out on the ratty couch in their apartment, flipping a football made of recycled junk, while Rock sat on a box that served as one of their two chairs.

Rock's back was straighter and more rigid than ever, his face lined with worry. "It just isn't logical," he said. "We simply cannot cut Pickaxe. If you cut him, Nugget will go as well. A single player would be hard enough to work in this late in the season. Replacing two would kill any chance we have of winning the Ultrabowl."

"I don't want to do it any more than you do," Strike said. He fought back tears of frustration. The Fireball Five had already lost one of its members in heartbreaking fashion. After today, only he and Rock would be left. Strike's world was imploding. But he had to find the strength to do what needed to be done—not just for his Miners, but for all of Taiko Colony. "As GM of the team, I have no choice. It's like what Berzerkatron and the Mad Mongol keep saying: Pickaxe will sooner or later end up costing us the season."

"It would take us at least a few games to work in two new players," Rock said. "Rookies are bound to make mistakes, and we cannot afford to lose our upcoming game."

"We can beat the Saladin Shock with two rookies."

"The Shock may be terrible, but they'll be hungry to take us down," Rock said. "White Lightning knows his season is already over. His quarterbacking career might be over, too. He would do anything to have something he could brag about. Beating the Miners would be exactly that."

"You, me, and Boom could take down the Saladin

Shock by ourselves, three on five. The Shock play like a bunch of chickens in Ultrabot suits."

"We couldn't play three on five. A team is automatically disqualified if they don't have five manned suits on the field." Rock looked up in thought. "Do you think a chicken could actually operate an Ultrabot suit?"

Strike squinted at Rock. "This hardly seems like a time to be joking around."

"Could we borrow a chicken from Yangju Colony's breeding facilities?" Rock asked. "Chickens do have extremely fast reflexes. I wonder if we could eventually train one to play rocketback—"

"Focus, Rock." Strike snapped his fingers. "We got a big problem on our hands."

"I'm certain that Pickaxe hasn't thrown any games." Rock took a deep breath. "It's become clear to me that much of the problem is that you've shown him little to no trust over the past two games. I think he's just crumbled under the pressure."

Strike launched the football across the apartment and then dropped back onto the old couch. He'd been rough on Pickaxe during the Neutrons game, no doubt, and even harder on him during the gut-wrenching loss to the Flamethrowers. But if Pickaxe was clean, he would have stepped up and delivered. His terrible play was proof that he was in Raiden Zuna's pocket. As much as it killed Strike to break up the Fireball Five, cutting Pickaxe was the only possible choice. He had let his general manager duties take a back seat to his personal loyalties for far too long. Tomorrow, Strike would start trying out people from the backup list.

They both jumped at a bang on their door. "Open up in there!"

"Boom?" Rock said. He opened the door, nearly getting thrown to the floor when she burst in, her face twisted into a furious scowl.

Boom jabbed a finger at Strike. "You're going to single-handedly cost us the Ultrabowl."

"Me?" Strike said. "I'm not the one who missed all those blocks. Remind me, how many times did Asbestos sack me from my blind side?"

Boom picked up the toy football and whipped it at Strike. It smacked him in the face, his head snapping backward.

"Hey!" Strike said, his eyes watering from the blow. "What are you trying to do, blind me?"

"You're already blind if you can't see that you're the frakkin' problem, not Pickaxe." She glared at him. "After the first play of the Neutrons game, did you call him Axepicker?"

"What?" Strike said. "No. I'd never do that."

"I talked with Pickaxe this morning, and that's what he told me. And that just happens to be when he started falling to pieces."

Strike strained to recall the start of the Neutrons game, but so much had been going on. There was Chain Reaction's taunting. The terrible first kickoff return. Strike nearly getting thrown out of the game for insulting a ref. Slapping Pickaxe's helmet . . .

He groaned, dropping his head into his hands. He *had* called him Axepicker. "How could I have been so stupid?"

"This makes much more sense now," Rock said. "It's one thing to be called a horrible nickname by Berzerkatron or the Mad Mongol. It's an entirely different thing when it's your own quarterback."

Boom bounded over and yanked Strike off the couch by the front of his jumpsuit, shaking him. "Did you call him Axepicker on purpose? Are *you* the frakkin' traitor TNT's been trying to root out?"

Strike's fists rose, trembling with rage. "You'd better be joking."

Rock jumped between them. "Stop it," he said. "As if things weren't bad enough. All we need is for one of you to get hurt. I don't know what TNT is up to. But all these rumors he's bringing up are messing with your head, Strike. And Boom. I guarantee that Strike will never have anything to do with Raiden Zuna. Is that correct, Strike?"

"Do I even have to reply to that insane question?" Strike said.

"For Boom's sake, yes."

Strike locked eyes with Boom. "I've never taken money from Zuna. I never will."

"So why have you been treating Pickaxe like dirt?" Boom asked. She pushed Strike down to the sofa. "All your talk about how tight you Fireball Five guys are, and you call him Axepicker? And then you start a fight with him after yesterday's game? You can't really think he's on Zuna's payroll, do you?"

Strike steeled his jaw. "Maybe I do."

"Can't you see how stupid that is? Pickaxe and Nugget follow you around like you're their big brother. You're like God to them. Pickaxe will never be able to perform if you don't trust him. If you call him Axepicker."

"She's right," Rock said. "TNT is shutting down your ability to think logically. I know how close you and TNT used to be. I appreciate the chances he and his mother opened up for us. But you have to stop listening to all his stories."

Strike looked back and forth at his teammates ganging up on him. There was no doubt that he had been a complete and utter moron, going way too hard on Pickaxe. But he also knew deep down that TNT's warnings were spot-on. TNT had been right about Zuna planning on cratering Taiko Colony. He was right about there being a traitor, too.

"Pickaxe isn't on Zuna's payroll any more than Rock is," Boom said. "So knock it off. We have to win our last game, and we have to score a whole lot of touchdowns. Make things right with Pickaxe. You need to apologize to him, and you better frakkin' do it good."

Rock nodded. "Her arguments are sound."

"You would agree with your girlfriend," Strike said.

"Girlfriend? What? That's ridiculous." He whipped out his notebook. "As ridiculous as a man in an Ultrabot suit. I mean, a cat in a jumpsuit. Wait. I mean—"

"Stop talking already," Boom said. A thin smile came to her face.

The three Miners watched each other in an uncomfortable silence. Boom got up, shaking her head at Strike. "This is all on you. You're going to cost us the season. The title." She turned to leave.

"Boom, wait," Strike said.

"What now?" she muttered.

"I know it's true. There is a traitor. It's not only TNT who's said so."

She turned and narrowed her eyes. "Who else?"

"At the start of the Neutrons game, Fusion told me that someone was going to stab me in the back. A Miner." It took him a while to force the words out, to trust someone else with this critical piece of information and every thought it had triggered. His words came out soft, cracking. But as he got going, everything rushed out. He had been so stupid for not telling her all this earlier.

Boom rubbed her chin in thought. She sat down next

to Rock. "You believe this? One of us is a traitor?"

Rock took a deep breath, looking away from Strike. He frowned. "No, I think it's ridiculous. TNT might believe he's helping out. But look at all the problems he's caused. We can't play together as a team if we don't trust each other."

Boom turned to Strike. "If what Fusion and TNT said is true—and Rock, I'm not saying that it is—are you absolutely sure the traitor is Pickaxe?"

"Who else could it be?" Strike said. "Even before I called him Axepicker, he almost cost us a forfeit against the Explorers. And that offsides at the end of the Beatdown game. And he was so terrible yesterday." He shook his head. "There is no other explanation."

"Yes, there is," Rock said. "It could easily be that he couldn't handle all of your pressure and venom. There could be other explanations, too."

Boom studied Rock, her eyes slowly widening. "Hey. Can you do me a favor?"

"Of course," Rock said. "Anything."

"I need some . . . some research done. Right away." She leaned over and wrote something in his notebook. "Get everything you can find. Don't let anyone find out what you're doing. Make sure no one follows you. And hurry. Go now."

Rock's forehead furrowed in confusion, but he nodded. "Right away." He got up and ran out the door, slamming it behind him.

"Where'd you send him?" Strike asked.

Boom listened until Rock's footsteps died out. Boom motioned him in close and started whispering in his ear.

Strike pushed her away. "What are you doing?"

"Being careful. In case your apartment is bugged."

"No one ever is in here but Rock and me. You think the Blackguard somehow slipped in?"

"No. But just trust me, okay?" She leaned in tight and whispered.

A gut-wrenching tear ripped through Strike's chest. A jagged knife was tearing all the way from his throat to his stomach. "No," he hissed. "No way." His breathing went ragged, his lips quivering. His vision clouded over, blurred by hot tears he couldn't hold back. "Impossible. No frakkin' way. It couldn't be."

"Couldn't it?" Boom said. "Think about everything that's happened in the past few weeks. I know he's been close to you. Really close. But doesn't it make sense?"

Strike blinked, his eyes stinging. A horrible sickness churned up the hardtack bar in his stomach. How could he have been so stupid to let this happen all over again, putting his trust in the wrong people? He wished so badly that this wasn't true. It just couldn't be.

But somewhere deep in his heart, he knew Boom was right.

He lurched forward and threw up all over the floor.

19

GAME 7 VS. THE SALADIN SHOCK

INSIDE SALADIN STADIUM, the Miners came out hot. There was no way to prepare Boom for the jarring impact of Saladin Stadium's disruptor zones—electromagnetic fields that crackled with storms of electrical arcs, messing up an Ultrabot suit's sensors—but she adjusted quickly. After a huge kickoff from Strike, Boom blasted right through a disruptor zone, electrical arcs exploding around her Ultrabot suit, to smash the Shock return man with a devastating tackle. Crunching him right off his feet, she sent him flying into an uncontrolled spin, his armored limbs flailing wildly in swirls of orange. The ball popped loose, bouncing into the Shock end zone. When Pickaxe jumped on it, energizing his glove magnets a split second before a defender to secure the fumble, the Miners were up 7–0, after only twenty seconds. Just as he had done all week, Strike chest-bumped Pickaxe, yelling encouragement at him, slowly but surely rebuilding his confidence. There had been some rough days of practice, but the signs were all there: Pickaxe was turning it around.

The Miners kept rolling the Shock during the first half. Boom blitzed early and often, fighting her way through disruptor zones, her suit sparking with bolts of electricity. She crushed the Shock QB, White Lightning, with four huge sacks. Rock rumbled down the field on sweeps and up-the-gut rushes, scoring a personal record three touchdowns. Even Pickaxe and Nugget got into the action when Strike called an inversion for them, a trick play where both of them lined up backward, confusing the Shock defenders staring at their butts. Before long, the Miners were demolishing the Shock 49–7. Strike almost felt a little sorry for them.

Almost.

A gun sounded, signaling the end of the first half, and the Miners high-fived one another as they made their way to the locker room. Pickaxe pointed to a small section of blue amid the crowds decked out in Saladin orange, and the Miners fans went wild, stomping and cheering for him. He took a step away from the others and jumped high, doing a double backflip. A chant of "Pick-axe! Pick-axe! Pick-axe!" started in the stands, and he did a triple-twisting backflip for them, soaring twenty meters into the air.

Strike clicked his helmet off and smiled at Pickaxe. "You're on fire. Keep it up." He paused. "Hey. Again, I'm sorry about—"

"Enough with the apologizing already, QB," Pickaxe said. "That's, like, a hundred apologies in the past week. It's getting weird." He grinned. "But I'd take another compliment if you got one."

Strike gave him a deep bow. "You are the man, sir. The man." Apologizing never came easily to Strike, but it had paid off in spades, coaxing back the smashmouth Pickaxe of old.

After getting out of their suits in the changing area inside the tunnel entrance, the Miners headed toward the locker room, with Torch falling in behind them. Pickaxe and Nugget slugged each other while Strike relished the awesomeness of one of the best first halves in team history. The Miners were back. They would make the playoffs, and even if they didn't get home-field advantage for their semifinal game, the Miners would crush whoever they faced.

Assuming that Boom flushed out the traitor.

Strike put up a hand for Boom to high-five, struggling to keep on a poker face while all the time wondering what she had planned. "Gotta hand it to you," he said. "You got us back on track."

"I didn't do anything," Boom said, slapping his hand.

She cracked a smile. "Except get you to pull your head out of your butt."

"Speaking of head in butt," Rock said. He pointed ahead to where the tunnel opened into the visiting team's locker room.

Standing by the door was TNT.

Strike ran up, hissing into his ear. "Are you crazy? If a single Miners fan sees you, you're going to get torn to shreds. How did you get in here, anyway?"

"Strike," TNT said. His words came out as if he was being strangled. "I really have to talk to you. In private." TNT grabbed the front of Strike's jumpsuit. His eyes flicked to Boom. "Please. I have proof."

A voice yelled out from the far end of the tunnel, and two guys in black jumpsuits came running toward TNT. "Hey, you!"

Strike yanked TNT into the locker room ahead of everyone else and ushered him out the back way. "Meet up at our spot at the usual time. Now get out of here. Use the left emergency exit. Run!"

"Watch your back, Strike. I'll bring the proof tonight." TNT slipped out and took off.

One of them barged into the locker room a few seconds later. He grabbed Torch by the front of his jumpsuit and shook him. "Where did that intruder go?"

"It's okay," Strike said. "Just a fan wanting an autograph, that's all."

The other Blackguard shoved Torch against a wall

and then glared at Strike. "Careful of how you speak to a Blackguard, boy. Now, which way did the intruder go?"

Strike pointed to the back of the locker room. "Took the right exit."

"You better hope we find him." The Blackguards knocked hard into Strike as they took off, heading the wrong way.

"You let TNT escape?" Rock said after the Blackguards disappeared. "Not a logical decision."

"Or was it?" Boom asked. "Maybe TNT is actually on to something."

Rock scratched his head. "Really? But with the confidence Strike has shown in Pickaxe, he's back on track. Outstanding play in the first half."

"That's right," Boom said. "Pickaxe is a true Miner." She grabbed Rock's shoulder with her left hand and shoved him down onto a bench.

"What are you doing?" Rock asked. "Why did you push me—"

"Just shut up and sit down."

Rock looked at her and then at Strike, his face quizzical. "Strike?" he asked. "What's going on?"

Boom shot a glance at Strike before he could respond. "That was an awesome first half," she said. "But did you catch the score on the Flamethrowers game?"

"Flamethrowers are up, 42–28," Pickaxe said. "We have a lot of work to do if we're going to pass them in total points."

"That's exactly right," Boom said. "We have to pull out all the stops. If it's okay with Strike, I think we should roll out the new dual quarterback sets. All of them." She raised an eyebrow at Strike.

"Good idea," Strike said, straining to keep his words relaxed and easy. "I like Boom's thinking. Let's do it."

The rest of the Miners looked at each other, exchanging bewildered glances. "But I thought we were going to save them for the Ultrabowl," Rock said. "That's when we'll really need our secret weapons."

"Rock has a point," Torch said. "Is now the time to pull them out?"

Rock nodded. "This is absolutely the wrong situation to—"

"Quiet!" Boom shot Rock a look that stunned him into silence. She nodded at Strike. "We're agreed, then. Roll out all the new dual QB sets. We need to put a lot of points on the board."

"Go big or go home," Strike said. "I bet each one of those plays will score us a quick touchdown."

"This is insanity," Rock said. "We must save these critical plays to use against the Neutrons—"

"I said, shut the frak up!" Boom's icy stare made Rock shrink down into his bench seat.

"But Rock is right," Torch said. "You're on a roll right now. Just keep doing what you've been doing. Keep those dual QB sets in your back pocket, Strike. If you use those plays now, the Neutrons will know exactly what to expect."

"Or do they already know exactly what to expect?" Boom asked.

The locker room went quiet. Pickaxe and Nugget looked at each other, their foreheads wrinkled in confusion.

Boom pulled something out of her left jumpsuit pocket. She held up a picture of the inside of a late-night tram, showing it to everyone. It was dark, bathed in the shadows of the Tunnel Ring, making it tough to see much detail. Two were people sitting next to each other. One was wearing a dirty Taiko Colony jumpsuit, with a gray star-shaped blotch on the back. Another was a big guy in the bright red jumpsuit of North Pole Colony.

Pushing over a briefcase.

Boom stepped in front of Torch, tilting her head up, locking onto him with a fiery gaze.

All eyes focused on Torch. He pushed his black hair into a curtain over his eyes. "Why are you all looking at me?" he asked.

Boom took deliberate steps toward him, cracking her knuckles. "The last play of our game against the Neutrons. It was like they knew exactly what play we'd be running. Because they did."

"What are you talking about?" Torch said. He squeezed his hands together, fidgeting with the front of his dirty blue jumpsuit, caked nearly gray with moon dust. "How would the Neutrons know what to expect?"

"Because you sold Raiden Zuna those plays," Boom said.

Nugget sucked in a sharp gasp.

Torch froze in stunned silence before shaking his head. He let out a nervous laugh. "You're joking, right? I mean, come on. Strike, what is she talking about? This is ridiculous. Frakkin' insane." His eyes darted about the room, at all the Miners staring at him. His breathing went shallow. "Wait. Are you saying you think that guy in that picture is me? What the frak has gotten into all of you? Are you all crazy?"

Boom's right hand shot out, grabbing Torch's shoulder to spin him around. "Look." She pointed to a gray blotch on the back shoulder of his jumpsuit.

It was the same star shape as in the picture.

"Rock," Boom said. "When I sent you out the other day, what did you find?"

Puzzled, Rock squinted as everyone turned to him. "I located a record of admission into Salaam Colony's hospital for Torch's little sister. Jasmine Tariq is currently in treatment for a severe case of dust poisoning. But what does that have to do . . ." His eyes widened. "Oh."

Strike's vision blurred through the tears welling up in his eyes. He couldn't bear to look at his boyhood idol, the QB he'd grown up wanting to be exactly like. He had seen

Torch do amazing things on the field. He had watched in astonishment as Torch ran up walls as if gravity had somehow been turned off, made the first superjump off an opponent's back, and even skimmed along the steel ceiling of Beatdown Stadium using his electromagnetic gloves. Hot tears streaming down his cheeks, he forced himself to stare at Torch. "How could you, man? I trusted you. And you sold me out. You sold all of us out."

Torch's face crinkled. A tortured moan rumbled from somewhere deep inside him, and he slammed an open palm into a locker. "I told you not to use the highball bounce during the Neutrons game. Strike, I pleaded with you not to use it. Why didn't you listen to me?"

Pickaxe's eyes narrowed as he connected the dots. "This entire time, you let Strike believe I was the traitor," he said. "You skated along while I took all the heat." He curled his hands into fists. "I'm going to kill you!" He charged at Torch.

Jumping in his way, Boom wrapped Pickaxe up, Rock stepping in to help.

"Let me go!" Pickaxe said, spittle flying from his mouth as he fought like a wild animal to tear into Torch. "I'm going to rip his throat out!"

"I never thought it would hurt the team," Torch said, his voice hollow. "You have to believe me. I had to find a way to take care of my little sister. She had dust poisoning. What was I supposed to do? She was going to die. I just sold Zuna a few plays. Just a couple. Only the ones that I thought you would never actually use."

"But you didn't say anything during the Neutrons game, did you?" Strike said. "We're fighting for our playoff lives right now, because of you. And I was saving the dual quarterback sets for the Ultrabowl. I thought they would be our secret weapon."

"I would have come clean if it had come to that. Honest, Strike, I would have."

"You would have single-handedly cost Taiko Colony its future. Three thousand people, with no place to live. Three thousand people, dead. Because of you."

"What?" Torch said. He took a step back, his lower lip trembling in horror. "Three thousand people, dead? What are you talking about?"

"If Zuna becomes Taiko Colony's governor, he's going to crater it," Strike said. "So he can harvest all the ice deposits underneath."

"No," Torch said. "That's frakkin' crazy. Zuna is shady, but he's no murderer. He couldn't do that, anyway. No one could." He looked around the room for support. "Right?"

Rock turned away, his eyes closed. He shook his head.

Boom clenched her jaw tight. Veins in her neck throbbed.

"Oh my God," Torch said in a low rasp. "Oh my God. What have I done? I didn't know, Strike. Honest. I didn't know."

Strike spoke through gritted teeth. "Get out of here."

"But, Strike—"

"Get out!"

Pickaxe writhed in fury, thrashing in an attempt to shake loose from Boom and Rock. "We teach him a lesson," he growled. "The traitor deserves a beatdown."

Torch closed his eyes and slumped onto a bench. "You're right. I deserve to be beaten to a pulp. I won't fight back. Hurt me. Knock me unconscious. Kill me. Please. I deserve to die."

"I get the first punch," Pickaxe said.

Strike studied the broken teenager, his head turned to the side as he braced for the beating to come. "Leave."

"Please, Strike," Torch said. "Hit me. Hard. I stabbed you in the back."

"You did," Strike said, his tone eerily gentle. "But you did it for your sister. And you didn't know about Taiko Colony. So get lost. Don't ever let us see your face again." He grabbed the shoulder of Torch's jumpsuit and pulled him to his feet. He led him to one of the emergency exits.

Torch took a step through the doorway. He looked over his shoulder at Strike, tears pooling in his eyes. He opened his mouth to speak, but nothing came out. Finally, he dropped his head and ran.

"Why didn't you at least let me throw one punch?" Pickaxe said. "I would have floored him."

"And why did you keep me in the dark?" Rock asked.

"For a horrible moment, I thought you were accusing me of being a traitor."

"Sorry, Rock," Boom said. "But you have a terrible poker face."

"The worst," Strike added.

"I couldn't risk you asking questions," Boom said. "I had to make Torch confess."

"But why?" Rock said. "You had the evidence you needed to prove his guilt . . ." His eyebrows shot up as he pointed to her right hand. "Oh. I see."

All eyes locked onto Boom's hand. She raised it, holding out her palm to show everyone gritty gray debris.

Shaped like a star.

"You tricked him?" Strike said. He looked at his own hand, covered with traces of a sticky gray sludge, from when he had grabbed Torch's shoulder to lead him out. "You planted a pattern of dirt on his back when you spun him around?"

Boom nodded. "I'm so sorry about keeping you in the dark, Rock. But you would have given away my plan with just one look." She took another look at the grainy picture of the two guys inside the tram. "It took my friends so much to get this. I was almost positive it was one of Zuna's guys giving Torch a payoff. But it's fuzzy enough that Torch could have denied it. So we had to doctor up the picture, to add that gray star to the back of his jumpsuit. To trap him."

"Clever thinking," Rock said. He exchanged glances with Strike, raising his eyebrows again. "I'm sure glad Boom's on our side."

Boom glanced at the wall clock, ticking down. Just five minutes until the start of the second half. "We need to work on the game plan."

Although Strike wanted to do nothing more than crawl into bed and forget everything he ever knew about Torch, he would have plenty of time to mourn the betrayal later. Now was the time to rally his team to victory. "Okay, guys. We have to move out of the fourth playoff seed and up to the third. Let's figure out how we're going to score a record number of touchdowns." He gathered everyone around the monitor, motioning for Boom to draw Xs and Os.

Nodding as he watched Boom sketch out plays, Strike tried his best to concentrate on the game plan. But part of him kept on thinking about how awesome it was going to be to meet up with TNT at the junk hole at midnight.

Strike allowed the tiniest glimmer of hope to grow in his chest. TNT had been wrong about Boom being a traitor, but he had been right about something critically important. He had saved the Miners, tipping Strike off about a real plot against them. Maybe if TNT would just tell him why he had done it last year, things might—in time—go back to the way they used to be.

Maybe someday, the Fireball Five would be back. Stronger than ever.

Fireball Five forever, he thought.

Strike barely heard Boom as she gathered everyone up for the "Miners together, Miners forever" chant, his smile growing bigger and bigger at the thought of TNT one day becoming his best friend, his sworn brother once again.

During the second half, the Miners gambled with trick defenses, including five-man nuclear blitzes, spearing double slingshots over the line of scrimmage, and sneak jumps out of disruptor zones for interceptions. Some of those gigantic risks led to Shock touchdowns, but that was okay—it meant that the Miners got the ball back quickly for more chances to score.

Strike kept a close eye on the Beatdown and Flamethrower game updates on the scoreboard. The Beatdown were racking up TDs. They were going to lock up the second seed in the playoffs, so the Miners turned their attention to catching the Flamethrowers, who were still within reach.

Deep into the fourth quarter, the Miners huddled up on defense. "The Flamethrowers just scored again," Boom said, pointing to the standings at the top of the scoreboard. "That puts us into a dead tie. Only thirty seconds left on the clock. We have to get the ball back and score again."

"We have one chance to cause a fumble," Strike said. "Stunt blitz motor right. Hit low, hit hard. Do whatever it takes to knock the ball loose."

The Miners jogged to the line of scrimmage. Boom went into motion as the Shock got set. Anticipating the count perfectly, she rushed around the right side as the Shock QB, White Lightning, handed off to High Voltage. Boom slammed into the lead blocker and tried to spin off him, but another blocker came in to pancake her.

Strike hurdled over the pile Boom had made, and slammed High Voltage backward. He wrapped him up and punched, trying to wrestle the Ultraball away, but High Voltage had his glove electromagnets engaged at full. Strike pushed his Ultrabot suit into its highest gear. Red lights flashed in his helmet, warning him that his power level was critically low. But everything came down to this one play. Driving his legs hard, he brute-forced High Voltage toward a disruptor zone. They tumbled in. Strike's heads-up display went berserk, fireworks of lights popping in front of his eyes. He swung away blindly at High Voltage, his fists connecting like jackhammers. He lurched forward as someone leapt on top of him, and then others dog-piled them. His helmet hit the ground, and soon, he couldn't move.

A whistle sounded. The disruptor zone turned off, suddenly clearing everything in front of Strike's eyes. Someone pulled him to his feet as the pile got untangled. He groaned when he saw High Voltage curled up on the ground. He had a death grip on the Ultraball.

The Shock started to huddle up. But after looking up

to the scoreboard, their QB waved them off. With just twenty seconds left and the clock still running, White Lightning shrugged and motioned his team toward their sideline. Waves of fans in orange and blue jumpsuits began to head for the exits.

Strike fell to his knees in despair. They had come so far. Everything had gone their way today. But the Miners had fallen short at the last minute. Having already used their one and only time-out earlier in the game, the Miners could do nothing to stop the final seconds from ticking away. The game was over. Because the Miners had scored exactly the same number of points as the Flamethrowers over the course of the season, losing to them in their head-to-head matchup meant the Flamethrowers had earned the third seed in the playoffs.

The Miners had fallen into the dreaded fourth seed. It was what Berzerkatron and the Mad Mongol called "The Seed of Death." Next week they'd have to play a brutal semifinals game against the North Pole Neutrons. At Neutron Stadium.

Boom raced to White Lightning and flipped her visor to clear. "Where do you think you're going? Get back here and finish this game."

White Lightning put a hand in Boom's face and walked away.

"Coward. The mighty White Lightning, running away. From a Dark Sider."

He flipped his helmet to clear, glaring at her over his shoulder. "You sure got a big mouth."

"Let's go," Boom yelled. "You and me, one-on-one. I'll beat you down so hard you'll cry to your mama. Or are you going to let my butt in your face be the number one play tonight on *LunarSports Reports*? *SmashMouth Radio Blitz* is going to have a field day with this. Berzerkatron and the Mad Mongol are going to skewer you." She turned around and stuck out her read end at him, wiggling it back and forth. "This is how White Lightning's career is going to end. Well, you can just can kiss my—"

"That's it." The QB signaled for the Shock's time-out. Staring daggers at Boom, he snarled. "A hundred U-bucks says I score on you."

Strike inhaled sharply. A hundred U-bucks was a fortune.

"Deal," Boom said. "You and me, one-on-one in the open field."

They set up at the line of scrimmage as the time-out expired. The refs exchanged glances, but they stood in their regular positions on the field.

Strike and the other Miners cautiously approached Boom, but she waved them back. "One-on-one. Stay out of it."

An excited buzz lifted through the crowd. Nothing like this had ever happened before. Just two players lined up, face-to-face. The other eight Ultraball players stood out of the action near the sidelines, watching along with the rest of the spectators.

"Are you sure about this?" Strike asked through his helmet comm. In the open field, the offense always had the advantage. It was all too easy for a defender to miss a tackle or get juked the wrong way. And a hundred U-bucks was on the line.

"Quiet," Boom said. "I need to concentrate."

A ref in steel plate armor blew his whistle and circled his arm. White Lightning walked up to the ball and stood over it, waiting to see what Boom would do. He waved his hand forward, goading her on.

With fifteen seconds counting down on the play clock, Boom approached, coming to within a meter of him. She got into a three-point stance and raised her head. With her free hand, she pointed at the ball.

As White Lightning bent down over the ball, Boom jumped up and backed away as if she were dropping into coverage. She hit the edge of a disruptor zone, her Ultrabot suit crackling with giant arcs of electricity. She planted her back foot and charged at him.

White Lightning flinched at the sight, but he didn't hike the ball.

Stopping just before the line of scrimmage, Boom bent down into her three-point stance again. She jumped up to repeat her defensive drop-back. The moment she did, White Lightning reached down and snatched up the ball.

But this time, Boom had only backed up two steps before charging forward like a rocket to smash into White Lightning. The QB tried to throw a stiff-arm as Boom blitzed hard, his glove smacking her helmet with an echoing thud. But Boom drove into him, relentless in her charge.

White Lightning spun around in a frantic effort to escape. He punched wildly at Boom with his free hand. A tremendous uppercut crunched into Boom's visor, snapping her head back. White Lightning shook her off and started running. He almost broke loose, but with a mighty leap, Boom shot herself at him, catching one of his boots. He lost his balance for a split second, and that was all Boom needed.

Boom threw her arms around the QB, picking him up off his feet. Leaning back, she spun him in a circle, whipping him around faster and faster until he was just a blur.

Then she let him go.

White Lightning soared backward, landing in a disruptor zone, a storm of electricity lighting him up into an explosion of fiery orange sparks. He cradled the ball as he sprang to his feet, disoriented, trying to figure out which direction was up.

A split second later, Boom raced into the disruptor zone, her Ultrabot suit exploding into crackles. She threw a monster uppercut at White Lightning's glove, her aim dead-on. The Ultraball smacked loose, bouncing backward toward the Shock's end zone.

Boom's momentum carried both players clear of the disruptor zone, the storms of electricity dying out. They both scrambled toward the ball. White Lightning had the angle, but Boom threw a hard elbow into his visor to knock him off balance. She dove for the Ultraball, and it clanged to her electromagnetic glove. Leaping to her feet, she raced toward the end zone, diving just as White Lightning crashed into her side. They careened sideways, but Boom stretched to full extension. Writhing and twisting, she smacked the Ultraball into the end zone.

Kicking White Lightning away, Boom jumped to her feet, punching her fists into the air, screaming in elation. She did a double backflip and then kicked the Ultraball so high it cracked off the roof of Saladin Stadium. The Miners swarmed to her, whooping and hollering.

White Lightning crumpled to the ground, smashing his fists into the turf.

"Every radio, TV, and phone is going to be playing this all night long," Nugget said. "Number one on *LunarSports'* Top Ten Plays."

"Number one play of all time," Pickaxe said. "You fooled him good. Berzerkatron and the Mad Mongol are going to go to town on White Lightning."

"A hundred U-bucks," Strike said. "That's a ton of money. What would you have done if you'd lost?"

Boom shrugged. "Not my problem. Money stuff is handled by the general manager of the team." She pointed at him with a sly grin.

Strike's smile nearly split his face in two. He shook his head, grinning at Boom's gutsy plan. She might be insane, but she had just single-handedly moved the Miners up out of the fourth playoff seed into the third.

Next up on the road to the Ultrabowl: a semifinal game against the Tranquility Beatdown.

RESULTS AND STANDINGS, END OF REGULAR SEASON

RESULTS, WEEK 7

Miners	**112**
Shock	56
Neutrons	**84**
Molemen	21
Flamethrowers	**84**
Venom	56
Beatdown	**98**
Explorers	42

STANDINGS, WEEK 7

	Wins	**Losses**	**Total Points**
1 Neutrons	7	0	672
2 Beatdown	5	2	630
3 Miners	5	2	623
4 Flamethrowers	5	2	616
Explorers	3	4	504
Shock	2	5	294
Venom	1	6	287
Molemen	0	7	161

PLAYOFF SEEDINGS

1	Neutrons	*(at Neutron Stadium)*
4	Flamethrowers	
2	Beatdown	*(at Beatdown Arena)*
3	Miners	

Bet	⛾1 Bet Pays:
Neutrons Win	⛾0.37
Miners Win	⛾2.64
Neutrons Score First	⛾0.94
Miners Score First	⛾1.04
Chain Reaction as MVP	⛾0.65
Fusion as MVP	⛾1.45
Boom as MVP	⛾3.54
Strike as MVP	⛾5.49
Co-MVPs	⛾10
Anyone Else As MVP	⛾15
No MVP Chosen	⛾25
Over / Under: 150.5 Total Points Scored	⛾0.98
Over / Under: 1675.5 Total Meters Gained	⛾0.98
Game Has 1 Overtime Series	⛾1.75
Game Has 2 Overtime Series	⛾2.12
Game Has More Than 2 Overtime Series	⛾2.27
At Least 1 100-Meter Passing or Rushing TD	⛾5
At Least 1 Passing TD Thrown Through Slingshot Zone	⛾7
At Least 1 Passing TD Bounced Off Roof	⛾10

No Four-and-Out Series During Entire Game . . . . . ₩500

One Player Drains Suit Power . . . .₩50
Blackout in Neutron Stadium During Game . . . . . . ₩100
Two or More Players Drain Suit Power . . . . ₩250

Any Ultrabot Suit Malfunction During Game. . . . . ₩1,000
Solar Flare Hitting Moon During Game . . . . ₩5,000
At Least 1 Pass Breaking an Impactanium Barrier . ₩100,000
Meteor Strike (Class 3 or Higher) During Game . . ₩250,000

20

ULTRABOWL X

RIDING THE MOMENTUM of their huge win during their last regular season game, the Miners rolled the Beatdown during the semifinals. Even facing a hostile crowd at Beatdown Stadium, the Miners came out in full attack mode, burying the Beatdown 49–21 by halftime. The spanking accelerated into the second half, the crowd actually heading toward the airlock exits halfway through the second half. The final score of 84–70 didn't tell the story of what a blowout the game had been, as the Miners eased up on the Beatdown during the last minutes of the game.

For a fourth straight year, the Ultrabowl would be a showdown between the Miners and the Neutrons.

The Miners' reversal of fortune took the moon by storm, reporters from *LunarSports Reports*, *SmashMouth Radio Blitz*, and the *Touchdown Zone* converging upon Strike and Rock's apartment building, permanently camping out in hopes of getting an interview. The *SmashMouth Radio Blitz* broadcasted continuously, Berzerkatron and the Mad Mongol going for twelve hours a day, and Genghis Brawn taking the other twelve. It seemed like everyone on the moon was trying to get to Strike, which was no surprise, given how much money was riding on the game— *LunarSports Reports* estimated that over fifty million U-dollars had been placed on hundreds of different bets. Strike hardly had a chance to get outside, except to and from practice, and that was always with an entourage of Taiko Colony citizens acting as their bodyguards.

Strike tried to keep things light as the Miners prepared for the game of their lives. Things were going great— Pickaxe getting his mojo back, the Miners on a roll, Torch flushed out as the traitor—but one thing kept eating away at Strike: TNT had never come to the junk hole. Strike had gone there at midnight every day for a week, but TNT hadn't shown.

Strike had to find TNT. He put feelers out through friends from the Tao Children's Home and from the apartment building. Every single one came back empty. With each passing day, Strike felt more certain that the Blackguards had chased TNT down and arrested him. It made him sick to think about TNT in a prison cell—or worse—after everything he had put himself through to make things right with Strike.

The day of Ultrabowl X arrived, and the Miners sat in the visitors' locker room inside Neutron Stadium. "We've been through a lot together," Strike said. "And this game will be the biggest challenge that we've ever faced. That crowd is almost one hundred percent Neutron fans. We're not going to be able to hear anything."

"We have to trust each other," Boom said. "That's when we've been unstoppable."

"Boom's right. Trust each other. And Miners, about the season. About trust." Even though he had said the words a hundred times to Pickaxe, they stuck in his throat yet again. "I'm so sorry."

"For clarification purposes, he's sorry about being an idiot for thinking that you could possibly be a traitor," Rock added.

Everyone laughed.

"What's so funny?" Rock asked in bewilderment.

The announcers' pregame routine blared outside the locker room, the crowd roaring so loud the Miners could hear the chanting through the door. "All right, guys," Strike said. "We'll huddle up with clear visors so I can give you the plays. Duck down low so no one can steal our plays using telescopes or whatever. I bet Neutron Stadium has all sorts of high-tech spy equipment. Hands in."

Everyone put their hands on top of his.

"Neutron Nation is going to boo us like crazy," Strike said. "They're going to throw rocks and trash at us. Just remember, none of that matters. We got this. We're the better team. We've prepared more. We've studied more. We've practiced more. We showed the Beatdown who's the best team in the league last week. And today, we're going to teach the Neutrons that same lesson. It's our time, Miners. Ultrabowl X champions. Let's go do this thing. Win it all. For Taiko Colony."

"For Taiko Colony," everyone repeated.

"Oh yeah," Strike said. Love and pride for his teammates surged through him, and he bellowed out a joyous scream. "Miners together!"

"Miners forever!" everyone shouted back.

As the announcer read off introductions for the Miners, Strike opened the airlock door to a sound wave that nearly slammed him backward. Nugget and Pickaxe went first, then Rock. Before Boom went out, she held out a fist. "Leave it all out on the field," she mouthed.

Strike emerged last out of the tunnel as his Miners were getting pelted with rocks, bouncing off the players' helmets. Blackguards were in the stands to stop it, but they weren't trying very hard. Almost the entire stadium was decked out in Neutron red, making it look like the stands were flickering with the flames of hell.

Only a small section was wearing Taiko Colony blue, Governor Katana surrounded by a team of bodyguards at the fifty-meter line. Even in the midst of a sea of Neutron fans swearing and booing at them, Governor Katana and his bodyguards screamed out the Miners' slogan at the top of his lungs, leading the Taiko Colony section in a chant of "Miners together, Miners forever." Holding out a fist with his thumb sticking straight up, he smiled broadly at Strike. But it was too big of a smile, like that of a hostage being told to say they were fine.

Strike nodded back, trying to look confident. The Neutrons were a five-person wrecking crew. In their semifinals game, they had annihilated the Flamethrowers in a 105–56 rout that was over even before halftime. The next sixty minutes would be a battle royale, ten Ultrabot tanks pounding one another into submission, with nothing less than the fate of three thousand people hanging in the balance.

From the very first play, the Neutrons' Radioactive Waste defense was relentless. Fusion kicked off, putting heavy backspin on the Ultraball. Strike tracked it as it soared halfway up to the roof, seeming like it would smash into the protective barrier behind them. But the crazy spin on the ball made it start curving upward, then almost stop in midair. It dropped down with an eerie slowness, right over Strike's head.

Strike's visual targeting system locked on easily. But as he waited for the Ultraball to come down, all five Neutrons shot themselves through magnetic slingshot zones simultaneously, accelerating and blasting out like nuclear missiles. They cracked into Strike's blocking wedge, exploding the tight formation backward into Strike. It was all he could do to catch the Ultraball and yank it into his chest plate before Nugget and Rock both smashed into him, everyone whomping backward into the clear protective barrier before crunching down to the turf.

He pushed his teammates away and jumped back to his feet. But a bright red arm smashed into his throat and whipped him back to the ground. Other Neutrons piled in, smothering Strike in his own zone. Underneath it all, the lead defender grabbed Strike's throat as if he were choking him, pinning Strike to the turf.

Touchdown, Neutrons.

Not even thirty seconds had passed, and the Miners were already down, 7–0. The Neutron crowd went insane, all ten thousand people on their feet, stomping and roaring for blood. The throbbing waves of sound slammed into Strike's ears, his helmet yellow, alerting him to potentially dangerous noise levels.

The lead Neutron was still on top of Strike. He flipped his visor to clear. Chain Reaction's cracked and peeling face loomed over Strike as if he were the grim reaper. A ref came in to clear the scrum. Just before Chain Reaction got yanked off, he pulled back his cracked lips into a ghoulish smile and smashed a double-fisted rabbit punch directly into Strike's helmet.

The Miners' first few possessions were more

demoralizing. Even with Pickaxe and Nugget giving Strike solid blocking on the line, there was no way the Miners could defend against the Neutrons' array of swarming blitzes coming from crazy angles, from above, off side walls, even sliding low between Pickaxe's and Nugget's legs as they expertly used the magnetic slingshot zones to rocket in. After the first four sacks, Strike placed Rock in the backfield as an extra blocker, but that barely slowed the Neutrons. The Radioactive Waste defense racked up hurried throws, batted balls, interceptions, and sack after sack after sack.

On offense, Chain Reaction was an unstoppable force, scoring TDs on the Neutrons' first three series. For the third one, he launched himself through a slingshot zone and superjumped off Fusion's back, soaring so high and fast that he smashed into the roof, kicking off hard to ricochet like a bullet into the end zone.

It was the highball bounce play that Torch had sold to Raiden Zuna.

A couple of big touchdown throws from Strike to Boom kept the Miners in the game. But not having as much practice with the slingshot zones as the Neutrons, they fell behind by as many as twenty-eight points. When the whistle blew for halftime, the Miners jogged to the tunnel amid the crowd's deafening roar, people pelting them with trash and rocks again. Strike looked up at the scoreboard, shaking his head: Miners 35, Neutrons 49.

The Miners were lucky to be down only fourteen points, but the way the Neutrons were playing, that fourteen-point lead looked bulletproof. The Miners were dead men walking.

Inside the locker room, Strike stood in front of his team, sweat dripping off his brow, trying not to look shaken in front of his teammates. What his team needed now was strength. And a plan. "It's rough out there," he said. "But we can do this. We've come back from a lot worse than this. Boom, awesome TD grabs. Rock, fantastic blocking. Big hit on Chain Reaction a couple of plays ago. Pickaxe and Nugget, you're doing a great job keeping me alive out there. But the Neutrons' defense is chasing me all over. I need more time. More protection. Ideas?"

"What about Torch's dual quarterback sets?" Boom asked.

"Can't use those," Strike said. "He sold some of them to Zuna."

"I'm counting on that." A devious smile came to Boom's face.

Rock jumped up in excitement. "A fake-out. We'll line up in the exact dual QB sets Torch drew up. We'll have to maintain a careful balance so they believe they know exactly what we're going to do, while always staying one step ahead of them." He pulled out his notebook and wrote out statistics, mumbling to himself.

"We'll make it look like we're improvising off broken

plays," Boom said. "But it'll all be planned. Strike will still take all the snaps, just like usual."

"Good thinking," Strike said. "Except that we should take it one step further. Boom, you're going to get some snaps."

"Are you sure?" Boom asked. "You're our QB."

"I need you to be my QB2 today. The Neutrons will quickly figure out what we're doing if every snap goes to me. We'll mix it up so you get some, too."

Strike and Boom rushed to sketch out a series of plays using Torch's two-quarterback formations as a starting point. When the horn sounded, Strike brought everyone into a huddle. "All right," he said, with confidence that he didn't really have. "Miners together."

"Miners forever," everyone said.

Pickaxe and Nugget looked at each other, both green in the face. "We can do this, right?" Pickaxe said.

"Thirty minutes to victory," Strike said. "We got this."

"Leave it out on the field," Boom said. "It all ends tonight."

After a short return to open the second half, the Miners lined up in a dual shotgun formation, with Nugget over the ball at center. Sure enough, the Neutrons signaled to each other, setting up a defense that looked like it was specifically designed to stop the two QB set. Strike yelled and stomped a foot, and the ball came quick-snapping into his hands. Already in motion, Strike swept in front of Boom, flipping her the ball as he passed. He charged at a blitzing Neutron defender, going low and upending the guy, sending him head over heels.

Another Neutron raced in toward Boom from the backfield, and Pickaxe blocked him. But there was no room for Boom to scamper around the edge. Cornered, she backtracked and spun toward the middle of the field. Two Neutrons came in hot pursuit of her.

Leaping to his feet, Strike cut upfield and jumped through a slingshot zone, cannonballing out the other side. Just as he was hoping, Boom jumped high and threw the ball over a defender's outstretched fingertips, firing it like a missile. The laser pass traveled fifty meters and came in hot. Strike leapt for it, snagging it one-handed with his glove electromagnet, the ball's momentum twisting him into a hard spin. He tucked the ball in as he tumbled back to the turf in a roll. He popped to his feet and raced for the goal line, leaping in for the score.

Strike tossed the ball to a ref, relishing the crowd's stunned silence. The rest of the Miners sprinted in and mobbed Strike, cheering and yelling via helmet comm, able to hear each other for the first time in the game.

After a four-and-out stop, the Miners got the ball back near the fifty-meter line. Still using their dual quarterback set, Nugget hiked the ball to Boom, who ran an option play to the right side, with Strike trailing her. After a fake pitch to Strike, she vaulted clear over a defender, kicking away his magnetized glove before it could latch onto her suit, and took off for the end zone. With a huge block from Nugget and another one from Pickaxe, she sprinted clear to the ten-meter line before a defender shot himself through a slingshot zone to spear her. But Boom protected the ball like it was a fresh potato as they hurtled into the protective barrier and smashed into a pile at the five-meter line. She fought and wrestled her defender for the last five meters, dragging Ion Storm into the end zone with her, collapsing over the goal line for a score.

In less than five minutes, the Miners had tied it up. Strike took advantage of the stadium going dead quiet to talk to his team through helmet comm. "Awesome run, Boom. And great blocking and coverage, Pickaxe and Nugget. We have to turn it up even one notch further, because the Neutrons will figure out a way to defend this."

And they did. After using their only time-out to regroup, the Neutrons came back out with a vengeance. Two plays later, Chain Reaction went seventy meters on a double reverse, launching himself through two slingshot zones before hurdling clear over Nugget into the end zone.

The Neutrons stopped the Miners on the next series, adjusting to the dual QB sets by coming even harder with their atomic blitzes, five defenders rushing in or thrown in by their teammates from all angles. Then Fusion scored another TD on a naked bootleg, his fake handoff to Chain Reaction so convincing that none of the Miners figured out what happened until the QB had launched himself through a slingshot zone to the end zone for a score.

The game went back and forth, the Miners and Neutrons trading TDs until halfway through the fourth quarter, when the Miners scored two straight. On the first, Boom beat out Chain Reaction in a flat-out footrace through a slingshot zone. The second, she outleapt both Chain Reaction and Meltdown, who were draped all over her, kicking and punching as they all fell in a tangle of flailing limbs, just managing to fight her way into the end zone.

With only three minutes left, the Miners were ahead by seven, 91–84, and the Neutrons had the ball on their own forty-two-meter line. A defensive stop would give the Miners the ball back, along with the chance to ice the game.

As the Neutrons came to the line of scrimmage for first down, Strike scanned the five players and their formation. His eyes went wide. In a moment of perfect clarity, it was like everything he had learned from four years of Ultraball crystallized. He could see the play unfold in his head: *Fusion with a fake scramble to the slingshot zone, then Chain Reaction on a sweep.*

He signaled to his teammates to set up like they were in a passing defense, and then charge in to stop the run.

Boom signaled back, asking if they shouldn't keep one person deep at safety in case it was a long bomb.

Strike shook his head. The thousands of hours of practice and study had prepared him. There was zero doubt in his mind.

The Neutrons got into their three-point stances. Fusion stomped once. Twice. He hiked it, scrambling back off the line. He jumped right, as if he were heading toward a slingshot zone. Chain Reaction came around from the far side, setting up as if to block for his quarterback. As Fusion ran by, he stuffed the Ultraball into Chain Reaction's gut. The rocketback took off on the sweep, sprinting toward the sideline, ready to turn the corner and hit a slingshot zone after outracing everyone there.

But Nugget came out of nowhere, leaping over a Neutrons blocker, timing his jump perfectly. His knockout punch rammed into Chain Reaction's helmet, snapping the rocketback to the ground. Stunned, Chain Reaction rolled away and tried to spring to his feet. But Strike came flying in with a spearing punch, smashing him right back down to the turf.

Second down, on the Neutrons' thirty-six-meter line.

Inside the huddle, Strike said nothing as he watched the Neutrons from across the line of scrimmage. The other Miners waited for their leader to make his call. Deep in the zone, Strike studied Fusion as the Neutrons' quarterback set up in the shotgun. And again, Strike could see everything unfold. He grinned, tapping his helmet and then chest plate in a series of motions, calling for Pickaxe and Nugget to delayed wave blitz from the right side.

Pickaxe and Nugget both flipped their visors to clear. Pickaxe cocked his head.

It was as if Strike could read Pickaxe's mind. After four years of being together day in and day out as the Fireball Five, all it took was one glance to tell Pickaxe to go launch Nugget over the line, sending him blasting into Fusion.

The Miners broke their huddle, setting up in a pass protection scheme, with only Pickaxe up at the line, across from the Neutrons' two crackbacks. Radioactive crouched over the ball, with Ion Storm next to him. The crowd roar ratcheted up as the play clock counted down.

Radioactive snapped it to Fusion, who faked right away to Meltdown on a slant. But the play was going to Chain Reaction, who had juked Strike and was racing long. Fusion bounced on the toes of his boots. He reared his arm back, ready to launch it up for grabs. As good as Strike was on defense, a one-on-one matchup would always favor the top rocketback in the league.

At the line, Pickaxe got creamed by Radioactive and Ion Storm. Nugget raced in as if he were coming around from the far side. But he suddenly changed direction, heading straight at his brother. He took a mighty leap as Pickaxe jumped up to catch his arms and sling him forward. Hurtling in like a bazooka shell, Nugget cracked into Fusion's arm just as the quarterback was throwing his pass. The ball nearly popped loose, but Fusion managed to hold on as he twisted, falling to the turf. Nugget grabbed Fusion as the quarterback tried to wriggle free. But Pickaxe came racing in to jump on them, smashing Fusion's butt to the turf.

Loss of nine. The hometown crowd grew quieter. At their own twenty-seven-meter line, the Neutrons had a long way to go. But there were still two plays for Neutron Nation to make things happen.

On third down, Strike went in hot pursuit of Chain Reaction, who streaked for a slingshot zone. Strike locked a glove onto Chain Reaction's boot as the rocketback leapt in. Both of them shot forward, accelerated by the powerful electrical field. But Strike had slowed them down, giving Boom time to get into position at the other side of the slingshot zone. Chain Reaction and Strike still launched forward like two connected cannonballs, but they blasted straight into Boom, for only a short gain.

Fourth down on their own forty-two-meter line brought up an obvious passing situation—the Neutrons had to score on this play or they would turn the ball over. But as the Miners set up, Strike signaled hard: let the primary receiver go and charge in to stop the reverse. He had never felt more confident, never more sure of himself. The Miners would let the play fake unravel, making it look like they had bit on the passing play. And then they'd race in to blast the ball carrier off his feet.

Fusion walked to the line, the quarterback waving to his players, motioning Ion Storm to give him more protection. He met Strike at the line of scrimmage. For a short moment, the two quarterbacks exchanged glances from behind their reflective visors. Strike said a silent thanks to Fusion for the warning he had given Strike before their regular season game. *But now we have to stop you*, Strike thought. *Stop Zuna.*

Fusion crouched and quick-hiked the ball, back-pedaling. Ion Storm and Radioactive blocked hard, creating a pocket for their quarterback. Fusion cocked his arm like he was going to fire a pass. But he jerked it back down and flipped it to Meltdown, who ran right behind him toward one sideline.

The Miners went in hard pursuit to stop the sweep. Meltdown skidded to a stop and raised the ball as if he was going to lateral back to Fusion. But just as Strike had called it, Meltdown instead flipped the ball to Chain Reaction cutting the other way on the reverse.

Strike leapt out of his hiding place behind Nugget. He slammed into Chain Reaction a split second after he got the ball, sending the rocketback crashing backward. The ball jarred out of his hands. Strike dove for the bouncing Ultraball, but he crunched into the field surface when someone landed on top of him. The ball pinged off boots and gloves, taking crazy bounces back toward the Neutrons' end zone.

Chain Reaction scrambled to his feet. He scooped up the ball after it took a high bounce, and ran toward the far sideline. Turning the corner behind a blocker who creamed Nugget, there was only one Miner between Chain Reaction and the end zone: Boom.

Crouched and ready, Boom waited as the top rocketback in league history charged at her. He juked hard. He threw his best double spin move, making her guess.

But Boom read it perfectly. She launched herself to match his move. With a great *clang*, one of her glove electromagnets clapped to the ankle of his Ultrabot suit. With Chain Reaction's incredible speed and strength, he dragged Boom along the ground. But no matter how hard Chain Reaction shook her, Boom never let go. She slapped at his legs with her other hand until her other glove locked on. She somehow got to her feet as Chain Reaction bucked and swung wild punches at her with his free hand. With a huge yank, she pulled Chain Reaction's legs out from underneath him. She lifted the rocketback into the air and turned him upside down. With a great jump, she pile-drove his helmet into the ground. The thunderous crunch echoed throughout the stadium.

Chain Reaction crumpled, his limbs splayed out.

Flipping her visor to clear, Boom stood over the dumbfounded Chain Reaction. She said nothing. Did nothing. Just stared at him, her gaze intense. Burning.

The crowd in fiery red fell silent, stunned into disbelief. It was the changing of the guard. The new top rocketback in the league had put the old one in his place. And worse yet, it didn't matter that the oddsmakers had given the Neutrons a 76 percent chance of winning. There would be no fourth straight title. Neutron Nation's dynasty was over.

The Miners raced in and jumped at Boom, high-fiving and forearm bashing. But she shrugged them off. She pointed to the game clock on the scoreboard, showing less than two minutes left. "Close out the game first, and then we'll celebrate," she yelled over the helmet comm. "Line it up."

Strike nodded and motioned everyone to the line of scrimmage. All the Miners needed to do was to run the ball four times, just hard enough to not get called for a stalling penalty. Having already used their time-out, there was no way the Neutrons could stop the clock. The Ultrabowl X trophy was theirs. Taiko Colony was saved.

The Miners started to line up in their dual quarterback formation, but Boom motioned to Strike. "You do the honors," she said. "You earned this one."

Strike paused. He had always imagined himself being the one taking the last carry to win the Ultrabowl. But there was no way the Taiko Miners would be in this position without the help of Boom. Heck, she *was* the

Taiko Miners. Just seconds ago, it was her brilliant open-field tackle of the Neutrons' star rocketback that sealed the game. "You earned it," Strike said. "I want you on these carries."

"Let's split them. You take the first two."

Strike nodded. He lined up over the ball, snapping it and running around the right side. Chain Reaction wrapped him up, punching at the ball, but Strike's glove electromagnets were engaged at full power.

Another run by Strike on second down. Same result.

On third down, Strike handed off to Boom. Neutrons tackled her, but she cradled the ball with a death grip and went down.

The Miners went over to congratulate Boom, but she waved them off. The crowd was dead quiet, people heading for the airlocks. Boom stared up at the luxury skyboxes at the very top of Neutron Stadium. Her arms spread out, she flipped her visor to clear and yelled up, "Neutron Nation dies today. It dies! Miners forever!"

The Miners lined up for the last play of the game. Boom was still jawing away at the skyboxes, taunting Raiden Zuna, wherever he was. As Strike got into his stance over the Ultraball, he turned to Boom. "Same play?"

"Same play," she said, not turning away from the stands. She took her place in the backfield, ready for the handoff. Taking a knee, she yelled up at the skyboxes. "As soon as Strike hands it off to me, I'll be down. Miners win. Nothing you can do about it, you old frakkin' fool!"

As the play clock ran down, Strike glanced over his shoulder to see Boom screaming into the stands. *Why does she think Zuna is going to hear her?* he thought. He followed her gaze, looking up at the skyboxes. A bright red circle of light glowed in one of the highest boxes, making Strike squint.

Strike jolted as an ear-piercing explosion rocked Neutron Stadium. The ground rumbled beneath his feet, throwing him off balance. He ducked, throwing his hands over his head. Every light in the arena crackled in a shower of blue and yellow sparks before winking out. Even the emergency lights cut out, total blackness blanketing everything. The pitch-dark stadium filled with screams, the pounding of feet on bleachers, people scrambling in the chaos.

The heads-up display in Strike's helmet flickered in a storm of static before blinking out. A second later, a red initialization sequence came up. Green lights finally flashed across his display, showing his suit's power level at only 1.4 percent. "Rock," he said into his helmet comm. "Where are you?"

"What happened?" Rock replied.

"What's going on?" Nugget yelled.

Blackouts weren't uncommon given the moon's shaky electricity. But Neutron Stadium, powered by two separate nuclear reactors and a solar farm, was a different story. Raiden Zuna had guaranteed that a repeat of last year's Ultrabowl blackout would not happen. And Zuna never broke his promises.

He was up to something big. And it wasn't good.

Nugget's shaky voice came on the helmet comm. "I'm scared. What's happening?"

"Just stay put," Strike said. "Everyone okay? Pickaxe?"

"I'm okay," Pickaxe said. "But I can't see a thing. My suit power is only at 1.7 percent. What's going on?"

Strike threw his hands over his face as the arena lights snapped back on at full force. His eyes burned before his visor automatically snapped back to tinted mode. He looked to see his teammates were around him, the Neutrons not far away, the steel ball still on the ground at the line of scrimmage. Frenzied hordes of people in the stands stampeded for the exits.

A crackle of static blared over the loudspeaker, Strike clapping his hands to his helmet at a shrill cry. "Strike! Stop her!"

Strike furrowed his brow. The voice was so familiar. A jolt of panic shot through him as he realized it was TNT. But how could TNT be on the Neutron Stadium loudspeaker?

TNT cried out, the sounds of a scuffle amplified across the stadium. "Strike, get to Boom! You have to stop her, now!" Then there was a sickening punch. Then the thud of a body hitting the floor.

The announcer came on. "Ladies and gentlemen, we apologize for the blackout. Please remain calm, as emergency power has been routed from secondary sources. The game will continue shortly."

"Boom's gone!" Nugget said. He pointed to the sideline.

Strike's stomach tightened. He whirled around to see Boom's number 3 Ultrabot suit lying on the ground. It was open. Empty. The field turf next to the suit was scratched, scuff marks heading toward one of the airlock exits. "Boom!" he called out. "Where are you?"

And then a wave of despair crashed over him, dropping him to his knees. Strike slapped his hands to his helmet. He slammed his head into the turf, pounding it over and over. The realization hit him like a roundhouse punch to the stomach. He collapsed.

"Player out of suit and off the field," the announcer's voice blasted over the loudspeaker. "The Miners are automatically disqualified. Congratulations to the champions of Ultrabowl X, with their fourth championship in a row . . .

"The North Pole Neutrons!"

UNDERGROUND ULTRABALL LEAGUE: ULTRABOWL RESULTS

Year	Ultrabowl	Champions	Losing Team	MVP	Score
2343	I	Kamar Explorers	Saladin Shock	Berzerkatron	35–14
2344	II	Tranquility Beatdown	Farajah Flamethrowers	The Mad Mongol	49–28
2345	III	Saladin Shock	Tranquility Beatdown	Electrify	56–42
2346	IV	Farajah Flamethrowers	Kamar Explorers	Beastfire	70–63
2347	V	Farajah Flamethrowers	Tranquility Beatdown	Beastfire	63–56
2348	VI	Tranquility Beatdown	Farajah Flamethrowers	Genghis Brawn	77–70
2349	VII	North Pole Neutrons	Taiko Miners	Chain Reaction	70–56
2350	VIII	North Pole Neutrons	Taiko Miners	Chain Reaction	77–70
2351	IX	North Pole Neutrons	Taiko Miners	Chain Reaction	98–91
2352	X	North Pole Neutrons	Taiko Miners	Chain Reaction	DQ

21

THE FATE OF TAIKO COLONY

STRIKE AND ROCK had racked their brains with Governor Katana and his advisors, trying to come up with some solution, some trade, some arrangement that Zuna might accept. Part of the deal was that Governor Katana could call off the bet by buying Zuna's oxygen recycler outright, thus saving Taiko Colony. But coming up with ten million U-dollars was laughable.

Strike paced in front of the eastern airlock to Taiko Colony, waiting to intercept Raiden Zuna when he arrived. Taiko Colony was doomed. Raiden Zuna would take control, and then the blast fracking and explosion mining would start. The giant cavern would collapse, destroying the colony. In the distance, a low background buzz of people desperately evacuating filled Strike's ears.

All night long, Strike had kicked himself for being so stupid. How could he have trusted Boom? She made such a good show of being his star RB1, his teammate—even his friend. And then she sold him out, getting out of her Ultrabot suit to get the Miners disqualified. The scratch marks in the field turf around her suit were signs of her scrambling away in the dark. The traitor had signed Taiko Colony's death warrant.

So much for all of Boom's talk about trust. Whatever it took, however much it cost him, Strike would find the dirty rat.

And then he'd make her pay.

Strike turned at the sound of footsteps from behind. Rock shook his head, dark circles under his eyes. "I scoured the law books at Copernicus College library all night."

"Any miraculous ideas?" Strike asked.

Rock glumly shook his head.

Strike's last shred of hope shriveled and died. If Rock couldn't figure a way out of this, no one could. He clenched his fists, picturing the dead Earth swirling with nuclear fallout. Earthfall had happened because of ultrapowerful tyrants battling to gain control over the planet. Raiden Zuna had to be stopped.

It was time for the nuclear option.

"You did everything you possibly could," Rock said.

Strike closed his eyes, seeing the toxic clouds covering Earth. Taiko Colony would soon fall in Earth's footsteps, a rotting graveyard. Where would three thousand people go? They would wander the Tunnel Ring, begging one of the other twenty underground colonies to take them in. Maybe set out for the Dark Side. Many of them would die.

"Strike?" Rock said. "Did you hear me? You did all you possibly could."

A dizziness filled Strike's head. "Get going, Rock," he said. He reflexively touched his right jumpsuit pocket. "I need to meet Zuna by myself. Alone."

Rock furrowed his brow. "I should stay."

"I don't want you here," Strike said. "Go."

"Promise me you won't do anything crazy," Rock said.

Strike kept staring forward, silent.

Rock grabbed his shoulders and shook him. "Strike. I know what you're planning. It's stupid. Zuna will kill you for sure. And that can't happen. You're the only friend I have left."

At the bottom of Strike's jumpsuit pocket, the hilt of a knife pressed into his leg. His brain spun, trying to think of a way to make this promise to Rock and still carry out his plan.

Rock shook him hard. "Promise me you won't do this. On your parents' graves."

"Someone has to stop Raiden Zuna."

"But this won't achieve anything. It'll only end with you dead. The people of Taiko Colony need you more than ever right now. Governor Katana needs you. I need you."

Strike had to do something. Anything.

But like always, Rock was right.

Strike screamed in frustration. Attacking Zuna was pointless.

Everything was pointless.

He dropped his head in defeat. So much for going out in a blaze of glory. So much for showing Zuna that some people still had fight in them.

"I'm going to stay right here with you," Rock said. He reached into Strike's pocket and took the knife. "And I'm going to hold on to this."

They both turned at the sound of the metal airlock door squealing open.

But it wasn't Zuna. A scrawny boy in a filthy jumpsuit tripped through the gateway and stumbled, falling to the ground in a heap.

"TNT?" Strike said. "Where have you been?"

Breathing hard, TNT struggled to catch his breath.

Strike recoiled at the sight of his face, bony and ashy gray. His eyes were sunk into sockets darkened black. TNT was no longer human. He was a skeleton.

"Zuna bribed two Blackguards to haul me in," TNT said. "They got me after I tried to warn you." He broke into a spasm of coughing. "He had me locked up in a prison cell under Neutron Stadium for two weeks." He shook his head. "I failed you, Strike. I couldn't get you the message."

"You got locked up," Strike said. "So that's why you never showed up at the junk hole."

A look of relief appeared on TNT's face. "You actually went. I wasn't sure you'd show up. I tried to escape from my cell to get there, but it was no use. At least until the power went out during the Ultrabowl. I busted out right then and ran straight to the announcers' booth to warn you about Boom. But I was too late." TNT clawed at his cheeks. "I told you I had proof, Strike. It cost me everything to get this." He pulled a grainy picture out of his jumpsuit pocket.

Strike leaned in. It was tough to make out the two figures in the blurry shot. But the angular black weapon strapped to the man's side and the shoulder-length hair framing the girl's face made everything clear.

It was Zuna and Boom, shaking hands inside an apartment building.

Strike paused, but he reached down to give TNT a hand. He pulled him up easily, TNT's bony frame shockingly light.

TNT sobbed. "I had a chance to stop this. But I failed you. All I wanted was for things to go back to the way they used to be. And now they never will."

Memories came flooding back to Strike. The day they first met. So many all-nighters, planning practical jokes on their teammates. Thousands of hours at practice. Dozens of high-pressure games. Strike had thrown over one hundred touchdown passes to TNT. They had fought together to make three straight Ultrabowls. Even after a full year, the pain of losing his best friend still stabbed at his heart.

A phone rang, startling them all. "Where's that coming from?" Strike asked. Hardly anyone in Taiko Colony had a phone, everyone having hocked anything of value long ago. He followed the sounds to Rock. "Is that you?"

"No." But Rock patted his pockets, and pulled out a tiny phone. "Where did this come from?" He answered it, and a scratchy picture appeared.

It was Boom, flanked by people in white jumpsuits.

But this wasn't the Boom who Strike knew. Lying in a cot in a dim room, she looked even worse than TNT. Her face was charred and raw, skin peeling off her cheeks, covered by oozing red sores. Big clumps of her hair had fallen out, and the rest was so thin you could see her scalp through it.

She took a raspy breath. "Rock. I'm calling you because you're my friend. Remember that, no matter what."

"Where are you?" Rock said. "You look terrible. Are you okay?"

"Always the charmer, aren't you?" She let out a pained

sigh. "They say I could get better, but . . ." She shook her head, tears running down her cheeks. "Tell Strike I didn't plan for it to end this way."

Strike jumped in front of the phone. "Liar. You took a payoff from Zuna, didn't you?"

She paused. "Yes. But—"

"I knew it. You screwed us. Taiko Colony is going to die because of you. You deserve to die, you frakkin' traitor."

"You're right," Boom said. She squeezed her eyes shut.

"Wait." Strike glanced uneasily at Rock and TNT. "What?"

"This will explain some things," she said.

A second later, the phone in Rock's hand beeped. He pushed a button, and a document came up. He squinted as he read through it. "This transfers ownership of Raiden Zuna's oxygen recycler . . . to Governor Katana?"

Strike pushed in to look at the document. He ran his fingers through his hair as he studied it, hardly understanding a word of the legal mumbo-jumbo.

Rock pored over the details, hardly blinking. "It appears that Zuna has been paid the ten million U-dollars needed to buy the oxygen recycler and cancel the bet."

A corner of Boom's mouth curled up.

"This doesn't make any sense," Strike said. "Someone explain to me what the frak is going on."

Rock held up the phone, a giant smile on his face. "Look."

Strike studied a photo containing dozens of pieces of paper. "Betting slips?"

"That's right," Rock said. "A total of one hundred thousand U-dollars in bets, all placed at one-hundred-to-one odds. Boom turned one hundred thousand into ten million."

"But . . ." Strike shook his head, dumbfounded. "Where did you get one hundred thousand U-dollars?"

"I told you," Boom said, with a wry grin. "I took a payoff from Zuna. A big one. My friends then placed all those bets for me. They already collected all the winnings and sent them to Governor Katana." Her smile widened. "What I wouldn't give to see Zuna's face when he finds out what happened."

"She rigged it all," Rock said, bouncing with excitement. "Everything. She's been pulling the strings all along." He zoomed in on one of the slips. "Her friends bet all that money on a blackout happening during the Ultrabowl. Zuna was so sure that his two nuclear reactors and his solar power backup wouldn't all go off-line at the same time, he set the odds at one-hundred-to-one."

"Didn't count on me and my friends," Boom said. "We Dark Siders pride ourselves on having all sorts of different skills. Tunneling. Electronics. Explosives." She paused, looking expectantly at Rock, waiting for him to figure it all out.

Rock slowly put the pieces together. "You tunneled

underneath Neutron Stadium?" he asked. "And then set off a massive electromagnetic burst? But how?"

"Remember the day we met?" Boom said. "I stole that Blackguard's ID badge?"

Rock flipped through his notebook, studying a page titled "The Day I Met Boom." "You said you had some shopping to do . . ." His face lit up. "At Saladin Colony. You said you needed some big-ticket electronic items."

"People in Saladin Colony love two things," Boom said. "The Saladin Shock, and high-powered electronics. Making a gigantic electromagnetic explosion is easy, if you have the right equipment."

Strike rubbed the back of his neck, still trying to make sense of it all. "But this is crazy," he said. "Why did you do all this complicated stuff? Why not just help us win the Ultrabowl? That would have been a much easier way to save Taiko Colony."

"Vengeance," Boom said.

Rock and Strike looked at each other, puzzled. Then Rock's eyes widened. "Did you blow up the Meltdown Gun?"

She nodded. "I finally destroyed the weapon that . . ." She choked up. "That . . ."

"The weapon that killed your parents," Rock whispered.

"I don't get this," Strike said. He shook Rock in frustration. "Dumb it down for me."

"An electromagnetic burst blows up all things electrical," Rock said. "But only if they're running. The Meltdown Gun had to be operating in order for that massive electrical blast to destroy it. At the end of the Ultrabowl, Boom made it look like she was going back on her agreement with Zuna. All that yelling, up toward the luxury boxes at the end of the game? She was goading him."

"I had to convince him that I was double-crossing him," Boom said. "I only left him one way to stop me: to pull the trigger."

Rock gulped. "To nuke you with the Meltdown Gun."

A cold shiver shot down Strike's back as he remembered the bright red circle he had seen up in the stands. It was the Meltdown Gun, firing at Boom. No wonder she looked like she had been burned to a crisp. Ultrabot suits could withstand almost everything, but nothing could stop the focused nuclear radiation blasting out of the Meltdown Gun. Even impactanium armor could only block it for a few seconds. "But wait," Strike said. "Zuna still becomes governor of Taiko Colony because we didn't win the Ultrabowl, right?"

Rock broke out laughing as he studied another document that popped up on the phone's screen. "No. Boom's Dark Sider friends already sent that ten million U-dollars to Governor Katana, allowing him to buy Zuna's oxygen recycler outright. That will officially cancel their bet. Governor Katana will remain governor."

"But won't Zuna somehow weasel his way out of all that?" Strike asked. "Still take over Taiko Colony?"

"No," Rock said. "Not even he has enough power to welch on a bet this huge. Taiko Colony is saved. Everything went exactly to Boom's plan."

Boom's smile melted away. "Not everything."

Strike and Rock waited for her to explain, but Boom didn't speak. Her jaw trembled.

"What do you mean . . ." Rock startled. "Wait. The scratches by your Ultrabot suit. You weren't scrambling to get away. You were fighting to stay put. You tried to die out on the field?"

Boom closed her eyes. She nodded.

"What?" Strike said. "That's insane. Why?"

"Disqualification only happens if a player gets out of their Ultrabot suit during the game," Rock said. "If she had died inside her suit, we would have been allowed to play, as long as her body was suited up and on the field. We could have run out the clock and won."

"You tried to stay on the field," Strike said, a lump clogging his throat, "so we could win?"

Boom nodded again. "I tried. But I couldn't stop my friends from evacuating me. From trying to save my worthless life. Once I destroyed the Meltdown Gun and saved Taiko Colony, I accomplished my mission. But my friends cost you your Ultrabowl title, Strike." She turned away, her eyes pinched tight.

Strike stared at the phone, trying to process the horror of it all. Boom had orchestrated a grand plan to get her vengeance, save Taiko Colony, and get Strike the title he so badly needed, all in one fell swoop. She had been planning to die in order to make it all happen.

But as he tried to process everything, something didn't sit well. His hands balled up into fists. They began to quiver, then tremble. "You're a coward," he said through gritted teeth. "Nothing but a frakkin' coward."

Boom's eyes popped open. She scowled, and her jaw tensed. "What did you just call me?"

"You heard me," Strike said. "You're not even going to fight to stay alive, are you?"

She looked down before shaking her head.

"You think destroying the Meltdown Gun means anything?"

"Of course it does," Boom said. "It's the source of Zuna's power. I blew it up. Avenged my parents. I saved Taiko Colony, too. Shouldn't you be thanking me?"

Strike took several deep breaths, struggling to hold his rage in check. "Yeah. Okay. That's big. But don't you see? Zuna won't stop until he gets at those ice deposits underneath Taiko Colony." Although Strike had only wanted one thing his entire life—to win an Ultrabowl for his Miners, thus guaranteeing their futures—he could no longer ignore what had been staring him in the face.

"This is a major setback for him. But he'll regroup. He's going to come at Taiko Colony even harder. And it won't be just Taiko Colony. His alliance will be gunning to take over the entire moon. Zuna has to be stopped for good. No one's standing in his way. Someone has to take him down." He glanced nervously at Rock. "I think . . . as crazy as it sounds, I think it has be us. And we need your help, Boom."

"But I'm a disgrace—"

"Stop saying that!" Strike yelled. "What you are is brilliant. Amazing. You die, and Taiko Colony dies along with you. Frak! I don't know what chance a couple of kids have of stopping the most powerful person on the moon. But one thing is for sure: without you, we'll go down in flames."

Boom stayed quiet for a long moment. She peered nervously at Rock. "Can you ever look at me again?"

Rock's face screwed up in confusion. "What are you talking about? You're my friend. You'll always be my friend. Strike is right. We can't stop Zuna without your help. We need you to survive." He choked back a sob. "*I* need you to survive."

Boom turned away, tears freely flowing down her cheeks. She wiped at her face. "Way to make it awkward, doofus."

"What?" Rock said, turning red. "I didn't mean to—"

"Just yanking your chain," she said with a tiny grin.

"You have to hold on, Boom," Strike said. "Get better. Get back to full strength. Then help us fight Zuna. Help us take him down. For good, this time."

She took several weak, rattling breaths. "I don't know if I'll ever be in Ultraball shape again. Or what I can do to help stop him. But . . ." Her voice lowered to a whisper. "I'd be honored if you'd still let me call myself a Miner."

Strike turned to Rock. "Miners together?" he said.

"Miners forever," Rock replied.

A million-U-dollar smile came to Boom's face. She keyed a code into her phone. "We won't be able to talk on this phone again—too much risk of Zuna picking up the signal and locating us—but I'm sending Rock an emergency code. If there's ever a dire need, punch it into the phone. I'll come running."

"But you'll never be able to return to the UMC," Strike said. "Zuna will be gunning to kill you."

"I'll figure out a way. Dark Siders cast no shadows." She bit her lip. "It might be a long time before I see you again. I have no idea how we're going to do it. But we will take down Zuna. Together." She nodded to them, a glimmer of hope in her eyes. Then the screen blinked out.

"Miners forever," Rock whispered.

Strike turned back toward the cavern, listening to the sounds of Taiko Colony preparing for evacuation. "We should go find Governor Katana. Make sure he understands all of this. I gotta admit, I'm still a little confused. The only thing I know for sure is that Boom is a genius."

Rock nodded. "Taiko Colony is saved. Although not exactly how you planned."

"I was so sure we were going to raise that Ultrabowl trophy," Strike said. "My last chance at an Ultraball title. It's all over now."

"You probably have another year left before you outgrow your suit."

"Even if I could play another year, Boom is gone. We'd have to find a new rocketback 1. We'll never find another superstar to replace her."

Rock pinched his lips into a taut line. "There is a possible solution to that problem." He pointed at TNT, still in a heap on the ground.

Strike stared down at the boy who once had been his best friend in the entire world. *Can I ever trust him again?* he thought.

"It is true that TNT sold you out to Zuna last year," Rock said. "But look at everything he's done to try to make up for it."

His grudge hardening deep in his gut, Strike glared at TNT. "He won't even tell me how much Zuna paid him to stab us in the back."

"That is true," Rock said. "It does seem very odd to make such a promise to Zuna."

Strike kicked at the cavern floor. If only TNT would come clean. With Torch, Strike at least understood why he had sold plays to Zuna. Anyone might do that, if the life of someone close to them was at stake.

A realization hit Strike like a meteor blasting into the moon. He turned to TNT. "The promise you made. Was it to Zuna?"

TNT slumped. With the barest of motions, he shook his head.

"Your mom," Strike said. "You promised *your mom* you would never say anything?"

TNT grabbed the front of Strike's jumpsuit. "She's so ashamed of what I did. Of me. But what was I supposed to do? Zuna offered me one hundred thousand U-bucks to throw the game. When I refused, he threatened to hurt my mom. To kill her."

Months ago, Strike would have scoffed at the idea of a Colony Governor threatening to kill someone.

Now it seemed all too real.

"Please don't say anything, Strike," TNT whimpered. "She made me swear that no one would find out."

"Why didn't you go to the authorities?" Rock asked. He closed his eyes, pinching the bridge of his nose. "Sorry. What a stupid question. Zuna is one of the authorities."

Strike gently pried TNT's hands off his jumpsuit and turned away. Sadness and regret sat heavy in his stomach as he tried to process everything.

Rock cleared his throat. "Strike. I think you know what the answer has to be."

Strike stuffed his hands into his pockets and stared into Taiko Colony's flickering roof lights off in the distance. He had been living so long with this hate, this thirst for revenge against his former best friend.

But as always, Rock was right.

Strike punched Rock's shoulder. "TNT will have to earn back his spot. We'll have to try him out all over again."

"Really?" TNT said. "Thanks, Strike. I'll never let you down, ever again."

Rock flipped his notebook open to the pages of jokes and chuckled to himself. "If TNT does make the team, he'll need to go through rookie initiation."

Strike smiled. "Yeah. The Taiko Arena locker rooms are sure in need of a good cleaning. The waste collectors are disgusting. They need to be scrubbed. By hand."

TNT's face fell. "Hey. You're just kidding, right?"

"Another secret trapdoor pit on the one-meter line would play to our home-field advantage," Rock said. "Someone would need to dig that."

"He could scrape it out with his fingernails," Strike said. "On hands and knees. With 'KICK ME' written on the back of his jumpsuit."

"TNT's butt is about the same size as an Ultraball," Rock said. "It would make a good target."

"I could use some kickoff practice," Strike said. "A *lot* of kickoff practice."

"Hey," TNT said. "Come on, guys. That's not funny."

"No, it's definitely funny," Rock said. Cackling out his machine-gun laugh, he scribbled into his notebook.

Strike extended TNT a hand. "Never turn on me again?"

"I swear it," TNT said. "Miners forever."

They shook hands, softly at first, but then with a firm squeeze. "You'd better get started," Strike said. "That new pit isn't going to dig itself."

TNT grinned. "How deep do you want it?"

Strike put one arm around Rock's shoulders, the other around TNT's. He wasn't sure how they would fight someone as powerful as Raiden Zuna. But it was just like Boom said. They would find a way to defeat him. Together.

Maybe even win an Ultrabowl along the way.

The three of them headed back toward Taiko Colony to reassemble the Fireball Five. To prepare for the coming war.

ACKNOWLEDGMENTS

Writing can be a lonely, soul-squashing process. Thankfully, I've been incredibly lucky, getting immeasurable support from friends, family, and community.

Alec Shane, my literary agent, gave me my first big shot. His multiple rounds of thoughtful notes expanded my manuscripts and improved them tremendously. Locating the right home for this book was just one of the many factors that make him The Man.

Speaking of The Man, Ben Rosenthal worked tirelessly with me to pump up, shape, and hone the book into fighting trim. I'm embarrassed to look back upon the draft I originally sent him—it feels like a thin shadow of what it's grown into under Ben's careful guidance. If you enjoyed anything about the book, there's a huge chance it's due to his editorial brilliance. The entire team at HarperCollins has been amazing, somehow managing to stay in Beast Mode 24/7.

So many people have read for me over the years, both for this book and for my dozen or so "practice novels" (also known as "fart-odored wordsplosions"). I've learned something from each and every critique. Thank you so much to Abby Cooper, Alec Shane, Alex Chen, Allison Denny, Amie Paradise, Andrew Chen, April Wall, Becky Appleby, Ben Brooks, Bill Malatinsky, Bonnie Perfetti,

Brian Murphy, Brian Sargent, Brooks Benjamin, Cam Earles, Chris Brandon Whitaker, Colten Hibbs, Dan Lazar, Dana Edwards, Dee Garretson, Diana Buzalski, Elise Mebel, Ella Schwartz, Erin Earles, Erin Reece, Fred Lee, Frewin Hermer, Gail Nall, Glenn Bradford, Grace Jurkowski, Heidi Schulz, Jason Nelson, Jean Giardina, Jen Malone, Jennifer Skutelsky, Jessika Fleck, Jill Denny, Jim Horne, Jo Marie Bankston, Karen Hallam, Kathryn Crawford Saxer, Kathy Berla, Katrina Earles, Kieran Trudel, Ki-Wing Merlin, Laurie Litwin, Liesl Shurtliff, Lindsey Becker, Marissa Burt, Mary Lou Guizzo, Melanie Conklin, Mirjana Reams, Paul Adams, Rachelle Lopp, Rebecca Cianci, Rebecca Sutton, Rhonda Battenfelder, Ronni Arno Blaisdell, Ryan Hancock, Sara Wilson Etienne, Sarah Chen, Shannon Duffy, Shannon Schuren, Sloan Ginn, Spencer Lopp, Stefanie Wass, Wendy BooydeGraaff. I'm sure I've forgotten some people—apologies to those I've accidentally left off.

Special props to my writing group, MG Beta Readers, a collection of hardworking novelists at every stage in the process. Commiserating and celebrating with all of you has helped me keep whacking away at the words, even when it felt hopeless. You can find us at our blog, www .kidliterati.com.

A huge shout-out to my twin brother, Alex Chen, who somehow managed to read my earlier FOWs all the way through. All the way! Amazingly, he never once gagged on the stench or used the word "crapulific," even though it was dead nuts on. Much appreciation to Andrew and Sarah Chen, who eagerly listened to me read those works of (f)art with excitement and laughter. And to Kate Kerkering, for always being there with a kind word, even when the manuscripts were less than kind to behold.

Similarly, Lorenzo Stubbs, my decades-long little (through Big Brothers), kept on telling me he was certain I'd eventually get one of my books published. Not sure why he believed in me so unwaveringly, but it drove me to make sure that his confidence wasn't for naught.

Thanks to my parents, Fu-mei Chang and Winston Chen, for setting a great example, pushing me hard, and filling me with grit. I hope to do the same for my kids, Tess and Jake. I love you two, tons. Now for the eleventy-ninth time, get your fingers out of your noses!

Finally, none of this would have been possible without the enormous encouragement, never-ending support, and insightful advice (both literary and life in general) from my wife, Jill Denny. I always tell people how much smarter she is than me, but it's also true that she's funnier, wiser, tougher, more tactful, better smelling . . . pretty much everything. She's the best.

The Best.

I'm a lucky man.